BOOKS BY TINA FOLSOM

Ace on the Run (Code Name Stargate, Book 1)

Fox in plain Sight (Code Name Stargate, Book 2)

Yankee in the Wind (Code Name Stargate, Book 3)

Tiger on the Prowl (Code Name Stargate, Book 4)

Samson's Lovely Mortal (Scanguards Vampires, Book 1)

Amaury's Hellion (Scanguards Vampires, Book 2)

Gabriel's Mate (Scanguards Vampires, Book 3)

Yvette's Haven (Scanguards Vampires, Book 4)

Zane's Redemption (Scanguards Vampires, Book 5)

Quinn's Undying Rose (Scanguards Vampires, Book 6)

Oliver's Hunger (Scanguards Vampires, Book 7)

Thomas's Choice (Scanguards Vampires, Book 8)

Silent Bite (Scanguards Vampires, Book 8 1/2)

Cain's Identity (Scanguards Vampires, Book 9)

Luther's Return (Scanguards Vampires, Book 10)

Blake's Pursuit (Scanguards Vampires, Book 11)

Fateful Reunion (Scanguards Vampires, Book 11 1/2)

John's Yearning (Scanguards Vampires, Book 12)

Ryder's Storm (Scanguards Vampires, Book 13)

Damian's Conquest (Scanguards Vampires, Book 14)

Grayson's Challenge (Scanguards Vampires, Book 15)

Lover Uncloaked (Stealth Guardians, Book 1)

Master Unchained (Stealth Guardians, Book 2)

Warrior Unraveled (Stealth Guardians, Book 3)

Guardian Undone (Stealth Guardians, Book 4)

Immortal Unveiled (Stealth Guardians, Book 5)

Protector Unmatched (Stealth Guardians, Book 6)

Demon Unleashed (Stealth Guardians, Book 7)

A Touch of Greek (Out of Olympus, Book 1)

A Scent of Greek (Out of Olympus, Book 2)

A Taste of Greek (Out of Olympus, Book 3)

A Hush of Greek (Out of Olympus, Book 4)

Venice Vampyr (Novellas 1 – 4)

Teasing (The Hamptons Bachelor Club, Book 1)

Enticing (The Hamptons Bachelor Club, Book 2)

Beguiling (The Hamptons Bachelor Club, Book 3)

Scorching (The Hamptons Bachelor Club, Book 4)

Alluring (The Hamptons Bachelor Club, Book 5)

Sizzling (The Hamptons Bachelor Club, Book 6)

IMMORTAL UNVEILED

STEALTH GUARDIANS #5

TINA FOLSOM

To my mother
You left me too soon. I miss you.

PROLOGUE

Closing her eyes, Kim turned her face into the spray of the shower and allowed the warm water to rinse away the soap. The water pressure wasn't quite as strong as she was used to from her own condo. After all, her childhood home, which Kim's mother now occupied alone, was an old house with aging pipes, creaking stairs, and oodles of character. Her own place in a turn-of-the-century warehouse-turned-condo-building was currently undergoing some minor renovations after her upstairs neighbor's negligence had caused water damage to several floors in the building.

Kim had opted for staying with her mother while the work to her condo was being done rather than staying with her fiancé, Todd. He'd been taken aback by her decision to stay with her mother. Her excuse that the commute from his suburban home to the internet news blog she worked for as an investigative journalist was too long hadn't quite convinced him.

"You work remotely half the time anyway," Todd had said.

He had a point. A good one.

Still, she hadn't let him talk her into staying with him and instead taken up residence in her childhood bedroom. Maybe it was a sign that their relationship had moved into a direction she wasn't ready for.

Though they were engaged, no date for the wedding had been set. The fact that she was fine with that didn't exactly make her a model fiancée. She should be browsing bridal magazines and planning her dream wedding, but she couldn't get into the mood for it.

To Kim's surprise, her mother had brought up the matter only a few nights earlier over a late glass of wine.

"Maybe Todd isn't the right guy for you."

"Mom? Are you drunk? You adore Todd."

"Of course, I do, but do you?" her mother had retorted so quickly that Kim had been stunned into silence.

She'd been unable to give an answer to that question. And even now, several days later, the question remained unanswered. Not that her mother had pressed her for a response. Maybe the question had been simply meant as a thought-provoking exercise, part of a game her mother had played with her when Kim had been a teenager. A game that had fueled her inquisitive nature and taught her never to accept anything at face value.

Kim sighed and turned off the water. She pushed the curtain back and reached for the towel when she heard a loud thud from downstairs. Had her mother come home?

Instinctively, she ripped the towel from the rack and pressed it to her front.

"Mom?"

She didn't expect an answer. If her mother was downstairs, she wouldn't be able to hear her calling out from the upstairs bathroom. Not with the door closed. Kim shook her head. She was used to her condo, where everything was open plan, and the partitions in the loft-like space weren't soundproof.

Another thud followed by shattering porcelain or glass sent her heartbeat racing. She tossed the towel on the hamper, snatched her bathrobe from the hook on the door, and slipped it on quickly, already opening the door.

"Mom, what's going on?" she called out toward the stairs, hurrying toward them.

Grunting sounds drifted upstairs, then a high-pitched yelp.

Panic flooded her now. Was her mother having a seizure of some sort?

"Mom, hold on, I'm coming."

Kim flew down the stairs, having to hold onto the railing so she wouldn't slip with her wet bare feet. She missed the last step, slipping on the landing, and would have slammed into the front door had she not been gripping the old mahogany rail.

A whooshing sound made her snap her head to the right, where an open arch led into the living room. Kim froze. The area of the living room she could see from her vantage point was in disarray. Broken porcelain was strewn over the carpet, a lamp lay on the ground, the coffee table was turned over. But while she noticed those things, her focus was drawn to something else.

At the spot where the coffee table had stood, a mass of smoke was swirling in a circle. But there was no fire. No heat. No smell. Just smoke or black fog swirling around as if it were a tornado or a black hole. Only it wasn't a vertical tornado but a horizontal one. And in the middle of it she noticed a leg disappearing, as if a person had stepped into the fog hole.

Kim gasped and shivered at the same time, suddenly feeling the cold from the odd phenomenon. She took a step toward it, and the swirling mass shrank. Another step, and it shrank even more as if it was being sucked into nothingness. A second later it was gone completely, leaving no traces of its existence behind, except that it now revealed what it had hidden.

Her mother.

She lay several feet behind the spot where the mysterious tornado-like mass had manifested.

Kim barreled toward her and crouched down. "Mom! Mom!"

There was no response.

"No! No, please no!"

She looked into her mother's pale face, felt her skin, searched for her pulse.

Kim's heart beat into her throat. But it was the only heart in the room that was beating. Because her mother's had stopped.

She gripped her mother's shoulders, shook her. Her head rolled to the side, her long hair falling to the floor, away from her neck. That's when Kim saw why her mother's heart wasn't beating anymore, why her lungs weren't drawing another breath. Strangulation marks.

Something wet dripped onto her mother's cheek. A tear. Kim's tear. Another followed until rivulets streamed down Kim's face, running along each side of her nose, touching her lips until she tasted the salt on her tongue. Numbness engulfed her. Or was it desperation? Grief? Pain? Rage? Whatever it was, it reverberated inside her, asking the same question again and again: Who or what had killed her mother? Who or what had snuffed out her life in such a violent way?

Zoltan punched Frederic, his underling, in the face. "You did what?"

"She wasn't talking." The coward lowered his eyes, too scared to face his master. And so he should be. Because what he'd done demanded punishment. Severe punishment.

They were alone in Zoltan's private study in the Underworld, the vast system of caves and tunnels the Demons of Fear called their home and expanded daily. The smell of sulfur was strong in the tunnels, but the caves Zoltan had chosen for himself smelled less pungent. For some reason, he'd always hated the smell of the Underworld even though he was a demon through and through. And not only that, he was the strongest, the fiercest, the most brutal and ruthless among them. Because that's what it took to be their leader, to be the Great One, the ruler of the Underworld. Because only ruthless men got to rule the world. Everybody else would collapse under the weight of it.

"Of course, she wasn't talking." Zoltan grabbed his subject by the throat and started squeezing his windpipe. "Would you be talking if you were being strangled?"

The idiot fought against Zoltan's hold, a futile measure if there ever was one. His defiance alone would cost him dearly.

Zoltan loosened his grip and let go of his demon subject. Frederic coughed instantly and sucked air into his lungs. He appeared relieved.

"Did you search her place for it?" Zoltan asked gruffly, already guessing the answer. After all, the man had returned from his excursion up top empty-handed.

"I did. Turned the house upside down. It wasn't there."

There was a flicker in the demon's eyes, one Zoltan didn't miss. He rarely missed anything, particularly not a bold-faced lie. All his demons lied. Whether it was inbred or out of fear of him, he didn't particularly care. No matter the reason, a lie was a lie and a breach of loyalty. And he demanded absolute loyalty from his subjects and didn't care how he got it. And how he kept it. If it meant killing one of his underlings in order to impress the importance of obedience on his subjects, so be it. Because no Great One could rule the Underworld without blindly obedient subjects who didn't ask questions.

"It wasn't there, you say," Zoltan repeated now, keeping his voice even. "Did you search her office?"

"Her home office? Yes, of course."

"I mean her office at the museum, you idiot," Zoltan ground out from between clenched teeth. A liar and an idiot. The demon's chances of surviving this interview diminished with every stupid word coming out of his mouth.

"Nobody said, I mean, I wasn't told..."

No initiative either. No redeeming qualities whatsoever.

"I see. Tell me again which rooms you searched in the woman's home before she surprised you."

"Uh, I got in through the kitchen. The door was locked, but I could see inside, so I used a vortex."

"A vortex, you idiot? If you could see inside, it means the door was glass. You could have smashed it rather than take such a risk." If a human saw the vortex, questions would be raised. And the Stealth

Guardians would be on their ass again. "Stupid!" Zoltan pounded his hand against the mantle of his fireplace.

"But, but I thought... I didn't want them to hear me. I'm sorry."

"Sorry?" Zoltan let out a growl. Then he suddenly snapped his head toward Frederic. "Them?"

The demon's head whipped back, and his eyes widened. "Uh..."

Zoltan grabbed him by the collar. "She wasn't alone? You left a witness alive?"

"Yes, no. Uh..."

"Which is it?" Zoltan bared his teeth. "Who was with her?"

"Her daughter. But she didn't see me. I'm sure of that."

"How can you be sure?"

"She was taking a shower upstairs when I entered. I never went upstairs. And I was gone before she came downstairs. I swear."

Zoltan shook his head. He'd just caught the idiot lying. "You said you turned the house upside down and searched everywhere."

"Yes, I did."

"So, you insist on continuing to lie to me." Zoltan slammed his underling against the wall. "You just said you never went upstairs. So, you never searched the entire house."

Frederic swallowed visibly. "I can go back," he offered hastily. "The daughter won't be a problem. I can kill her, if you want."

Zoltan lifted his hand to stop him. "I'll send somebody." Somebody more capable than this imbecile. "The daughter will do the search for us. We'll just need to watch her."

"Huh?" Frederic asked, clueless.

"She'll be handling her mother's estate and go through all her possessions. We'll just need to be patient." And not do anything else stupid that could draw the Stealth Guardians' attention onto them.

"Good idea."

Zoltan stared at his subject. "Yes indeed." And he'd just had an even better one. He put his hand on the mantle and pressed an indentation. Soundlessly, a flat stone in the oversized fireplace slid back and revealed what was beneath it: a lava pit.

The smell of sulfur alerted his underling to it, and he turned his head toward it. Too late. Zoltan already had him by the throat and tossed him toward the opening. Frederic fought against him, trying to grip the stone surrounding the fireplace, but his hands didn't find purchase.

"Next time, don't lie to me."

With a kick in the stomach, Zoltan sent his subject backward.

Screams of pain filled the study, but not for long. Within seconds, the demon's body was burning up and sinking deeper.

Zoltan pressed the indentation in the mantle again and watched the slab of stone slide back in place.

For today, his work was done. Tomorrow, he would send his best demons out to watch the dead woman's daughter. This time, the Stealth Guardians wouldn't get their hands on what Zoltan coveted: a treasure trove of secrets that could spell the end of the guardians' reign.

1

Three months later

"How did I get stuck with you guys again?" Manus looked at Grayson and Ryder, the two vampire hybrids who were currently residing within the Stealth Guardians compound in Baltimore. Their fathers, Samson, the owner and founder of Scanguards, and Gabriel, the second-in-command at the San Francisco security company, had sent them to intern with them as part of the alliance the Stealth Guardians had forged with the vampires.

The two twentysomethings had come to join them on various missions against the demons in order to learn all about the Stealth Guardians' capabilities and help out where the guardians needed a vampire's natural skill: to literally sniff out their enemies, the Demons of Fear.

Both Grayson and Ryder, who'd trained as bodyguards at Scanguards, were fitting perfectly into the motley crew at the compound, a group that, in addition to the warriors stationed here, now included two human women, one female psychic—all three mated to Stealth Guardian warriors—and two almost five-year-old twins. It was getting a little crowded and rather domesticated at the compound. Just as well that there were a few single men left to shoot the breeze with.

"I think it's the other way 'round," Grayson said and jabbed Ryder with his elbow, then winked at Manus. "*We* got stuck with *you*."

Ryder, the quieter of the two, chuckled. "Yep, that's how I see it too. But hey, we're good with it. At least you're not a stickler for the rules, right?"

No, he wasn't. In fact, Manus was known for skirting the rules whenever he could. Which was probably why the two hybrids preferred getting assignments with him rather than one of the other guardians at the compound. But he wasn't supposed to let the two youngsters get away with shit. At least not with too much.

"Well, let's get started then," Manus suggested and motioned to the hallway that led from the kitchen and great room, the social center of the compound, to the command center. "Let's see what they've got for us today."

The two hybrids fell into step with him. Their boots clacked against the stone floor and echoed from the walls that were adorned with runes to ward off magic and protect its inhabitants.

"It better be something good," Grayson said. "It's been a little quiet here lately. I need some action."

Manus rolled his eyes and exchanged a look with Ryder, who smirked. "Be glad that it's quiet. You can't fight demons all the time."

"I can!" the hotheaded hybrid protested.

"Yeah? Let's talk again in a hundred years, and then you tell me if you still think the same way."

That seemed to shut him up. Just as well. The kid—and he was still a kid compared to Manus's own age of just over two hundred, and a spoiled one at that—still had a lot to learn.

For a few moments they were walking in silence. Manus cast a quick glance at Grayson and noticed how tight his jaw was. Yep, the heir of Scanguards didn't like to be told off.

"Hey, don't get me wrong," Manus started. "I like a good fight with the demons like the next guy, and I know you both are more than capable of fighting them... But there's more to defeating the demons than simply bashing their heads in. There's strategy, there's tactic, there's planning. And just because you don't get action every day, doesn't mean what you're doing here isn't important."

"Whatever," Grayson said.

"You're such a dick as usual," Ryder said, tossing a glare at his friend. "You begged your dad to let you come here to learn from the Stealth Guardians, and then you pout like a little girl every time things don't go—"

Ryder didn't get to finish his sentence. Grayson pounced and slammed him against the wall, growling ferociously with his fangs bared. "I don't pout!"

Ryder wasn't intimidated. He pushed the aggressive hybrid off him, catapulting him against the wall opposite.

Manus didn't interfere and stepped aside in order not to get caught in the crossfire. He'd seen this coming. For weeks now, those two had been launching verbal barbs at each other. They needed to get this out of their system.

"You know what, Grayson?" Ryder ground out, his eyes glaring red now. "You're an ass. You've always been an ass. And it's about time somebody beat it out of you before it becomes permanent."

Ryder swung his fist and punched Grayson in the face. The counterpunch was almost instantaneous and hit him on the chin, whipping his head to the side.

"You want a fight? I'll give you a fight," Grayson spat and aimed for his colleague's head again, but Ryder was faster, diving to the side so the fist merely grazed his shoulder.

Still, for a human, the impact would have been painful; not so for the half vampire. He absorbed it as if he'd been touched with a feather. Just like Grayson seemed to feel nothing when Ryder delivered another blow, this time lower, hitting the arrogant Scanguards' heir in the abdomen.

Folding his arms across his chest, Manus leaned against the wall to watch the fight. It was a thing of beauty, he had to admit. Two half vampires punching and kicking each other was like an intricately choreographed martial arts performance. They were agile, strong, and incredibly fast. They also had a high threshold for pain, and neither of the two was inclined to give up first. Their grunts and groans filled the hallway and bounced off the thick stone walls of the old building. At least they couldn't damage anything here. In a regular house, they would have already left holes in the drywall.

The sound of footsteps suddenly drifted to him, and Manus turned his head. He saw Hamish running toward him.

"What the fuck's going on here?"

Manus lifted his hand, stopping him. "Nothing."

Hamish reached him and stopped, his eyes focused on the two vampire hybrids. "Doesn't look like nothing to me." He made a motion to march past Manus, but Manus grabbed his shoulder and held him back.

"Don't. They need to have it out."

Hamish raised an eyebrow. Then he slowly nodded. "'Bout time, I guess." He leaned one shoulder against the wall, crossed his ankles, and exhaled. "So, who's winning? Should I be putting my money on one of them?"

Manus shrugged. "Your guess is as good as mine. They're pretty equally matched, if you ask me."

"Pretty good form too," Hamish noted. "Light on their feet."

Manus gazed at the two Scanguards bodyguards. "Hmm. Not bad. A bit unrefined. But trainable. Give 'em a few decades, and they'll be almost as good as us."

"Yeah, almost," Hamish said, smirking. "Shame they're using up their precious energy on each other rather than on creatures that really deserve it."

Both hybrids' heads suddenly whipped toward Hamish, and they stopped in mid-punch. Their eyes narrowed.

"Did they just say *almost* as good as them?" Grayson asked, exchanging a glance with Ryder.

"I heard that too," Ryder said, tilting his head and tossing Hamish and Manus an assessing look. "Wanna rephrase that, guys? You should know by now that vampires are physically stronger and faster than you."

Manus grinned. "Yeah, vampires. But last time I checked, you were only *half* vampires."

"Yeah, half-breeds," Hamish tossed in, barely suppressing a chuckle.

"Maybe we should give them a taste of our strength," Grayson suggested, "since they don't seem to know what we're capable of."

Manus knew only too well what vampire hybrids were capable of. They were as strong as their vampire fathers or mothers, yet their human genes made them less vulnerable. Though they could be killed by silver bullets or a stake through the heart, the rays of the sun couldn't hurt them. But instead of acknowledging that, Manus turned to Hamish.

"They're way too easy to rile up, don't you think, Hamish?"

"Yeah, barely a challenge," his compound brother admitted.

Outraged huffs reached Manus's ears. He turned his head to look at the two youngsters. "You guys done now? Or do you want to go another round?"

Both tipped their chins up in defiance.

"Good," Manus said. "Then let's see what Pearce has got for us today. Can't stand around and play all day." He turned and walked toward the command center. "And put your fangs away."

He didn't wait for a reply but continued walking, and seconds later, he heard the two guys follow him and Hamish retreat in the other direction. Manus opened the door to the command center. Pearce, their resident IT genius, sat in front of a bank of monitors. He turned his head briefly and nodded.

"About time. You oversleep or something?"

Manus marched toward him. "Nope."

"Hmm. Got some work for you."

The door closed behind the two hybrids.

"Yeah, an assignment?" Grayson asked eagerly.

Pearce glanced over his shoulder. "Oh look, the kids are here—" He stopped himself when he noticed their bloodied noses. "Run into some demons on your way here?"

Manus slapped Pearce on the shoulder. "More like run into some egos."

Pearce chuckled and turned back to his monitor. "Figures." Then he mouthed to Manus *Who won?*

I did, Manus mouthed back and winked at his colleague.

Pearce rolled his eyes, then he pointed to a file he'd just pulled up on the screen. "Got something for you."

"Demon activity?" Manus asked, trying to sound casual when he, too, just like the two vampire hybrids, was eager for some action.

"Not recent. Remember the emissarius that was murdered about three months ago?"

Manus nodded. Stuff like that was hard to forget. "Nancy Britton? Curator at the Museum of Antiquities?"

Pearce nodded. "Yeah."

"Do we have new leads in her case?"

Grayson and Ryder came closer, interested.

"Other than that we know it was a demon? No."

"Then what—"

"It's about her daughter. She can't let it go. She's convinced her mother's death has supernatural causes."

"Well, she's right," Manus said.

"You know that, and I know that, but the Council is concerned that she's getting too close to finding an explanation that's actually coming close to the truth. And we can't let that happen." Pearce swiveled in his chair. "They figured you could take care of this."

"Take care of this?" Ryder echoed and took a step toward them. "Are you saying the Council wants you guys to kill the daughter?"

"Fuck!" Grayson let out.

Shocked, Manus stared at the hybrids. "Kill? Are you guys for real?" Then he glanced at Pearce, letting out an exasperated breath.

"Would you please tell these jokers what our procedure in cases like that is?"

Pearce shook his head at Grayson and Ryder. "Honestly, guys, I know that killing is constantly on your minds, and that there hasn't been any decent demon killing lately, but really..." He sighed. "Anyway, no, we're not killing the daughter. We're just sending Manus out to convince her that whatever supernatural cockamamie theory she has is totally loco, so she'll stop pursuing it and drop the whole thing before it goes viral."

"Viral?" Manus asked.

Pearce looked at him. "Yep, she's posted all kinds of crap on this forum for paranormal buffs, hoping to get answers. Her description of a vortex is pretty damn accurate."

"She saw a demon vortex?" Manus asked. "I don't remember that from the file."

"'Cause it wasn't in there. The police didn't put it in the murder book, or at least not in those words. So, we missed it."

"Fine, I'll take care of it," Manus said.

Ryder asked, "How?"

Manus let a smile widen his mouth. "The gift of the gab."

"Charm? You think you can talk her out of believing what she's seen?" Grayson asked in disbelief.

"Piece of cake." Manus winked at the two hybrids. "And so you'll learn something, I'm gonna let you watch."

It would be a nice diversion for one day.

2

———

Kim switched off her computer and grabbed her handbag. She hadn't been so excited and hopeful in months. Finally, a lead! Finally, a light at the end of the tunnel. She could only hope it wasn't another oncoming train like those other leads that had looked promising at first. But somehow, she had a good feeling about it.

With a spring in her step, she left her condo, locked the door behind her, and sauntered down the stairs. Midway, she already pulled out her cell phone and navigated to her recent calls, then hit the number for her friend Jennifer. Two rings, and the call was answered.

"Hey, what's up?" Jennifer asked.

"I got news," Kim said.

"What?" Some shouting and overlapping voices coming through the line accompanied Jennifer's question. "Can you say that again?"

"Where are you?"

"On the bus. You've gotta speak up, so I can hear you. Or do you want me to call you back when I'm in the office after lunch?"

"No, no! Don't! I've gotta tell you now," Kim insisted.

"Okay, shoot!"

Kim barely knew where to start. "I'm on my way to meet some guy who's got information for me. He replied to my thread on the forum."

"Oh," Jennifer said, sounding a little deflated. "For a moment there I thought you were going on a date."

"A date? Why would I go on a date?"

She had no time for men. Particularly not if they turned out to be like Todd, her ex-fiancé. She'd thought he'd be supportive after her mother's death, helping her find the killer when the police had practically given up. But he'd dismissed the phenomenon she'd seen the night of her mother's murder, trying to convince her it was the result of the shock she'd suffered. After all, the police hadn't taken her seriously either.

A botched burglary had been their guess. For a few weeks, they'd followed all the leads, checked out her mother's friends and co-workers at the museum, but they'd found nothing. The case had gone cold.

When Todd had sided with the police and begged her to accept what had happened and stop chasing a phantom—as he'd called it— Kim had broken off the engagement. She couldn't be with a man who didn't stand one hundred percent behind her.

"Just saying," Jennifer said. "So, what does this guy claim to know?"

"He said he's dealt with the same phenomenon before." There, if that wasn't a step in the right direction.

"Dealt as in how?"

Kim shrugged. "Not sure. He said he needed to explain everything face-to-face. He suggested we meet."

"You're not meeting him at his place, are you?"

"Of course not!"

"Did you give him your address?"

"I'm not stupid, Jennifer. I'm meeting him at a busy coffeeshop. That's why I'm calling you, so you'll know where I am."

"Good girl." Jennifer sounded satisfied. "Which coffeeshop?"

"Auntie's Java Shop on Main."

"Good. If you don't check in with me in an hour, I'm calling the cops," her friend said.

"Make that ninety minutes. I first have to get there."

"Okay, ninety minutes, and not a minute longer. And if it's some creep who thinks he can take advantage of you because you've seen weird stuff, then run. There are all kinds of weirdos out there, particularly on that forum. It attracts the worst kind of people."

Kim sighed. This wasn't the first time they'd had that conversation. "Just because these people have seen stuff they can't explain? I'm one of those people. Would you call me a weirdo too?"

"You're the only normal person on that forum. That's why I'm telling you to watch out."

"I will."

"Good, and oh, almost forgot: what's the guy's name?"

"Manus."

"Manus what? No last name?"

"I didn't give him my last name either."

"Okay then. Call me in ninety minutes or I'm mobilizing the troops."

"Thanks, Jennifer."

"And Kim?"

"Yes?"

"Don't expect too much. I don't want you to be all crushed again when it turns out that this guy doesn't know anything useful either. Promise me that."

"Promise," she said quickly and ended the call before Jennifer could say anything else.

Still, Kim couldn't tamp down her excitement. She had to continue believing that she could solve her mother's murder. She owed it to her. And she needed the closure because even three months after her mother's death, the pain was as raw as on the first day.

MANUS RECOGNIZED Nancy Britton's daughter the moment she entered the coffeeshop though the picture in her file didn't do her justice: Kim was no woman to be overlooked. She was beautiful in that mysterious way that could drive a man insane. Not him, of course, because he'd had plenty of beautiful women and considered himself immune to their charms. Sure, he'd fuck them, but that didn't mean they could lure him into a relationship.

No, not even the thought of looking into those sky-blue eyes and feeling that black hair caress his face while she rode him into oblivion would make him reconsider—no matter how hard his cock was growing under the table just by thinking of the possibility of passing time with Kim between the sheets.

Fuck, this was bad!

Manus shook his head. Better cool down. He was here to do a job, and he would do it. And nothing more.

Making sure his jacket covered the front of his pants, he rose and waved to Kim. She'd told him that she would be wearing a red top, so he pretended to recognize her by her clothing.

She looked at him, hesitated for a moment, then slowly walked toward him. She stretched out her hand. "Manus?"

"Kim?" He took her hand and shook it, then released it quickly before the touch could reignite his cock.

He motioned to the chair opposite his. "Thanks for coming."

When she sat down, Manus took his seat again and rested his folded hands on the tabletop. For a moment, there was an awkward pause.

"I'm so glad you replied to my thread on the forum," Kim started. "I have so many questions."

There was definite excitement in her voice, and for a second, he regretted that he would have to squash that glimmer of hope that it represented. But it was for the good of his people, and first and foremost, he had to protect his kind.

"Yes, I'm sure. But before I answer any of your questions, do you mind telling me in more detail what happened and what you've seen? I want to make sure we're on the same page and actually talking about the same phenomenon." He pasted a smile on his lips, making sure to look open and receptive so she wouldn't suspect that he was about to deceive her.

"Yes, of course, sure. Uh, where do I start?" She appeared a little nervous. Her face was flushed. "It's not easy for me to talk about it. You know, losing your mother, losing her in such a violent way... there aren't the right words to describe that." She stared right at him. "Do you understand?"

Manus understood only too well. The pain of losing a parent never vanished, no matter how many years passed. He put his hand on her forearm before he knew what he was doing. He felt a tiny jolt, but then Kim smiled at him, and their eyes locked.

"I'm sorry," she murmured. "How long has it been for you?"

Manus's chin dropped. How could she know? "Many years." Too many years to count.

"Does it ever get easier?" she asked.

He felt the connection, the shared pain, and shook his head. "No, but you learn to live with it." Then he pulled his hand away and broke eye contact. He couldn't get drawn into whatever this connection between them was. Because if she kept looking at him like this, he wouldn't be able to lie.

Quickly, Manus cleared his throat. "On the forum you said that you saw a storm-like phenomenon on the night of your mother's murder," he prompted her to bring her back on target.

Kim straightened in her chair as if to steel herself to withstand the painful memory. "I heard some noise from downstairs." She motioned with her hand to explain. "I was upstairs taking a shower when I heard sounds. You know, as if stuff was falling on the floor, furniture being turned over. So, I called out to my mother and ran downstairs."

Her breathing was accelerating.

"I reached the living room, and that's when I saw it." She spread her arms, making a circular motion. "It was massive. Like a tornado, only it wasn't vertical. And it was right inside the house. A swirling mass of dark air and wind. Like a black hole that would suck you into its depth if you got too close."

"Hmm." Kim was describing the demon vortex perfectly, only it wasn't a black hole but an entrance into the Underworld. "What else did you see?"

"A leg."

"A leg?"

She nodded, her expression serious. "Somebody was stepping into that thing, that vortex, you know, but I'd just missed him, so all I saw was his shin and foot as he disappeared. And then that phenomenon closed. It got smaller and smaller and just vanished." She swallowed. "That's when I saw my mother on the floor. The vortex had obstructed my view of her. She was already dead when I got to her." A wet sheen covered Kim's eyes now, and she sniffled, then pulled herself together. "I couldn't do anything to help her."

He nodded. He understood helplessness. "What did the police think happened?"

She shrugged. "They believe it was a burglar. But how can it be a burglar? Nothing was stolen."

"Nothing at all? But didn't you say that furniture was turned over? Was somebody looking for something?"

She gave him an odd look. "Why does that matter?"

Manus sighed. "Everything matters. As an investigator, I have to look at everything to see what's important."

"Investigator? You're an investigator? You didn't mention that."

He quickly gave her an apologetic look. "Sorry, I meant to introduce myself properly, but somehow we got right onto the subject matter, and I didn't get a chance." When she nodded, he continued, "Yes, I'm a private investigator, and I deal with all kinds of weird occurrences. That's why I replied to your thread. Because I've dealt with something like your case before."

Kim leaned forward. "So, you know what this is?"

"I think I do." He hesitated. "But I need to confirm a few more things. So, would you mind answering a few more questions, just so I can be sure?"

"Fine."

"Thank you. Does your mother's house have air conditioning?"

Kim nodded, looking perplexed.

"And nothing at all was stolen then?"

She shook her head, then stopped herself. "Actually, just one thing. My mother always wore a gold bracelet. It's gone. It wasn't on her, and I can't find it anywhere. But it wasn't really worth much, certainly not worth enough to kill her for it."

"I understand." Demons liked shiny things. And it wasn't unusual that a demon took a little memento with him, particularly one made of gold. "But could it be that your mother interrupted a burglar before he could take anything of greater value?"

"And take what? My mother didn't own anything worth stealing. Besides, there were no signs of a break-in."

"Could your mother have let the person in?"

"Sure, but if he got interrupted, then do you really think he'd close the front door on his way out?" She tossed him a combative look. When he said nothing, she added, "Exactly. Besides, it still doesn't explain the vortex. What burglar can do something like that? No, it has to have a different explanation. A supernatural one."

He sighed. Time to deliver his bogus explanation. "You're not the only one who thought that after what you've seen. I was hired by a family a while ago, a wife who'd seen what you've seen, some kind of vortex appearing in her house, leaving her husband dead."

Kim's eyes widened, and he noticed her chest rising in anticipation. "What did you find?"

"Well, at first, I did my usual questioning, and then I examined the house, looked at everything that could give me an answer. Like in your mother's case, the police suspected a burglary gone wrong. Nothing was stolen there either. And the wife insisted she saw the vortex. I was inclined to believe her."

"Inclined?"

"Yes, I kept an open mind, until..."

"Until what?"

Now it was time for the blow. Manus leaned forward. "Don't take this the wrong way. You believe what you've seen. And I believe that you believe it. It's just, there's a logical explanation for what you've seen. A technical one, actually."

"What are you saying?" Her eyes narrowed by a fraction.

"It's a rare occurrence, but when the weather conditions are just right, and the air conditioning is running in the house, a negative airflow can be created that will suck dust particles through a vent into the house and whirl them around. Because of the different pressure inside and outside the house, the particles are electrically charged and therefore create in effect a vortex that's visible by the naked eye."

Kim stared at him, her mouth slowly opening as if she wanted to say something, but no sound rolled over her lips. Her luscious red lips. So plump, so kissable.

Focus! Focus! Don't lose your head. You're not on a fucking date. This is a job.

"I mean," Manus added, "it's unusual, I admit that. And I was thrown myself at first, but I checked it out with a few professionals, you know, an air conditioning contractor and a meteorologist. And they both assured me that it's possible. And then, of course, when the police finally found the burglar in that case, it all fell into place."

"Did it?" Kim's voice was stiff and cold. Not a good sign.

"Yeah, it all made sense. Just give the police a chance to do their investigation. You'll see that it all has a normal explanation. I just don't want you to fall down this rabbit hole and get lost in something that has no basis in reality."

"You know what?" she asked, and he knew it wasn't a question. He could tell from the pissed-off tone in Kim's voice. She pushed the chair back and rose in one fluid movement. "How stupid do you think I am? An air conditioning system creating a vortex? I don't know what kind of Kool-Aid you think you can dish up and what your motivation for this crap is, but let me tell you one thing: I know when somebody is full of shit, and you, buddy, are about to spill over. If this is how you get your kicks, then do it with somebody else. Jerk!"

She spun around.

"Kim, I'm not—"

But she'd already reached the door and swung it open. A moment later, she was gone.

Fuck!

This hadn't gone at all how he'd expected. And on top of it, she'd called him a jerk. He had to correct that. Manus rose, pushing the chair back, when he heard suppressed chuckles coming from the table next to his.

3

Manus pivoted and took a step toward the two hybrids who were having a laugh at his expense. He glared at Ryder and Grayson.

"Piece of cake, huh?" Grayson said.

"So that's how it's done, yeah?" Ryder added.

Grayson turned his head to Ryder and lifted his finger like a schoolmaster. "Lesson number one: how to get a woman to believe your lies. First, roll out the charm—"

"Shut up, Grayson!" Manus snapped.

When Ryder opened his mouth, Manus cut him off with a glare. "Same goes for you."

For a moment, the two sat there stone-faced, then Ryder lifted his hand as if he were sitting in a classroom and asking the teacher for permission to speak. Manus felt like catapulting him through the window, but there were too many witnesses.

"What?"

Ryder lowered his hand. "You're not gonna give up, are you? I mean, we still have to convince her that what she's seen has a logical explanation."

"Duh!" Manus huffed. "Apparently she hates men. Had I known

that, I wouldn't have gone in with a charm offensive. Guess we'll have to do it the old-fashioned way and deliver evidence that will make her believe my explanation."

Now Grayson raised his hand.

"Would you stop that, you two?" Manus motioned to Grayson's hand. "Or you're gonna really piss me off."

With a grin, Grayson lowered his hand. "How're you gonna deliver evidence that your bogus air conditioning vortex is actually possible? We know that's not how it works."

"We don't have to prove the vortex explanation. We just have to give her something else that she can believe."

Both hybrids tossed him quizzical looks, then shrugged.

"Whatever you say, bro," Grayson said.

"Lead the way," Ryder added.

After determining that Kim wasn't going back to her mother's house, Manus hopped in the car, let the hybrids jump in, and drove to within a block of the house.

"I'll go in invisibly. You'll meet me in the backyard, and I'll let you in through the back."

Manus had been to the house just after Nancy Britton had been killed and looked around to see if anything left in the house could expose her as an emissarius for the Stealth Guardians. He'd found nothing that indicated that she'd ever worked for them. Nor had he found anything else that could have helped them solve her murder. Not that it needed solving because they all knew that she'd been killed by a demon. He'd literally sucked the life out of her. To a medical examiner, it would look like strangulation with a side of heart attack. But any Stealth Guardian would recognize the truth.

It didn't matter which demon had actually done the deed. But what mattered was why she'd been killed. How had she gotten onto the demons' radar? How had they known that she was associated with the Stealth Guardians, that she was one of their trusted spies who would feed them information about demon activity she came across in her daily life? Unfortunately, neither Manus nor his brethren had found anything. In their books, too, the case had gone cold—until Kim had started making waves.

Maybe this was a good opportunity to go back over the facts and look at everything with a fresh eye. Perhaps they'd missed something. The demons had targeted Nancy Britton. Was it to get information about the Stealth Guardians out of her? Since there hadn't been any security breaches after Nancy's death, it didn't look like she'd talked before the demon had killed her. Had he wanted something else other than information? That theory wore thin too, since nothing—apart from a bracelet—had been stolen.

Invisibly, Manus walked through the locked door into the house. Nothing much had changed inside though it appeared that Kim had started packing up personal items. She was probably getting the house ready to be sold. However, she hadn't gotten far with her endeavors to clean out the house. He understood that too. It was hard to move on after a parent's death, and packing everything into boxes seemed so final.

Before he could go further down memory lane, Manus walked to the kitchen in the back of the house and opened the door to the small, fenced-in yard. The two vampire hybrids were already waiting for him.

He ushered them inside and closed the door behind them.

Both looked at him expectantly. Apparently, they'd learned their lesson not to piss him off anymore today.

"I need you to go through Nancy's stuff and find a photo of that bracelet Kim was talking about."

"But we don't know what it looks like," Grayson said reluctantly.

"According to Kim, she wore it all the time. So, find her photos. If she really wore it all the time, it should be on practically every photo that shows Nancy."

Grayson shrugged. "Fine. But what are we gonna do once we find it?"

"Just do as I say. You take her bedroom. Ryder, there's a guest room upstairs where she stores a lot of stuff. I'll search the living room. Bring me every single photo in which Nancy wears a bracelet."

Both hybrids sauntered up the stairs.

Manus heard their footfalls on the landing when they reached the second floor. The old wooden floors creaked. Downstairs in the living room, the demon attacking Nancy would have heard Kim coming, giving him ample time to cast a vortex and disappear. The fact that he'd left it to the last second to make his exit meant that Nancy hadn't just been a convenient meal. He'd risked detection in order to get whatever he'd come for.

Manus looked around the living room. In a glass hutch, a display of antique dolls shared space with a collection of carved wooden toys. Nancy's interest in anything old was evident. As a curator for the Museum of Antiquities in Baltimore, she knew her trade. It was one of the reasons the Stealth Guardians had made contact with her and convinced her to work for them. With her knowledge of and access to antiquities, she was extremely useful when it came to assessing whether something was of value to the Stealth Guardians or the Demons of Fear.

Systematically, Manus started going through the various drawers in the hutch, then moved on to the piece of furniture that housed the TV. The shelves were filled with books and DVDs of TV shows and movies. Some DVDs didn't carry labels but were marked with a Sharpie, indicating they held photos and videos of recent trips. Nothing out of the ordinary. Manus leafed through a stack of old magazines and newspaper clippings. Again, nothing stuck out.

He turned and looked around. His gaze caught on the spot where Nancy's body had lain. He'd seen the police photos and recognized the signs of a demon kill. A visit to the morgue had confirmed his suspicion at the time. He shook off the memory. It wasn't the first time an emissarius had died, and it wasn't going to be the last. Nancy had known about the risks, nevertheless she'd agreed to help them.

"Got something," Grayson said from the entry to the hallway.

Manus lifted his head and marched toward the young hybrid. Grayson handed him a bunch of photos.

Ryder was coming down the stairs at the same time. "I found stuff too."

Manus looked through the photos. In some of them, the bracelet Nancy was wearing was obstructed, in others it was too far away to make out any details. But two of them showed the piece of jewelry much closer. He kept those two, then handed the others back to Grayson. "You can put those back." Then he addressed Ryder, "Show me what you've got."

Ryder produced a photo as well as a piece of paper. Manus looked at the photo first. It wasn't any better than the two he already had. "Too far away. What's that?" He pointed to the paper, and Ryder turned it so Manus could see it.

"A receipt for it." He grinned. "Together with an exact description of the bracelet and sketches of the front, back, and sides."

"Perfect!" Manus snatched the piece of paper. "Excellent work. We're done here."

"I still don't know how that's going to help us convince Kim that the vortex wasn't anything supernatural," Grayson said.

Manus chuckled to himself. "That's why you're an intern and I get paid the big bucks." He shoved the two photos and the receipt into the inside pocket of his jacket and motioned toward the kitchen. "Let's get out of here. We need to get a rush order in with a goldsmith."

"A goldsmith?" Ryder asked.

Manus nodded. "And I know just the guy who can get this done in less than twenty-four hours."

And then Kim would have to believe that a burglar had killed her mother, and the vortex had nothing to do with it.

4

———————

It was late evening the next day when Manus picked up the replica bracelet from a goldsmith who'd done work for the Stealth Guardians before and was extremely discreet. Manus inspected the gold bracelet and compared it to the photos and the sketches.

"Excellent work, George." He stuffed the bracelet into his pocket.

"Anytime," George replied and accepted the cash Manus laid on the counter. Then Manus turned and walked out of the shop, flanked by the two hybrids.

"Looks great," Ryder admitted. "You really think it's gonna work?"

"Yep. Now we just need a fresh body," Manus said and motioned to the car. "I think a trip to drug alley is warranted." Drug alley, as he and his brethren liked to call it, was a shitty area in downtown where the druggies of the city preferred to conduct their business. Shootings in that part of town were a nightly occurrence, and invariably somebody died there almost every night.

In the car, Grayson said, "You don't think it's creepy that we're going to search for a dead body we can pin the bracelet on?"

Manus shrugged. "If some gang bangers kill each other, or some druggie overdoses tonight, what do you expect me to do? Save him?

I'm not a social worker. It's not like I'm doing the killing. At least that way some poor schmuck's life will have had a purpose."

"Helping us keep the Stealth Guardians' and demons' existence a secret?" Ryder offered.

Manus glanced at Grayson. "See, your friend gets it."

Grayson growled softly. "I get it too. I'm just not quite as callous as you are."

Manus took the stab in stride. "Wait until you get to my age and go through all the shit I've been through. Then we can talk about being callous. I do my job. I do what's right for my people. And for the human race." And if that meant he'd take advantage of somebody's untimely death, so be it.

"Whatever." Grayson turned his head to stare out the window.

"Wow, he's moody tonight," Manus said, his gaze connecting with Ryder's in the rearview mirror.

"He's just pissed that he didn't come up with the idea first," Ryder said. "Which, by the way, is brilliant."

Manus grinned. "Thanks. I thought so myself."

For a few minutes, they drove in silence, then Manus made a few turns and brought the car to a stop at the entrance to an alley. "We're here. Let's spread out. Text me when you find a body. And don't get yourselves killed." He reached for the door handle. "Oh, and before I forget it: no midnight snacking, please. We don't want anything to look suspicious when the police arrive."

Grayson narrowed his eyes. "I already snacked earlier."

"I hope he was tasty," Manus said, rolling his eyes.

"He was a she, and yes, she was pretty sweet."

From the backseat, Ryder scoffed. "Really, Grayson, do I have to listen to another one of your little conquests? It's getting old. Besides, it doesn't count when you use mind control to seduce a chick so you can bite her."

Grayson turned in his seat and glared at his friend. "I wasn't using mind control. She wanted me."

Manus huffed and opened the door. "Whenever you guys are done with your bitching, I'd appreciate some help with finding a fresh body." He hopped out of the car and shut the door behind him. Not waiting for the two hybrids to follow him, Manus marched down the alley, making himself invisible in the process. He wasn't worried about keeping the car unlocked, since nobody could start the engine without the sophisticated control system that was installed in any car owned by the compound.

Manus followed his instinct and roamed the neighborhood, watching and listening. A drug dealer stood in the entrance to a building, handing a customer a tiny bag with white powder in exchange for a few bills. A few doors farther down, two guys were arguing, but they both appeared unarmed. Around the corner, a taxi let out a guy who then quickly hurried to a dark building, pressed a buzzer, and swiftly disappeared inside. For an hour, nothing much happened. A few more drug deals went down, a few drunks passed through, but there were no shootings, no stabbings, no fights.

It was a quiet night. Maybe they would have to come back tomorrow night to find a body. You couldn't force these things.

His cell phone vibrated. Manus stared at the display. The message from Ryder said, "Bingo."

A moment later, he texted an address.

"Coming," Manus messaged back.

Manus reached Ryder at the same time Grayson came around a corner. The body was that of a white man. He was casually dressed, and his clothes were relatively clean. Probably not a street person. His wallet was still in his back pocket, and a cell phone lay next to him. He lay on his face. There were no visible wounds.

"You sure he's dead?" Manus asked.

Ryder nodded. "Checked his pulse. Besides, I could smell the blood from a block away. He must have bled to death."

"Okay. Let's turn him around." Manus rolled the body on its back, revealing what the body had hidden: a pool of blood. The victim had been stabbed in the heart. "Yep, dead." Manus reached into his pocket and pulled out the gold bracelet.

"Put it in his front pants pocket, so it won't fall out when they transport the body," Ryder suggested.

Manus nodded and shoved the bracelet into the pocket of the dead guy. Then, carefully, he turned the body back into the same position he'd found him in.

"And now for some extra insurance," Manus added and took the man's cell phone, unlocked it with the dead guy's thumb print, and navigated to the contact app, added an address to it, then navigated to the map app from there before closing the phone again and placing it back on the ground.

From his own pocket, Manus retrieved a burner phone and dialed 9-1-1.

"911, what is your emergency?" a woman's voice answered within a couple of seconds.

"Yeah, there's a guy on the street. I think he's dead. There's blood."

"Where are you calling from, sir?"

"I'm at the corner of Brooke and Franklin. Can you send the police? I think I saw a guy running away. Come quickly."

"We're sending the police and ambulance now. Stay on the phone. What's your name?"

Manus disconnected the call, then opened the back of the cell phone and pulled out the SIM card. A few hundred yards farther, he tossed the SIM card into a dumpster, then shoved the cell back in his pocket.

"Great, we're done," Grayson said and pivoted.

"Not yet," Manus said, stopping him. "I wanna make sure nobody touches our body before the police can pick him up. We'll wait."

"And let the police find us here?" Grayson asked.

"They won't, since we're already invisible."

"Damn!" Grayson cursed. "I wish you'd let me know when you make me invisible."

"What would that serve? It's not like you're going to feel anything."

"I'd just like to know."

"And now you know: you're invisible. There."

Finally, Grayson shut up, and the three of them waited in silence. It didn't take long until police sirens indicated the arrival of the police and ambulance. Once the paramedics determined that the man was indeed dead, they departed, and the police cordoned off the area and waited for the coroner's van.

Manus could have left at that point or at least sent the hybrids home, but he needed to see this through. He couldn't afford another screw-up.

It took a couple of hours before the police had collected forensic evidence and the coroner could take the body away. Only then, Manus nodded to the two hybrids to follow him back to the car. Their job was done. Later, Manus would visit the morgue and make sure that the technicians there would collect the evidence Manus had planted on the body. With a little luck, it wouldn't take too long until the police connected the bracelet to Nancy Britton. Then it would only be a matter of time until Kim would accept that her mother had been murdered by a burglar.

Case closed.

5

Kim jumped out of the Uber and rushed up the stairs to the police station's entrance. She'd been here so many times in the last few months that even blind she would know how to get to Detective Emmerson's desk. He'd left a message on her phone that they'd found something concerning her mother's case and needed her to come to the station.

Finally, they were moving their lazy asses and doing something. Her hopes were up again, and she needed that because only three days earlier, Manus, the private investigator who she'd met with, had thrown her off her game. He'd played with her, feeding her this idiotic lie about the air conditioning system. How stupid did he think she was? Who in their right mind would believe such a bullshit story? As if she didn't know the first thing about air pressure systems and air conditioning just because she was a woman. What a jerk!

She was glad she'd told him what she thought of him. It just proved that good-looking guys were full of themselves. Did he think his charming smile would lure her into believing a single word he was saying? And why had he even tried? Was this a way for him to pick up women, by crushing their hopes and then offering a shoulder to cry on? Disgusting!

She was still seething now, despite the fact that she'd let off steam and vented to Jennifer after the incident at the café.

Take a breath!

Slowly, she inhaled and exhaled. There, better. Now she was ready to meet with the detective who'd been working on her mother's murder from day one. She crossed her fingers that this time he'd found a viable lead, something important. Why else would he call her to come to the station and not just tell her over the phone what he'd found? It had to be something significant.

A few more steps, and she stood in front of Detective Emmerson's desk. He looked up from his files.

"Oh, Miss Britton, so good of you to come in so quickly." He pointed to the chair in front of his desk. "Take a seat."

Kim followed his invitation. "You said you had something important for me to look at, Detective?"

He produced a thick file and opened it, nodding all the while. "Yes, I'd like you to identify something for me." He pulled out an envelope from the back of the file and emptied it on the table. A piece of gold jewelry.

"You said your mother always wore a bracelet." He lifted the item up and held it out to her. "Is this your mother's bracelet?"

Kim took the bracelet from him. She stared at it, examined it longer than she needed to because within the first second, she'd already recognized it. "That's my mother's. Where did you find it?"

Emmerson reached for the bracelet again and took it back. "We found it on a murder victim we picked up two nights ago, Clive Mulvaney. We believe that he was the burglar who broke into your mother's home and killed her."

She shook her head. "How can you be so sure? What if she lost it and he found it somewhere?"

Emmerson leaned over the desk. "Miss Britton, Mulvaney had a rap sheet longer than my arm: grand theft auto, breaking and entering, drug possession with intent to distribute. You name it, he's done it. He fits the picture."

"But that proves nothing."

"There's something else."

She stared at him.

"We found your mother's address programmed into his cell phone. Looks like he used GPS to find the address. He must have cased the joint. It's just like we suspected: he broke in, your mother surprised him, and then in a panic, he killed her." He placed the envelope with the bracelet back in the file and closed it. "I'm sorry, Miss Britton. But at least you have the satisfaction of knowing that the culprit got his just punishment. And you won't have to go through a lengthy trial where you'll have to relive everything. Many people don't get that." He gave her a kind smile.

Slowly, she nodded. This wasn't how she'd thought justice would look like. No trial. No sentencing. She couldn't even look the guy in the face and spit in it. She couldn't wail at him and tell him how evil he was and what he'd done to her—because the man who'd murdered her mother was already dead.

"Are you sure it was him?" Kim locked eyes with the detective, wanting more than just confirmation. She wanted certainty.

"As sure as we can ever be in a case like this. Short of Mulvaney's confession, this is as good as it gets. Plenty of circumstantial evidence. Any grand jury would indict him for your mother's murder." He sighed. "I've been doing this job for over two decades. Believe me when I tell you that we've got our man."

Kim shifted in her seat.

The detective kept talking, saying something about his lieutenant having to sign off on his conclusion so the case could be put to rest, but Kim wasn't really listening anymore. Was it really over? Was this the end of her quest to get justice for her mother? She'd expected this moment to feel different, more satisfying and not as anticlimactic.

A burglary gone wrong. Everybody had suspected it. But Kim hadn't wanted to believe it. And the vortex she'd seen? Had that all been a product of her imagination, a result of the shock she'd been dealt? Had she made it all up in her mind, so she could cope with her mother's senseless death?

Slowly, Kim rose from her chair. "Thank you, Detective."

Her throat was dry, her voice scratchy. She needed a drink now. Something to dull the grief that suddenly overwhelmed her. She hadn't allowed it to surface until now, not truly, because she'd had a mission until now, a goal. To find her mother's murderer. And now that he was found, there was nothing left other than grief.

It was time to face reality. Time to let go of her mother. Time to accept that which couldn't be reversed.

MANUS TURNED on his heel and headed for the men's room in the police station. Still invisible, he passed through the door and looked around. He was alone. With a sigh, he made himself visible and looked in the mirror. What he should see was a satisfied expression on his face. He'd done his job. The police as well as Kim had bought the story he'd so carefully crafted. It was just a formality for the police to close Nancy Britton's case. Kim would stop digging into the possibility that supernatural forces were behind her mother's murder, and the Stealth Guardians were in the clear. Their secrets were safe.

So, why was he looking and feeling like a man who'd just run over his own dog? Why was he feeling like he'd betrayed someone who deserved better?

You're getting soft!

Better not let any of his colleagues know about his scruples, or they'd be ribbing him until they found another convenient victim to tease.

With a resolute move, Manus pivoted and marched to the door. It was best to forget the whole thing, forget Nancy Britton's murder and avenge her death by killing every demon he encountered, and forget Kim Britton and the lies he'd had to tell her. This wasn't the first time he'd had to lie to a woman, and it sure wasn't going to be the last. Besides, she meant nothing to him, and he meant nothing to her.

Manus pushed against the double doors that led out of the police station and bumped into somebody who'd had the same intention. Their hands met, the other person's landing on his. He whirled his head to the right, jerking back to apologize.

The words got stuck in his throat. Only a sound akin to a grunt a mute could make rolled over his lips, while his chin dropped. Even though he knew Kim was at the station, he hadn't expected to run into her. In fact, he'd thought she would have left while he'd been in the restroom.

"Uh, Kim..."

Very smooth, man, very smooth, his inner voice commented. Just as well that he didn't have the two hybrids in tow. They would have a field day seeing him act like a babbling fool.

"Manus..."

He couldn't tell if Kim was just surprised or annoyed, or maybe both.

"Yeah, uh." He motioned behind him to the corridor that led to the different departments. "Working on a case. Catching up with a detective." Could he not even form a proper sentence?

Kim looked away as if she couldn't bear looking at him. "Uhm, yeah, of course." He saw her swallow visibly.

"Excuse me, please," a man in a fine suit and looking like an attorney heading for the exit suddenly said, his cell phone clutched to his ear.

Manus stepped aside when the doors suddenly swung open, and a police officer dragged in a man. The filthy-looking drunk stumbled on the last step and catapulted forward, slamming into the man in the suit, who was caught unawares. He lost his balance and tumbled backward in Kim's direction. Without thinking, Manus jumped into action, vaulted behind the attorney, and caught him, thus preventing him from crashing into Kim and possibly taking her down with him.

While several police officers came running, alerted by the

commotion, Manus put the attorney back on his feet and turned his head to Kim.

"You okay?"

She nodded.

"Hey, watch your hands, man, that's a new suit," the attorney said, glaring at Manus.

Was the ungrateful idiot talking to him?

"Fuck, you made me drop my phone!" He bent down and picked up his cell phone. "Damn it, the screen is cracked! See what you did."

Anger welled up inside Manus. His hand curled into a fist. So much for being the good Samaritan. He made a step toward the guy he'd just saved from a fall when he felt a hand on his arm.

"Manus?" It was Kim. "Can we talk?"

As if stung by a hornet, he spun his head to her. "Talk?" Fuck, another incomplete sentence.

"Yes. Maybe a drink? If you have time, that is. If you don't, I'd understand. I mean, you must be busy with your cases and—"

"I've got time," he interrupted her before she could withdraw the invitation. He motioned to the door.

"Hey, what about my phone?" the suit called after him.

Manus looked over his shoulder. "You're welcome." Then he followed Kim down the steps.

6

———————

It didn't take long to get to a small wine bar with a happy hour sign outside and plenty of seating inside. After the waiter placed their drinks in front of them—a glass of red wine for Kim and a Scotch for Manus—Manus looked at his companion.

"Did you really wanna talk, or did you just say that to distract me so I wouldn't beat up that ungrateful little shit?"

Kim took a sip from her drink as if she needed a moment to come up with an answer. "He should have thanked you for your help."

Manus took a swig from his whiskey. Just as he'd thought. She'd only wanted to get him out of the police station. But then why hadn't she tried to ditch him on their way to the bar?

"But that's not why I asked you for a drink."

He lifted his eyes to meet her gaze.

"I don't like drinking alone, and today, after what I found out from the detective handling my mother's case, I need a drink."

"What did you find out?" Manus asked even though he already knew. He'd listened to most of the conversation she'd had with Detective Emmerson, standing only a few feet away, cloaked in invisibility.

Kim hesitated for a moment, then took another sip from her glass as if it lent her courage. "You were right. It was a burglar. They found him, dead."

"Dead?"

She nodded as if to herself. "Some lowlife with a long rap sheet. They found the bracelet my mother always wore on him. And her address." She looked down into her lap.

"I'm so sorry."

She lifted her head and looked at him. "I owe you an apology."

It was the last thing he'd expected her to say. "You owe me nothing."

"No, I do. You tried to tell me that my mother's death wasn't the result of something supernatural. And I called you an idiot because of it. That was ungrateful, when all you did was try to help me." She reached for his hand and squeezed it. "I'm sorry."

The warmth of her hand flooded his entire body. Simultaneously, he felt like a jerk. He was the one who should be apologizing to her. He was the one who'd lied to her. "There's no need—"

"I'm normally not such a bitch."

He put his hand over hers. "Please, you weren't. And you had every right to react the way you did. You've been through a lot."

Kim gave him a weak smile. "It's been hard. I haven't even begun to grieve yet. I think I held onto a supernatural explanation for so long because I didn't want to grieve. I didn't want to accept that she's gone, you know?"

"Grief is an important step in getting your life back," Manus said and slowly withdrew his second hand, giving Kim a chance to remove hers, but she continued clutching his.

"My life will never be the same again." She huffed softly. "I was engaged before all this happened."

Somehow, he'd forgotten about that fact, which had been mentioned in her file. "*Was?*"

She took a long gulp, emptying her glass. "Yeah. I drove him away with all that supernatural stuff. He didn't believe any of it and begged me to stop. But I couldn't."

"Surely, now that you know what really happened, you can make another go of the relationship." It was hard to get those words past his lips, but it was the right thing to say. If Kim was back with her fiancé, a man who didn't believe in the supernatural, she had no reason to ever doubt the version of events Manus had cooked up and the police had served her up—even if pushing her back into the arms of another man felt wrong.

"With Todd?" She shook her head. "No. If anything, everything that's happened has prevented me from making the biggest mistake in my life. Mom knew it, too. She knew it better than I did."

"Knew what?"

"That I wasn't crazy about Todd." She lifted her glass toward the bar and caught the waiter's attention. *Another one,* she mouthed, before turning back to Manus. "Don't you think you should be crazy in love with the person you intend to marry? I mean absolutely crazy, no-holds-barred in love and lust, and not just feel comfortable with someone like you feel comfortable in an old sweater?"

The tightness around his heart that he'd felt when Kim had started mentioning her fiancé suddenly eased. Manus smiled. "I certainly wouldn't want to be any woman's old sweater."

Kim chuckled unexpectedly. "You're not sweater material."

Was she flirting with him? He leaned over the small round table. "What are you trying to say?"

Kim's cheeks suddenly flushed.

"Cabernet for the lady," the waiter appearing at that moment said and placed a glass in front of Kim, forcing Manus to shift back again.

"Thanks." Kim seemed to welcome the interruption and reached for the glass as if it were a life raft and she were drowning. She took a drink, then set the glass back on the table and flicked her hair back over her shoulder. "So, what about you? You said you were working on a case?"

Manus shook his head, laughing. "That was so not smooth."

"What was not smooth?"

"You changing the subject."

"I wasn't changing the subject."

"We were talking about old sweaters, and I asked you a question, which you didn't answer. Instead, you're asking me about my job. I'd call that changing the subject, wouldn't you?"

"I thought men liked talking about their jobs." She chuckled. "Or talking in general."

Manus clutched his heart. "Direct hit! I'm wounded."

Kim rolled her eyes and laughed.

It was the first time he'd seen her truly relaxed and carefree, the first time he realized that there was more to her than just external beauty. She had a glow around her that radiated outward. A warmth that came from a fire deep inside her. A heart that was full with love and grief, with compassion and pain. A heart so vulnerable it hurt him just thinking of what he could do to it if he ever allowed himself to do more than just flirt with her. Because that's what they were doing: flirting. And that's where it had to end because he wasn't capable of being more than a fling, a one-night stand. That's all he'd ever been to anybody: a man for one night. A man incapable of allowing himself to love because all love ever got him was pain.

Still, he couldn't get himself to end the evening yet. Hell, it was still Happy Hour, so he ordered another Scotch. Kim needed an evening to relax and have fun, and fuck it, he needed the same. But what he didn't need was get drunk and do something stupid that he'd regret later. So, despite the fact that he liked his Scotch, he drank slowly. Happy Hour turned into evening, and a few bar snacks later, it was time to take Kim home.

From his observations, Manus knew that she'd moved out of her mother's house and back into her condo. The building was in a nice part of town but not pretentious. Manus took Kim's keys to unlock the door to her apartment, then pressed them back into her palm.

"Thank you for the great company," he said, ready to turn on his heel and leave.

A hand on his arm stopped him. "Why don't you come in?" Kim took a step toward him, her body almost brushing his in the narrow doorway. Her lashes fluttered, and her hand moved up his arm.

Manus swallowed hard. "Uhm, Kim, I, uh..."

She put her index finger over his lips, stopping his protest. And, hell, why was he protesting in the first place? His pants were already tight across his crotch, his cock hardening at the thought of what Kim was offering him. A night of sex, of passion. Hadn't he wanted that the first time he'd laid eyes on her in that coffee shop? So why was he hesitating now? Why was he having scruples?

"Manus," she murmured, her head drawing closer. Her lips were red and plump, her cheeks rosy.

He dropped his gaze in order not to have to look at the temptation her mouth represented. It was a mistake he realized too late: the view he got of her cleavage was more than any man with a heartbeat should have to resist. He ripped his eyes from the lovely sight and collided with her gaze. Immediately, he knew it would have been better to keep staring at her breasts because trying to resist being drawn closer by her eyes was harder, much harder. It was a battle he couldn't win.

"Fuck!" Manus cursed. It was the last thing he said before he sank his lips onto hers and kissed her.

There, standing in the doorway to her condo, he pulled her against his body and crushed her lips with his, sliding his tongue between them, finding no resistance. She welcomed him without restraint, pressing her body to his, moving her hands over his back, down to his ass, grabbing him in a way that left no doubt in his mind as to what she wanted from him. Which was exactly what he wanted from her.

He pressed her back against the door, grinding his cock against her soft center. Her moan vibrated against his lips, and her breath engulfed his tongue. He tasted the red wine, and it reminded him of the amount of alcohol she'd had. If she wasn't drunk, then she was at least tipsy. In any case, she wasn't in a state to make a decision. He had to make it for her. Or tomorrow, she would regret what had happened.

Another minute of this, and he wouldn't be able to stop, but he knew he had to, so he ripped his lips from hers.

"I'm sorry." Manus avoided looking at her. "We can't do this."

He felt Kim's stare on him but was already turning.

"I'm sorry," he murmured too low for her to hear because he was already walking away. "I wish I could make love to you."

But it wouldn't do either of them any good.

7

Kim attached the file to the email and pressed send. She was sure her editor wasn't too happy about her being late on yet another article, but she couldn't help it. Besides, what did it matter if her exposé on corruption in the city's utility department ran a day later than anticipated? The online news outlet she'd been working for during the last few months wasn't exactly on the cutting edge of journalism, but the job afforded her more flexibility. Of course, now that her mother's murder was solved, she could try to get a real job with a newspaper or a TV station again—if somebody hired her.

However, today, she didn't really want to have to think too hard. While she didn't have a hangover, she wasn't exactly on top of her game. Just thinking of how the previous evening had ended made her cringe with embarrassment. She'd thrown herself at Manus, a total stranger, and he'd rejected her. She should be glad that he hadn't taken her up on her offer of sex. Instead, she felt embarrassed. She'd acted like a hussy, like a two-bit floozy who slept with anything on two legs.

This wasn't like her at all. Why had she acted that way? Certainly, the wine had lowered her inhibitions, but that wasn't everything. Too much had happened in the last three months, and the knowledge that she wasn't going to see true justice done because her mother's murderer was already dead, had been the last straw. Everything she'd done in the last few months had been for nothing. All it had served was to delay the inevitable: to deal with her mother's estate, to sieve through the memories in her mother's house and feel the grief crashing over her.

Maybe that's why she'd thrown herself at Manus, to delay even further. But she couldn't shirk her responsibilities any longer. It was time to deal with reality. And forget the handsome private investigator once and for all.

When the intercom buzzed, Kim rose from her chair. She wasn't expecting anybody. Maybe a delivery? She walked to the entrance door and pressed the speaker button.

"Yes?"

"Kim, it's Todd."

She took a breath and stalled for a moment. Should she tell him that she was busy? "Yes, Todd?"

"Can I come up for a moment?"

"Uh..."

"It won't take long."

"Okay." Against her better judgment, she pressed the button to open the door to the building.

Moments later, Todd stood at the entrance to her apartment, a hesitant smile on his face. "Hey, mind if I come in?"

Kim stepped aside and let him enter, then closed the door and followed him into the living room. "What's so important that you couldn't call?"

Todd turned to her. "I heard that they found the guy. That it was a burglary after all."

She raised her eyebrows. "I found out only yesterday. How did you —" She stopped herself. "Of course..."

He shrugged. "Too many contacts in the police department. Comes with the territory."

Kim nodded. Working for the district attorney's office did have its perks, such as getting police officers to share information that wasn't public yet. "They connected the guy to Mom's murder. He had her bracelet on him. And her address. But you probably already knew that."

His facial expression confirmed that he did. "I thought I'd come by, see if you wanted to talk or something."

"There was no need to come."

"I thought you might need someone now, since it's all over."

He shifted his weight from one foot to the other while tilting his head to the side, a slow smile playing around his lips. She'd once fallen for that smile, thought it charming and non-threatening. But it wasn't working on her anymore. She knew what was behind it, an attempt to get her to come back to him now that her mother's murder was solved.

"I mean now that you realize you were wrong about all that supernatural stuff, I figured I could—"

"You could do what? Rub it in?"

His smile vanished, defense moving into its place. "No, of course not. You know I'm not like that. I just thought that now that this thing isn't between us anymore, we could mend things. Get back together."

"This thing?" Kim shook her head. "You think that me believing that my mother's murder had a supernatural explanation was the only thing that drove us apart?"

"Well, yeah, of course. I mean... wasn't it?" Todd stared at her, confused.

"If you have to ask that, then you're more clueless than I thought." She sighed. "We weren't meant to be a couple, Todd. We tried, but it didn't work out. Mom always knew it."

He gasped. "What? I thought your mother liked me. Did she turn you against me before she died?"

"No, my mother was too classy to do such a thing! In fact, I think she loved you like a son. She wouldn't have loved anything more than you being part of the family. But she also knew that I didn't love you the way a bride should love her husband-to-be. I'm sorry. You were like a comfortable sweater. And I need more than that."

"A sweater?"

She shook her head. Of course, Todd didn't understand. Manus would have understood. She motioned to the door. "Please leave before we both say hurtful things. I wish you the best. I wish for you to find a woman who truly loves you as much as you'll love her."

Disbelief in his eyes, Todd shook his head and turned. He marched past her and left, slamming the door on the way out.

It was best this way. What woman could truly remain friends with her ex-fiancé after telling him she had never really loved him? Jennifer would probably agree with her.

Kim reached for her cell phone and dialed her best friend's number.

"Hey," Jennifer answered. "Sorry I haven't replied to your text yet. You done with your article?"

"Yep. I've got time to talk now."

"So, they solved the case after all, huh?"

"Yeah." Kim sighed.

"I've just cleared my schedule for the rest of the day."

"You didn't have to do that."

"I know that, but what are friends for? So, what do you want to do now? Get drunk?"

The thought of more alcohol brought back memories of her evening with Manus. "Better not."

"Really? I figured after that kind of news, you'd want to dull your senses a bit."

"I kind of did that last night."

"You drank alone? Why didn't you call me last night? I could have cancelled my date and come over."

"I didn't drink alone."

"Who were you with?"

"Uh..."

A gasp at the other end of the line. "Oh, no, you didn't! You said you weren't getting back with Todd. Did you fall off the wagon? Oh, Kim, why? Why?"

"I wasn't with Todd. Why would you even think that?" she interrupted. "Though he showed up here just now. Somebody at the station told him about the case being solved."

"What did he want?"

"To gloat, probably!" Kim huffed. "And get back together."

"What an idiot. I hope you tossed him out on his ass."

"I did."

"Good for you!"

Jennifer's confirmation felt good. At least one person was on her side. A person who wasn't bringing up the fact that Kim had believed in supernatural forces being involved in her mother's death. She'd been proven wrong—however, she still wasn't sure about the air conditioning and pressure system explanation Manus had given her. Not that it mattered anymore.

"You still there?" Jennifer asked.

"Yeah, sorry. I spaced out."

"So, if you weren't with Todd, who were you drinking with last night?"

"Oh, uh..."

"Come on, if you can't tell me, whom can you tell?"

Jennifer had a point.

"That guy, you know, from the forum. The PI. Manus."

"The hottie you called an idiot?"

She cringed at the recollection of it. "Yeah."

"How did that happen? Did you call him? Did he call you?"

Kim let out a breath. Of course, now Jennifer wanted details. "It's really not that interesting."

"It is for me." Jennifer clicked her tongue. "Come on, spill."

"Fine. But not on the phone. Do you feel like meeting me at my mom's house? I need to start going through stuff there, cleaning out things. You can help me, and we can talk." At least then she wouldn't have to be there on her own. It still gave her the chills to walk into the living room and see the spot where her mother had died so violently.

"Wow, you're really gonna make me work for it this time, aren't you?"

"Gossip isn't cheap."

"Don't I know it? See you in about forty-five minutes?"

"That works."

"Cool."

A click in the line, and Jennifer was gone.

8

———————

"You kissed him, and he rejected you?" Jennifer dropped onto the couch and put her feet up on the coffee table. "What's wrong with that guy? Is he gay? Or impotent?"

"Well, he certainly isn't impotent," Kim replied.

"How do you know that if you didn't sleep with him?"

Kim felt herself blush. If only she hadn't blurted out the first thing that had come to her mind. "Well, you know, he, uh, he was... he had a..."

Jennifer laughed out loud and almost spilled her wine. "He had a hard-on?" She could barely get the words out amidst her laughter.

Kim sank farther back into the cushions of the overstuffed armchair. "Either that, or he was wearing a codpiece."

"A codpiece?" That caused Jennifer to have another laughing attack. "Unless he's a football player, I doubt he'd be wearing a codpiece. Oh, no, hon, I'm sure what you felt was a hard-on. And why not? You're a gorgeous woman."

"Clearly not gorgeous enough, or he wouldn't have rejected my advances." Kim shrugged though the rejection had stung. "Just as well. It's another complication I don't need in my life right now."

Jennifer chuckled. "That's exactly the kind of complication you need. And I would call it a distraction, not a complication."

"Talking about distractions… How about you help me with going through Mom's stuff?" Kim rose and pointed to a stack of folded moving boxes and trash bags. "Old magazines and newspapers, recipes, and whatever go straight in the trash. If you find anything that's worth donating to Goodwill, put it in a box. Anything you're unsure about, just put it on the dining table, and I'll go through it later."

"Yes, slave driver!" Jennifer said and got up.

"You've got your gossip, time to pay up," Kim said, turning to the stairs. On the second step, she stopped and looked back at Jennifer. "Thanks for doing this with me. It's hard, you know."

Jennifer gave her a kind smile. "I know, hon."

Upstairs, Kim went to work, starting in her mother's bedroom. Looking through all the closets, cupboards, and drawers felt like invading her mother's private space. She had to remind herself that she wasn't snooping around, looking for Christmas presents like she'd done as a child, but was instead sifting through her mother's personal effects in order to decide what to keep and what to throw out.

She couldn't keep all of it, as much as she wanted to. The house had to be sold, and her own condo wasn't big enough to hold even a portion of her mother's prized possessions. Much of it would have to be sold at an estate sale. She made a mental note to ask her mother's assistant at the museum where she'd worked whether she knew anybody reputable to take over that arduous task. Kim neither had the stomach nor the eye for it.

She was in the middle of looking through the boxes on the top shelf of the closet when she heard a sound at the door to the bedroom. She turned on the stepstool, careful not to lose her balance.

"Didn't you say that the police showed you your mother's bracelet?" Jennifer asked, walking into the room.

"Yeah, and they kept it in evidence for now. I'll get it back when they've officially closed the case."

Jennifer furrowed her brow. "Well, then I'd like to know what this is." She stretched her hand out, palm open.

Kim stepped down from the stool and walked to Jennifer, her eyes zeroing in on the item in her friend's hand. Her heart started pounding instantly. Instinctively, she reached for it. "That's impossible." It was her mother's bracelet, the very same the detective had shown her only the day before. "Where did you get this?" She lifted her head to stare at her friend.

Jennifer motioned toward downstairs. "I was going through the living room cupboard and dropped that bag of antique marbles your mother loved so much. The bag's fabric ripped, and some of the marbles rolled under the cupboard. So, I got on my hands and knees, and guess what I found behind there, stuck in a crack?" She pointed to the bracelet. "That." She braced her hands at her hips. "I thought the bracelet is a one-of-a-kind."

Kim nodded. "It is. She'd had it made after a drawing she'd seen in one of her antiques books."

"And she never had a second copy made?"

"No. Why would she?"

"In that case, I think we have a problem."

Slowly, Kim nodded. She knew exactly what Jennifer was thinking. "The police lied to me. They didn't find my mother's bracelet on that dead guy. They planted a replica on him."

Jennifer nodded fiercely. "And I can guess why."

"To close the case. They figured I'd never stop asking questions, so to get me off their backs, they made it look like they solved the case."

"Probably helps their stats too. Another murder case solved and off their desks."

Fury rose in Kim. "Now there'll never be justice." Tears started welling up in her eyes. "I have to do something. I have to prove that the police are corrupt and that my mother's murderer is still out there."

"I agree. You can't let them get away with that. Call Todd. He'll know what to do."

"I can't."

"Why not? Because of what you said to him this morning? Pfff!" Jennifer made a dismissive hand movement. "This is bigger than your pride. Or his. This is police corruption. Just sell it to him that this will be his big break-out case. Something that'll make him attorney general of Maryland one day. He's ambitious. He'll go for it."

Kim shook her head once more. "That's not it. I can't trust him. What if he's in on it? What if he's part of the corruption? Don't you think it's kind of convenient that he showed up at my place the day after Detective Emmerson presented me with news about my mother's murderer?"

"You said yourself he's got all these contacts in the police department, and that's how he knew."

"Yes, but what if he's the one who set all this up?"

"What's in it for him?" Jennifer asked skeptically.

"He wants to get back together. And what was standing between us was my mother's unsolved murder. Or so he thought until this morning. He must have thought that once it's all behind me, and I give up believing in a paranormal explanation of it, I'll take him back."

Jennifer dropped on the edge of the bed. "Oh my God, what a sleazebag!" She sighed deeply. "You can't let him get away with that. You have to do something. Tell somebody."

Kim ran both hands through her hair. "But whom? I can't go to the police. I can't go to the district attorney's office. I doubt a reputable newspaper is going to go for the story unless I have concrete proof, more sources and—"

"The PI!" Jennifer shot up from the bed. "You have to call Manus. He's a private investigator. He'll check into it for you. He'll find evidence that Todd conspired with his friends at the police department to trick you into believing that this poor dead guy was your mother's murderer. He'll help you."

Kim cringed. "Manus? I'm not sure. I think it'll be awkward."

Jennifer rolled her eyes. "Awkward? Do you want to get justice or not? Don't let a little awkwardness stop you."

"But what if he doesn't want to help me?"

Jennifer reached for the phone on the nightstand. "There's only one way to find out."

9

Manus didn't recognize the number, but it was local, so he answered his phone amidst the ruckus in the compound's kitchen, were Leila, Aiden's wife, was cooking dinner, and their twins, five-year-old Julia and Xander, were playing chase with their father. In the attached living area, Logan and Hamish were watching sports on the oversized TV that hung on the wall, and Enya, the only female Stealth Guardian in their compound, was wearing headphones while trying to read.

"Yes?"

Manus couldn't hear the other person's reply, so he said, "Hold on, can't hear you." He walked to the door and opened it. In the corridor, where it was quieter, he said, "Hello?"

"Manus. This is Kim Britton."

She wouldn't have had to say her name. He'd recognized her voice immediately. He hadn't expected her to call him. Not after the way he'd left things the night before. He'd kissed her as if he'd wanted to devour her—because he did—and then discarded her like a used toy he didn't want to play with anymore. What woman in her right mind would call a man who'd treated her like that?

"Manus, can you hear me? Do you need me to speak up?"

"No, yes, yes, I can hear you now. Sorry, bad reception and lots of background noise." Stalling, that's what he was doing.

"Listen, there's something I need to talk to you about..."

There it went. She wanted to know why he'd left so abruptly, why he hadn't taken her up on her offer of sex. Shit! He hated conversations like that. And she probably knew that he wouldn't have answered his phone had she called from her cell phone, a number he would have recognized. He had to hand it to her: she was smart to use a different phone. Now he was on the hook.

"Uh, Kim, I'm not sure... What happened last night..." How could he make it clear to her that there couldn't be anything between them, that despite the initial spark, whatever they tried would fail miserably? So why even go through it? Why start something that he knew was doomed to failure?

"Last night?" Kim's voice sounded as if she didn't know what he was referring to. "This isn't about last night. This is about the bracelet. My mom's bracelet."

"What about it?"

"I don't want to talk on the phone. Can you come by my mother's house? I need your help."

"Uh, yeah, sure. But why don't you want to tell me on the phone?"

"I can't be sure that the phone isn't being tapped."

He lifted an eyebrow. "Okay. What's the address?" he asked even though he knew it already.

After Kim gave him the street name and number, he said, "I'll be there in about an hour."

He disconnected the phone and shoved it in his front pocket. "Fuck!" Something was wrong.

From the other end of the corridor, Pearce approached. "Problem?"

"Hmm."

"Not in the sharing mood?"

Manus tilted his head to the side. "Nothing to share. Yet." He turned on his heel. "I've gotta go out for a few hours. Tell Leila to keep some food in the fridge for me."

"Will do, but I can't guarantee there'll be any leftovers. We have a full house tonight."

Manus was already at the end of the corridor. "Whatever." Depending on what issues Kim had about her mother's bracelet, he wasn't even sure he'd come back with an appetite.

Less than an hour later, Manus reached Nancy Britton's house and parked in front of it. Kim greeted him at the door, looked to the right and left, then waved him into the house and closed the entrance door behind him.

"So, what's going on?" Manus asked immediately.

"I told you that the police showed me a bracelet they found on that dead guy. Only, it's not my mother's bracelet. It's a fake."

Fuck!

This was the last thing he'd expected her to say.

Crap!

How had she found out? He'd covered his tracks expertly. Nobody apart from the two hybrids knew that he'd been the one planting the fake bracelet on the dead guy. It was impossible that she knew.

"A fake?" Manus echoed. "How would you—"

"I found the real one while I was cleaning out the house." She motioned him to follow her into the living room and pointed to a cupboard along the wall. "It had slipped underneath it. Maybe she lost it during the struggle. Or maybe she lost it even earlier. I don't know. But I'm telling you that the bracelet the police showed me wasn't my mother's."

Shit! After all the work he'd done on this case, the problem was still not taken care of. "So, the one the police have didn't look like your mother's after all?" he hedged.

"No, no, it did. It was an exact replica."

She walked to a sideboard and picked something up, then turned back to him and showed it to him. Manus recognized it immediately: the bracelet. "I was fooled, Manus. Completely fooled. The police lied to me. They planted an identical bracelet on that dead guy to make me believe that he killed my mother."

She was right about one thing: the bracelet had been planted, just not by the police. "Are you sure it's not just some mistake?"

"Mistake?" She tossed him a skeptical look.

"Yes. Maybe the guy had an identical bracelet to your mother's, and the police thought it was the same. Doesn't mean they planted it on him."

Kim shook her head. "It's a custom piece, a one-of-a-kind. They went through a whole lot of trouble to make me believe that my mother's murder is solved. And that tells me that there's something else behind it. I have my suspicions. I think my ex-fiancé is behind this."

"Your ex? Are you saying you believe he killed your mother?"

"No, of course not. But we broke up after Mom's death. He didn't believe my supernatural theory, and as a result, we fought all the time. I think he thought if my mother's murder was finally solved, we would get back together."

Clearly, Kim had quite an imagination. But he didn't like to send her down a path that only made things worse and more confusing. "But how would he even have done it?"

"He works at the district attorney's office. He's got lots of connections in the police force. It wouldn't have been too hard for him to stage this."

"Hmm."

For a moment, Manus wondered whether he could use Kim's new theory to his advantage, but he knew it wouldn't help for long. Even if he could finagle it so it looked like her fiancé had been the one planting the bracelet to close the case, it meant the case was in fact still open, and justice hadn't been served. Kim would continue to pursue her own investigations and probably return to her supernatural theory. They would be back at square one.

No, he couldn't let her do this. He had to be the one directing where she kept digging for information. And the only way he could do that was if he pretended to help her.

"So, you want me to help you figure out what's really going on?" Manus asked.

Kim nodded, a ray of hope illuminating her face now. "Yes. I need your help. I can't go to the police. They are obviously corrupt, and Todd has his own agenda. My mother's murderer is still out there."

"I understand."

Unexpectedly, she clutched his arm. "Oh my God, I was just thinking: what if the air conditioning expert and the meteorologist you talked to about the vortex were corrupt too? What if they were in bed with the police and made up that story so that you wouldn't investigate any further in that case you told me about?"

Ah shit! He had his work cut out for himself. "I don't know, Kim. They were pretty credible people. Besides, the murderer in that case was found. I'm inclined to believe the explanation of how that vortex came to be."

Kim slowly shook her head. "I think we were both fooled. Please keep an open mind. There is more to this than we both think. Something about my mother's murder is off. I mean, she had no enemies, and nothing was stolen. It just doesn't make sense."

Manus remembered something from the police report. "You're sure nothing was stolen? But was anything disturbed?" He waited for the answer he already knew.

"Well, disturbed, yes. A few drawers were open and had been rifled through, but nothing was missing."

"Nothing that you know of," Manus qualified, suddenly having a thought.

After all, why would a demon come to an emissarius's house, rifle through her stuff, and then kill her when he was disturbed? What if he'd been looking for something? Had he found what he'd been looking for?

"What do you mean?"

"I mean, what if somebody was looking for something in your

mother's possession? Didn't she work in a museum and was handling pretty expensive things? Did she ever take anything home?"

Kim immediately shook her head. "Never. It wasn't safe. Besides, all employees are searched before they leave the museum, so they can't smuggle anything out."

But what if she'd managed to do just that? What if Nancy Britton had found something in the museum that was of interest to the demons? It wasn't an angle the Stealth Guardians had thoroughly investigated yet, partially because they lacked manpower, partially because the chances of Nancy not having brought anything of interest to the Stealth Guardians' attention immediately were slim. She'd been a dependable informant.

10

K im noticed that Manus had gone silent. His impenetrable expression didn't give her any clues as to what he was thinking. Seconds ticked by, and she couldn't stand the silence any longer.

"Will you help me find out what really happened?"

She pinned him with her eyes and didn't have to wait long for a reply.

He nodded. "I can't promise you that we'll ever find out what all this is about, but I'm willing to try."

"I understand that. Now, to the money."

"Excuse me?"

"Your fee. I can—"

He lifted his hand, stopping her. "This will be pro bono."

"But I can't accept that."

"You'll have to."

"But you have to make a living. We all do. And that's your job: investigating things."

"Let me worry about that. This case intrigues me. And if the police really covered this up and there's something to your supernatural theory, then it's possible that they did the same in my previous case. In which case, my former clients will want me to look into this anyway."

Though she wasn't comfortable with Manus working for her for free, she said, "If you insist..."

"I do." He let out a breath. "I should probably talk to some people at the museum. Maybe they can tell me what your mother was working on before her death. It might give us some leads."

Kim nodded. "I can introduce you to her colleagues. They'll talk to you if I come with you." She looked at the clock to see if the staff at the museum would still be working when there was a loud knock at the door.

Surprised, she looked toward the door. Had Jennifer forgotten something when she'd left just before Manus had arrived? "Excuse me for a moment."

She walked to the door and opened it. Mrs. Fogarty, one of her mother's neighbors, stood on the stoop, holding a few letters in her hand.

"Oh, Mrs. Fogarty, is something the matter?" Her mother had always been on friendly terms with the older lady, and they had on occasion watered each other's plants when the other was out of town.

"Good afternoon, Kim. I thought I saw you arrive earlier, so I figured I'd quickly come over and bring you these." She pressed the envelopes into Kim's hand. "That new mailman keeps mixing your mother's mail in with mine. I meant to bring it over last week, but then my gout was playing up, and I couldn't get out of my chair. And you haven't been here much."

"Thank you, Mrs. Fogarty. No, I've not been here much. But I've just started clearing out the house to get it ready to sell."

The woman gave a sad smile. "Such a shame. Your mother was such a good neighbor. Why don't you move in yourself?"

Kim shrugged, not really in the mood to continue the conversation, but she didn't want to be rude to Mrs. Fogarty. The woman had always been nice to her mother. "Too many memories." In particular the one of finding her mother dead on the floor. There was no way she could ever live here again.

To her surprise, Mrs. Fogarty put her hand on Kim's forearm. "I understand." Then she looked past Kim into the house. "Well, at least you've got a young man here to help you with the task. Is that your fiancé?"

Kim looked over her shoulder and saw that Manus had followed her and stood in the archway to the living room. "No, no, just a friend."

"Well, I won't keep you any longer then," Mrs. Fogarty said.

"Thank you, Mrs. Fogarty." Kim lifted her hand as a goodbye and waited until the older lady had turned and was walking away before closing the door.

As she turned, she looked down at the two letters Mrs. Fogarty had given her. One was a solicitation to take out life insurance and clearly of no use anymore. The other letter didn't look like a mass mailing. Kim read the sender's name.

"ABC Storage Facility," she murmured.

"What's that?" Manus asked.

Kim pointed to the letter. "Something from a storage facility on the outskirts of town. It says *overdue* here." Possibly a clever ploy by a business to get somebody to sign up for something.

"A storage facility?" Manus stepped closer. "Did your mother use one?"

"Not that I know of."

"Open it."

Kim ripped the envelope open and pulled out the single sheet. "It's an account statement. Annual fee overdue," she read the heading. "If we don't receive your payment within thirty days of the date of this letter, the contents of your rented storage unit #136 will be auctioned off."

Manus reached for the letter and scanned it. "That letter is four weeks old." Their eyes met. "We'd better check this out before whatever your mother stored there is gone forever."

"I agree," Kim said and reached for her handbag. Then she stopped herself. "How are we gonna get a look inside? I mean, I haven't found a key for it."

"Don't worry. Just take this letter, a copy of your mother's death certificate, and your ID with you, and the staff there will have to unlock for us."

"Smart thinking." She was glad she had somebody by her side who did this for a living and kept a cool head. "I'm just surprised that Mom never mentioned a storage unit to me. I can't imagine what she would be storing there."

"We'll find out soon enough," Manus said confidently. "We'll take my car. I'm parked right outside."

"Great. Give me a minute to grab what we need."

MOMENTS LATER, Manus was pulling away from the curb with Kim sitting in the passenger seat of his car. He'd punched the coordinates for the storage facility into the navigation system and followed the directions. It meant he could concentrate on Kim. He didn't want to accidentally say something he didn't want her to know, so he had to keep his guard up. Forty-five minutes in the car together was a long time. A lot of things could slip out if he wasn't careful.

"So, you started packing up your mother's house, I noticed," Manus started, wanting to keep the conversation away from the investigation itself. "You told your neighbor you're planning on selling it. It's a shame. It's got a lot of character."

Kim nodded. "It does. I wish I didn't have to pack it all up. I don't even know where to start. My mother kept a lot of stuff."

"Did you grow up in that house?"

"Not really. I was already fourteen when Mom and I moved there."

"And your dad?"

She cast him a long sideways look. "I don't have a father."

He met her gaze. "So, you don't get on."

She shook her long dark locks. "No, I don't have one. Mom was a single mother. My biological father was a guy she had a one-night stand with. She didn't even know his last name."

"Oh."

Kim shrugged. "I didn't judge her for it. I didn't miss having a father. Though right now, it would help to have one, you know, to share the grief."

He understood that need. "It's hard going through it on your own."

"And you? You mentioned you lost a parent too?"

Manus gripped the steering wheel tighter. "I lost both of them on the same day."

"Oh no! I'm so sorry." She let out a soft breath. "Was it a car accident?"

"House fire." It was a lie. It wasn't the fire that had killed them, nor the massive explosion that had ripped apart their home. Still, it was the only explanation he could give her. Telling her the truth would mean exposing his people's secrets. "It was an inferno. It was the most terrible thing I've ever had to watch." He let out a bitter chuckle. "Guess at least I didn't have to go through all their belongings to decide what to keep."

"The house burned to the ground?" Kim asked, her voice filled with sadness.

"Down to the foundation."

"And you were there when it happened?"

"I got there too late. I couldn't get them out..." He pushed back the memory of the flames burning away his shirt, the heat entering his nostrils, the smoke obscuring his vision.

"I'm so sorry, Manus. I feel really selfish now."

He turned his head. "Selfish, why?"

"Because I'm complaining about how much work it is to pack up my mother's house when you never got the chance to go through your parents' belongings and save those things that have a special meaning for you."

"They're just things," Manus said, surprised at how understanding Kim was, and how willing he was to share things with her he'd never shared with any of his fellow Stealth

Guardians. "I still have my memories of them. No fire can destroy those."

For a moment they locked eyes, silent in their shared grief.

"They are worth more than anything in the world," she murmured softly. "I hope they'll never fade. That you'll always remember them happy and full of love for you."

Manus smiled. "I hope you can do the same."

11

A half hour later, arrived at the storage facility on the outskirts of town, Manus let Kim deal with the facility's employee to gain access to her mother's unit.

"I don't think anybody notified us that Mrs. Britton passed," the bored college-age man with the nametag that identified him as Brian said. He shrugged. "Maybe the manager knew, but Mr. Songhurst isn't here today."

"I didn't realize she kept a unit here," Kim said. "Do you know when she was last here?"

Brian shook his head. "The units are self-serve; the renters have their own keys. We don't keep tabs on their comings and goings. Maybe the manager knows. But as I said…"

"…he's not here. I guess we'd better check out what's in the unit then."

"You'll still have to pay the overdue fee."

Kim reached into her handbag and pulled out her wallet. "Do you take credit card?"

Brian nodded, and Kim handed him her card. While he processed the transaction, he said, "This will give you until the end of next month to clear out everything that's in there. After that, we'll have to re-rent it."

"I understand," Kim replied. "That'll be enough time, won't it?"

Manus nodded. "Well, let's see what she kept in there." Maybe the storage unit would provide clues as to why a demon had killed her.

"Oh, and the office closes in half an hour. Please drop the key back in the lockbox outside the office before you leave, since that's the office's key," Brian added.

"Will do," Kim promised.

"Oh, and if you can't find your mother's key, we're going to have to keep the key deposit," he added.

Key in hand, Kim walked next to Manus, following the directions the kid had provided. By Manus's estimate, the lot held approximately four hundred storage units. They looked like garages with wide walkways in between the rows so a van could drive up to each unit to load and unload. The property was surrounded by mature trees and bushes.

Kim's mother's unit was an end-unit in the third row. Kim stopped in front of it and turned to Manus. "I can't imagine why she didn't tell me about this."

"Maybe she didn't think it was important."

"What if she was hiding this from me on purpose?"

"Why would she do that?" Manus asked. "I thought you two were close."

"We were. But what if there was something in her life she didn't want me to know about? What if she had a secret?"

Kim had no idea how close to the truth she was getting. Manus put his hand on her forearm to calm and comfort her. He regretted it immediately. Touching her, even in this platonic fashion, brought back memories of the kiss from the night before. Of the way he'd pressed her body to his, of the way he'd reacted to her. He wanted to tell her why he'd stopped so abruptly, but what good would it do? He could never tell her the truth about himself, about who he was, about what her mother had done for his race and who'd killed her. And if he couldn't tell her the truth, then he didn't deserve what he was craving.

"Don't speculate. You're just driving yourself crazy." He let go of her arm and motioned to the lock. "Let's get this over with."

Finally, Kim unlocked the padlock and removed it from the door. Manus reached for the handle and rolled the wide steel door up toward the low ceiling of the unit. Several shelving units with banker's boxes lined one side, furniture was stacked up against the back wall, a stack of paintings and an antique-looking mirror were leaned against the other wall, and more boxes and smaller items were littering the center of the unit.

"Grandma's rocker," Kim exclaimed and pointed to a wooden rocking chair covered in dust. "I thought she'd sold it after Grandma's death." She walked toward it, then veered toward the left. "And that mirror is from Grandma's house too." She looked over her shoulder. "When Grandma died, Mom cleaned out her house. She said she didn't want to keep any of Grandma's things."

"Why not?"

"They had a difficult relationship. They fought a lot. I assume it was because Mom was a single mother, and my grandmother was very conservative, staunchly Catholic and all. You know, the whole no-sex-before-marriage thing. Guess Mom didn't have the heart to get rid of Grandma's favorite things after all and wanted to look at them occasionally to remind herself of her."

Manus shook his head. "My guess is she was keeping your grandmother's things for you."

For an instant, Kim fell silent. A wet sheen drew over her eyes, and she sniffled. "She knew how much I loved her. No matter how much the two fought, Grandma loved me unconditionally, and I her." Kim sighed. "Oh, Mom, if you can hear me, thank you."

Manus looked away and moved toward the banker's boxes, feeling himself get nostalgic and wanting to squash the feeling. "I wonder what's in those boxes."

Kim cleared her throat and sniffled once more, then said, "Let's look."

"I'll start at this end," Manus said and pointed to the far corner of the unit.

"Looks too dark back there," Kim said. "Let me see if there's a light switch."

A moment later, a neon light attached to the ceiling illuminated the unit. Manus glanced up. This was a good sign. No demon had been here yet, otherwise the neon light would have burned out as it always did in the presence of a demon. While the demons didn't have an aura by which to identify them, something about their presence reacted with mercury and neon, both ingredients in fluorescent and neon light tubes used in many industrial buildings. Flickering and burned-out neon lights had saved many a Stealth Guardian's hide.

"Thanks."

"I'll start up front. What are we looking for?" Kim asked.

"Anything a thief might have found valuable." By thief he meant demon, but of course Manus couldn't voice that thought. It meant letting Kim in on a secret few were privy to.

Manus lifted the first box off the shelf and opened the lid. It was filled with old files, too many to go through in detail. He leafed through them. They were mostly old tax files and receipts. He closed the box again and opened the next one. It was heavier and contained old books. Some appeared to be first editions. Manus knew that Nancy had been an avid collector of antiques and anything old, and first editions certainly seemed to fit the bill. But could any of these books be valuable to a demon? Since he couldn't inspect each and every one more closely while he was with Kim, it was best to call in reinforcements.

Manus looked over his shoulder and noticed that Kim was going through a box containing photos. Perfect. She would be occupied for a while. He turned his back to her and pulled his cell phone from his pocket, set it to silent, and typed a quick message to Enya. He pressed send and received a positive reply just moments later. Satisfied, he slipped the phone back into his pocket and glanced over his shoulder. Kim was still going through the box of pictures.

Manus went through more of the boxes. One contained antique dolls, another was filled with tin soldiers and other metal items, a third contained manuscripts and playbills. It appeared that Nancy hated throwing anything out. The next row proved to be more fruitful. One box contained artifacts that appeared to be genuine though he couldn't be sure. He rummaged through the box, lifting figurine after figurine out of it.

Had Nancy stolen items from the museum with the intent of reselling them later? Had she not been as honest a person as everybody assumed? Had she maybe even dealt with the demons, supplying them with artifacts they were looking for? He had to consider this possibility. What if Nancy had been a double agent? It was something he had to bring up with his colleagues. But he couldn't voice that suspicion to Kim. Just the idea that her mother could have stolen items from the museum would crush her. The possibility that she could sell them to the evilest creatures that existed would destroy her faith in humanity.

Making sure Kim hadn't seen the items, he packed them back into the box and closed the lid. "Are you finding anything?"

Kim turned her head toward him. "Old photos. Lots of them. But nothing a thief could want. And you?"

"Old tax records, bills, a doll collection, but nothing that looks valuable enough to warrant—" He stopped himself. It wasn't necessary to mention her mother's death again. "Nothing of real value." He glanced outside, where it had gotten dark. "It's getting late. Let's see if we can go through the rest of the boxes."

For over an hour, they continued searching the boxes, but nothing stuck out as important. Manus was glad when Kim started to yawn.

"Shall we call it a night?" Manus asked.

Kim rose and brushed the dust off her pants, and Manus couldn't stop his eyes from roaming over her slender legs. He could think of a lot of things he wanted her to do with those legs, all highly inappropriate yet deliciously tempting. If only they'd met under other circumstances. Then he could at least take her to bed for one night of passion.

"I think I'll come back tomorrow during the day," Kim said.

Manus swallowed away his sinful thoughts, hoping they weren't reflected on his face. "Good idea. I'll drive you home." Though it would be safer if he got her a taxi.

"Thank you. I appreciate all your help." She glanced around the unit once more. "I wish I knew what we're looking for."

"I'm sure if it's here, we'll find it." Whatever it was. "And if it isn't, then we'll follow other leads. I still think we should talk to your mother's colleagues at the museum."

It would give him an opportunity to figure out if there was any way Nancy could have stolen anything from the museum that subsequently got her killed. It was his best guess.

12

Zoltan slid farther behind the bush and peeked through the branches, making sure he didn't lose sight of the two people who were now closing up the storage unit. He'd struck gold: Kim Britton, whom his underlings had been surveying for the past three months, was accompanied by a Stealth Guardian warrior. What an extraordinary stroke of luck!

The moment his scout had notified him that a Stealth Guardian was visiting Kim at her mother's house, Zoltan had made his way to the human world and taken over surveillance himself. He didn't want his idiotic subject to screw anything up for him because the presence of a Stealth Guardian confirmed that his intuition had been right. The Stealth Guardians were looking for the same thing he was looking for.

He'd followed the Stealth Guardian and Kim, and they'd led him to a storage unit that nobody had been aware of previously. He'd watched them rummage through the contents of the unit and even listened to snippets of their conversation. Luckily, they didn't know what they were looking for, and they were leaving empty-handed.

Zoltan already congratulated himself. He just had to be patient and wait until the two were gone, then break into the unit and retrieve the one thing that would finally reveal all of the Stealth Guardians' secrets and thus deliver victory to him and his demons. He was so giddy he could barely contain his excitement. In a few minutes, he'd hold the key to his triumph in his hands.

Nobody would doubt him then. Nobody would question his leadership then. He wasn't blind. He knew what was going on behind his back. Somebody was vying for his throne. Somebody was sowing discontent amongst his demons, planting doubts as to whether Zoltan could truly lead the demons to victory and subjugate the human population.

He wasn't sure how long he would be able to keep his demons in line with threats and fear. What he needed was a victory, one that would not only squash the Stealth Guardians but also wipe out his unknown rival. Despite his best efforts, he'd still not found the traitor though he had his suspicions.

When he heard Kim and her Stealth Guardian companion drive away, Zoltan waited for another thirty seconds before readying himself to come out of his hiding place. But before he could make a single step, he froze in place. He wasn't the only one intent on exploring the storage unit.

A woman suddenly appeared out of nowhere and stopped in front of the locked unit. Her sudden appearance wasn't the only thing that identified her as a Stealth Guardian. Her aura, something only preternatural creatures could perceive, gave her away too. Not that he would have needed either clue to identify her. He knew who she was. He'd seen her before though she'd never laid eyes on him.

Enya, one of the Stealth Guardians assigned to Baltimore.

She wasn't the kind of woman one would ever forget. There were beautiful women, even beautiful demon females, and then there was Enya, a woman who had it all: beauty, sex appeal, power. He'd never watched a woman fight like her. Never seen a woman so wild, so ferocious, so savage. If he didn't know any better, he'd say she was a demon. She exhibited all the qualities he wanted in a demon mate, yet she was on the wrong side.

If he were a poet, he'd say she was the Juliet to his Romeo, but he wasn't a poet. He was a demon. The leader of the Underworld. The Great One. And as such, he desired a demon mate, a woman who would bear his demon children to populate the world once he'd overthrown it.

From his hiding place, he ran his eyes over her body. She was petite, and he was sure that many a demon warrior underestimated her because of her size. Zoltan wouldn't make that mistake. She was as good if not a better fighter than her male brethren. But his thoughts weren't with her fighting skills right now. He was more interested in bathing his eyes in the sexy sight she was.

Enya wore a tight black bustier that accentuated her small but shapely breasts. Her hips were slim, her waist slimmer. Her toned legs were encased in leather pants, her ass filling out the garment like she'd been sewn into it. If only he could get his hands on that ass and peel her out of that leather, bend her over the nearest flat surface, and sink his rock-hard cock into her, he'd find true satisfaction. Of course, she'd fight him because he was a demon, but that would only add to his pleasure. He'd hold her down, loosen the thick braids of her golden hair, and ride her until she submitted to him. Yes, one day, when he'd destroyed the guardians, he'd make her his slave.

But not tonight. He couldn't risk bungling this. It would take too long to get backup from his demons, and fighting her on his own might not have the desired outcome. After all, he couldn't be sure that she was the only Stealth Guardian here. For all he knew, one of her brethren was with her and had remained invisible to watch her back.

It irked him to have to content himself with watching Enya pass through the steel door into the storage unit as if passing through air. He hated the fact that demons didn't have that skill. However, he remained quiet in his hiding place, listening and watching. He wouldn't do anything to her unless she reemerged with the object of his desire. Only then, he would attack her and have to find out if she was truly alone, or if she'd brought backup. He hoped it wouldn't come to that and, just like her colleague from earlier, she would leave empty-handed.

13

This was the second time in as many nights that Kim stood at the entrance door to her condo, Manus by her side. However, this time she wouldn't make the mistake of inviting him in. Not because she wasn't attracted to him, but because she didn't want to deal with another rejection. To Manus's credit, he hadn't brought up the debacle from the night before, and she was grateful for it. They could both pretend that the kiss had never happened.

When Manus pushed the door inward and removed the key from the lock, she awkwardly reached for her keychain, but Manus moved, causing her to brush up against his fingers instead. She froze in mid-motion and snapped her head up to catch his look.

"Uh..." she uttered, trying to apologize, but her throat was as dry as a desert.

Manus pinned her with his eyes, and she realized in an instant that she'd caught him in an unguarded moment. Naked desire turned his eyes molten. Her heart began to pound out of control, her breath caught in her lungs, and heat shot into her cheeks.

"Kim, I..." he started, but his voice died.

She tried to move, take a step away from him, but her body didn't listen to her commands. She opened her lips to tell him to leave, but only one word came out. "Manus..."

At the sound of his name, he pressed the keys into her palm. "You should send me away," he murmured without conviction in his voice. "I don't do relationships. I can't. All I can give you is sex. And I doubt you'd be satisfied with that."

So that was why he hadn't taken her up on her offer the night before. He was a commitment phobic, and he feared that she would demand more than just sex. But she wouldn't let him get out of this situation so easily. Last night, she'd felt rejected; tonight, she needed to make up for it.

Collecting all her courage, she said lightly, "So you're saying the sex won't be satisfying?"

His jaw tightened, and his eyes narrowed at the same time. "That's not at all what I said! The sex will be more than just satisfying. For both of us. I'll guarantee it. It'll be out of this world, no-holds-barred, headboard-pounding, chandelier-swinging, mind-blowing, begging-me-not-to-stop amazing."

Her lips quirked at his over-the-top description. Clearly, she'd hit a nerve by suggesting that he might not be up to the task to satisfy her.

"What? You don't believe me?" Outrage colored his face now, and he moved even closer.

Kim shrugged. "The proof is in the pudding." What had made her so brazen? When exactly had she decided to seduce him? Because that's what she was doing.

Manus slid his hand to her nape and pulled her face to him. "Are you daring me to prove it to you?"

"Maybe not where the neighbors can watch, but..." She turned her eyes in the direction of the interior of her condo.

∽

MANUS SLUNG his free arm around Kim's waist and pulled her to him. "Oh, I'm all for privacy." He wanted no audience to the things he planned to do with her. Certain things were just not meant for sharing.

He backed her into the apartment and kicked the door behind him. As soon as it clicked shut, he sank his lips onto Kim's mouth and kissed her.

He'd wanted to do this since the very first moment he'd seen her in that coffeeshop. He'd expected the kiss to be hot. After all, what kiss with a beautiful woman such as Kim wouldn't be hot? What he hadn't expected was the explosive effect Kim's lips had on him. A flame of lust shot through his center, and his cock went from semi-erect to rock-hard in one point three seconds flat. A new world record even for him.

Kim's response to his kiss was immediate. She pressed her body to his, molding her chest to his hard muscles, letting him feel her softness. He didn't ignore the invitation and moved his hand up until he could stroke the side of her breast with his thumb.

He felt her gasp and stilled for a brief second, half expecting her to change her mind about sleeping with him now that she realized that he wasn't going to take it slow or pretend he was a gentleman. He'd been here before with other women. They'd expected a slow seduction, and when he'd gone right down to business, they'd shied away, and he'd let them go.

Manus released Kim's lips.

"Why are you stopping?" she asked, tossing him a confused look. "Don't tell me you're bailing again." Her jaw tightened, her eyebrows pulled together, her hands curled into fists. "Goddamn it! If you run out on me now, I swear—"

He captured her lips in mid-sentence, kissing her harder this time, his head tilted to the side for better access. With his tongue, he explored her, tasted her, played with her. At the same time, he slid his hands down to her ass and yanked her against his groin. With a groan, he rubbed his hard-on against her, making it clear to her that he wasn't going to go anywhere until they'd both had what they wanted.

It seemed to work because now Kim put his arms around him. She slid one hand to his nape and caressed his exposed skin with her tender fingers, making him shiver and sending another bolt of fire into his cock. Her other hand she put to good use too, placing it on his ass and grabbing him possessively. He didn't mind. When it came to sex, he liked his women possessive. What was good for the goose was good for the gander. Outside of bed, of course, it was a different matter. But then, he was getting ahead of himself. All this would be was sex. So, her possessive grip was fine by him.

The longer he kissed her, the hotter he got. And he wasn't the only one. Under his hands, he could feel Kim's body heating up too. He knew just what to do about that. Shifting slightly, he got to work on the buttons of her shirt. One by one he popped them open, encountering no protest from Kim. On the contrary, she seemed to like the idea and helped him. Taking his lips off Kim's for an instant, Manus pulled the shirt down her shoulders and stripped her of it, revealing her black lace bra.

Fuck, he hadn't expected something that sexy under her casual clothes. But he wasn't complaining.

Instead of capturing her mouth again, he dropped his head to her cleavage and pressed a kiss to the soft indentation. "Damn it, you're hot," he murmured and looked up at her face, meeting her gaze. Passion shone from her eyes. "I can't guarantee that the first time will last long. But I'll promise you that I'll be ready for a second time only a few minutes later. And then I'll last as long as you want me to."

"You'd better," she said and ran her hand through his hair and down his nape, making him shiver once more.

Eager to explore her, Manus brought his hands behind Kim's back and opened the clasp of her bra, then slid down the straps and freed her from the garment. Quickly, he cupped her breasts, fitting them perfectly into his palms. A soft moan rolled over Kim's lips. Impatiently, he licked over one nipple, sucking the little bud between his lips to taste it. Then he let it pop from his mouth and did the same to the other nipple. Kim's breasts weren't big, but they were perfectly shaped and firm. He sank his face between them, drinking in her scent.

He'd always loved the scent of a woman right there. It made him crave more. Just like he wanted more from Kim now.

His hands were already on her pants when he felt Kim's hands tug on the seam of his shirt, pulling it from his pants. He stopped her by grabbing her hands and backing her against the wall. "First you."

Quickly, he opened the button of her khaki pants and pulled the zipper down. Kim helped him and shimmied out of them while kicking off her shoes. Manus dropped down, helped her with her socks, then rose. He slid his hand into her panties and gently rubbed his fingers along her cleft. Warmth and wetness greeted him. Before she could stop him, he pulled her panties down and rid her of them. Then he pressed her against the wall again, kissing her deeply.

"I can't wait any longer," he said while he was already opening his pants. He pushed them down, then did the same with his boxer briefs. His cock sprang free, hard and heavy.

Kim tugged at his shirt, but he couldn't let her do it. He had to be inside her, take her right now, before she saw all of him, before she saw what he so desperately wanted to hide from her. Because if she did, she might reject him.

Before Kim could open any of the buttons on his shirt, he sank his lips back on hers and was already hooking his arms around her thighs, lifting her and spreading her open at the same time. Pressed against the wall at her back, she couldn't move. He stepped between her thighs and brought his cock to her center. When his cockhead touched her wet outer lips, he groaned. This would be better than anything he'd felt in a long time. He pushed forward and upward, parting her nether lips, thrusting into her and allowing her interior muscles to grip him tightly.

"Fuck!" he hissed.

Kim moaned against his lips. "Oh!"

He took her reaction as encouragement and confirmation that she wanted what he had to offer and withdrew his cock halfway. Then slowly and much gentler than before, he thrust back in, enjoying the way her tight pussy clamped around his cock.

Manus continued pinning her against the wall, his superior supernatural strength making the task easy, while he rocked back and forth inside her. He lifted his lips from hers for a moment and looked into her eyes. He saw only passion and lust in them, no discomfort, no regret.

"So hot, so sexy," he murmured and captured her lips once more.

He knew he would come soon, but he didn't want to be selfish, didn't want to leave her unsatisfied. So, he pulled out of her and set her back on her feet while releasing her lips. She opened them, presumably to protest, but she didn't get that far. He was already spinning her around, making her face the wall, while he pulled her hips back. He was pleased to see that she braced herself against the wall.

"That's it, baby," he murmured at her ear before slicing back into her.

He left only one hand on her hip while fucking her from behind. The other he moved to her front, placing it over her mound.

Kim gasped. "Oh, yes!"

"Mmm." He kissed the spot where her neck and her shoulder met, and farther down, he combed his fingers through her hair until he found what he was looking for. "There." He rubbed over her clit and found it wet and swollen.

Kim let out a breath. "Ohh!"

"Now, be a good girl and let me work my magic," he murmured at her ear and caressed her clit.

Kim moved with him, showing him how she liked it. He adjusted to her tempo and rhythm, while he continued to drive his cock in and out of her, his finger stroking her clit.

With every second, her breathing became more erratic, her heartbeat faster. Her body was covered with a sheen of perspiration, as was his. His shirt was getting damp, and he wished there were no barrier between them, so his naked chest would slide against her smooth back. Rough against smooth.

He grunted in frustration, but it was too late to change things now. Kim was at the cusp. He could sense it under his fingers. Another thrust, and he pinched her clit lightly between thumb and forefinger. Kim trembled, her orgasm like a volcanic eruption. The shockwaves hit his cock, igniting him. His semen shot through his hard length and spurted from the tip, his orgasm so powerful he felt his legs tremble. He slammed one hand against the wall, having to brace himself for a moment so he wouldn't collapse.

"Fuck!" he cursed.

He pulled his cock back, then thrust forward again, and again Kim's interior muscles squeezed his cock as if she wanted to milk the last drop of him.

"Oh God!" Kim cried out.

Manus dropped his forehead against the wall next to her head. "Yeah, you can say that again." Because what he'd just experienced with Kim was fucking amazing.

She turned her head. "No! We didn't use protection." There was panic in her voice now.

"You're not on the pill?" Manus asked. Not that he cared. As an unbonded Stealth Guardian, he couldn't impregnate a woman, human or otherwise. But in order to keep his cover, he pretended to be as concerned as she seemed to be.

"Of course, I'm on the pill."

"Then what's the problem?"

She pushed backward, shifting away. As a result, his cock dislodged from her. The moment was sobering. At the same time, he realized what her concern was.

"I'm clean. I just got tested," he assured her though the second part was a lie. He'd never gotten tested for sexually transmitted diseases because as a Stealth Guardian, he was immune to them. Hence, he couldn't pass on any illnesses either. She had nothing to worry about.

Kim stared at him, eyeing him up as if to check if he was telling the truth. "You just got tested?"

He nodded. "You can't catch anything from me." Then he paused for a moment. "Don't you get tested regularly?"

She froze all of a sudden. Then she shook her head. "I, uh... I was in a long-term relationship, you know... I don't really do..." She dropped her lids to avoid his gaze.

"One-night stands?"

She nodded.

Manus put his hand under her chin and lifted it, so she had to look at him. "Do you regret this?"

14

———————

Kim stared at Manus. Regret? Did she regret having had sex with Manus? For the first time in a long time, she'd felt passion and desire. She'd felt lust. This wasn't the lukewarm sex she and Todd had had in the months before the breakup. Todd had never taken her like this. Like he needed her, like he would die if he couldn't have her. In Manus's arms, she'd felt desired, wanted, needed.

"No. I don't regret a single moment," she said, meeting Manus's penetrating look. She took a step toward him and placed her hands on his shirt.

"Good, because being inside you was mind-blowing," Manus said with a soft smile.

Kim felt herself blush at the compliment and popped one button of his shirt open. "Well, then maybe we should repeat this."

When she attempted to open the next button, he captured her hands. "Uh, Kim…"

Something in his tone made her breath hitch. "What?"

"I'm not perfect."

"Nobody is," she murmured. "Now, get out of these clothes."

He kicked off his shoes and wiggled out of his pants, yet he didn't let go of her hands.

"The shirt too," she insisted.

"About that..."

"Oh, come on, what is it? You have a third nipple or something?" She chuckled and shook her head, then brushed his hand off and unbuttoned his shirt. He stood there like a statue, totally unmoving. When she peeled his damp shirt from his chest and down his shoulders, she knew why.

"Oh." The sound escaped from her mouth before she could stop it.

Her eyes were drawn to the skin on his chest. He didn't have a third nipple. In fact, he had no nipples at all. But she knew it wasn't a birth defect because he'd had nipples once, she was sure of that. However, they were gone now. Burned away. In fact, his entire chest was covered with third-degree burn marks. Scars. He'd survived a fire, a devastating one. She remembered his words suddenly. *It was an inferno. I got there too late.* But then why...

He suddenly moved, and she realized it was to pull the shirt back over his shoulders and cover his chest. "I'd better go."

The words sounded tight, and she recognized that sound. She'd hurt him by staring, by her shocked gasp.

She put her hands on his chest, gently but firmly, before he could cover it with the shirt. "No, don't leave." She lifted her head to look at his face. "Don't you remember what you promised me? It was something along the lines of out-of-this-world, headboard-banging, chandelier-swinging sex. And what we just had was a nice start in the right direction, don't get me wrong, but I don't think we're done here."

"We're not?" he asked, his voice infused with doubt. He dropped his gaze to her hands on his chest to point out the obvious. "You can't possibly want..."

He didn't need to finish the sentence. She knew what he meant.

"That's only on the outside." She began to caress his chest, feeling the uneven ridges under her fingers. It was an odd feeling, something so different from what she'd ever felt before. But she wasn't disgusted.

"You don't have to touch me there," he said, his voice still tight, still hesitant. "I know that it doesn't feel good."

"You mean you don't like it when I touch you like this?"

He shook his head. "I do like it. But you don't need to—"

"What if I want to?"

"I guess then I won't stop you."

She smiled, dipped her head to his chest, and pressed a kiss to it.

A sharp inhale was the answer.

"It doesn't hurt, does it?"

"God, no," he let out.

"May I ask you something?" She looked up at him and noticed his apprehensive look. "You don't have to answer if you don't want to tell me."

He swallowed visibly, hesitating as if fighting with himself. "You want to know how it happened," he stated.

How many times had he been asked that question? And here she was just like any other lover he'd ever had, wanting to know the same thing. What was it? Morbid curiosity? Mentally, she shook her head. No, that wasn't it. She wanted to know because she wanted to know him. Wanted to know what he'd been through, what had made him into the man he was.

"If it's too painful, then don't tell me. I didn't mean to open up old wounds and—"

"No, I want to tell you," he suddenly said firmly.

She smiled and took his hand. "Come, let's go into the bedroom. It's a little awkward standing around in the hallway, all naked."

Kim led him down the hallway, past the living room and kitchen and into the bedroom. She flipped a light switch. A single bedside lamp threw a soft glow over the room. When she slid under the covers of her queen-sized bed, Manus followed her. For a few moments, while they settled into a comfortable position, they were silent. Kim didn't press him. She knew he would talk when he was ready, when he knew how to start. She had the feeling that he'd never told any of his lovers. He'd probably never thought he'd tell her either. And truth be told, she wasn't sure why he'd decided to tell her. Had something happened between them that was different from the encounters he'd had with other women? And she was sure there'd been other women, many other women. A man looking like Manus and built like him surely got offers of sex all the time.

"I told you about the fire that burned down my parents' house and killed them," Manus started, his voice quiet and detached as if it was the only way he could tell the story. "The fire scorched my clothes, burned my chest..."

"I thought you said you weren't home and only got there later..."

"I did. I arrived when the house was already engulfed in flames."

"But then how..." When she caught his gaze on her, she stopped herself. Her pulse raced. She suddenly knew how he'd gotten burned. "You ran into the house... into the flames..."

Manus turned his head and looked off into the distance. "I was young. I thought I could save them. If only I could get to them... pull them out..." He shook his head slightly, as if only for himself. "They were upstairs. The staircase was burning. I raced up. I almost made it."

Kim held her breath, feeling fear grip her.

"The flames were faster. The staircase collapsed. I fell through it." He touched his chest. "A burning beam fell on me."

"Oh my God. How did you get out?"

"My father's friends." He gave a bitter laugh. "They risked their own lives to save mine. I put them all in danger by running in there when everybody could see that it was too late. I was foolish, irresponsible. But I couldn't bear losing the only people I ever loved."

"I'm so sorry you had to go through that." Kim took his hand and squeezed it, then pulled it to her face and pressed a kiss into his palm. "I'm sorry I made you relive that memory."

Manus turned his face to her. "I haven't spoken about it in a long time. But sometimes it's good to remind myself of what drives me. What makes me do what I do. So I don't lose focus of what's important."

"You mean in your work as a private investigator, helping other people get closure by solving murders?" she asked.

"In a way."

"You're a good man, Manus," she murmured and pulled his head to her.

"You can't know that. There's so much you don't know about me."

"Then let me get to know you." She brushed her lips to his, and he accepted the invitation and kissed her.

She understood so much now. She understood why he didn't want to get close to anybody, knew that it wasn't just his physical disfigurement that had made him build a wall around him but the emotional toll his heart had taken. But maybe together they could heal and get over the loss of those they'd loved.

15

"**W**here the fuck is Enya?"

Manus slammed the door to the command center shut behind him and marched toward Pearce, who was sitting in front of the computer console.

His compound mate looked over his shoulder, shrugging. "I'm not her babysitter."

"She's not in her quarters."

Pearce raised an eyebrow. "You went in there? Then you're braver than most of us."

Everybody in the compound knew that Enya valued her privacy more than anyone. Being the only female Stealth Guardian assigned to the Baltimore compound probably had lots to do with that. Living with a bunch of male warriors, who had all been single until a few years ago, meant she had to establish boundaries.

Manus wasn't proud that he'd breached one of those boundaries—entering her private rooms uninvited—but when she hadn't replied to his call and text message, he'd decided to risk her wrath.

He'd entered the compound in the early hours of the morning, having taken the long way home, walking much of the way invisibly so he could think and not have to worry about a demon spotting him while he was less vigilant than usual. The place had been relatively quiet at that time of night, with most of the warriors in their beds, their mates by their sides.

He'd surprised himself by telling Kim about his scars, something he'd never talked about after that fateful day. Though his compound mates and many other Stealth Guardians knew the story, Manus wasn't the one who'd told them. The demon attack on his family's compound when Manus had been a teenager and therefore still rather vulnerable had become part of their common history, their lore. And everybody knew not to bring it up in his presence. He'd tested his brethren often enough when in a bad mood, showing up shirtless in the kitchen, daring them to stare at his scars or make any comments. But they were a fierce lot, and they'd seen their fair share of ugliness. Nobody had ever taken the bait. Nobody ever would.

Anxious to find out whether Enya had found anything in Nancy Britton's storage unit, he'd first sent her a text message, then called but only gotten her voicemail. He'd waited, thinking that maybe she was asleep, taken a quick shut-eye himself and showered before trying it again. When he'd still not gotten a response, he'd gone to her quarters to look for her.

"Her bed looked unused," Manus now told Pearce.

"Fuck, Manus, if she finds out you were in her bedroom, she'll slice you open like a fat pig ready for slaughter," Pearce warned with a shake of his head.

"Yeah, well, we'll see about that." He paced behind Pearce.

Finally, Pearce swiveled in his chair, facing him. "Man, what's your problem?"

Manus ran a hand through his hair. "I sent Enya out to do some work for me last night. It's not like her not to report back."

"What was she supposed to do for you?"

"Remember the daughter of the emissarius that was murdered by the demons about three months ago?"

Pearce nodded. "Nancy Britton. I thought you dealt with her

daughter. Kim, right? Grayson mentioned you went all out to make her believe the murderer was a burglar."

"I did. But it backfired." Manus sighed. "She found her mother's bracelet at the house and knows that the one the police have is a fake."

Pearce blew some air through his pursed lips. "Bummer."

"Yeah. So, she contacted me. Wants me to help her find out why the police are covering things up."

"Well, looks like you made a royal mess of it. Wouldn't wanna be in your shoes. Have you told the Council yet?"

"What do you think?"

"Ah, I see. You think you can fix it on your own," Pearce said. "When will you ever let go of your ego and just admit that you can't fix everything?"

"It's got nothing to do with that!" Manus huffed. "Listen!" He approached and rested his butt on the massive desk. "I think we overlooked something when we investigated Nancy's murder."

"What was there to overlook? A demon killed her. End of story."

"Yeah, but why? Why did he kill her? What did he want?"

Pearce shrugged. "It happens. Demons kill a lot of humans. It was only a matter of time until they killed an emissarius. Doesn't mean they knew she was one."

"They knew. I think they were looking for something. And I'm trying to find out what it was."

"You're wasting your time. And apparently not just yours. What did you have Enya do for you?"

"She was supposed to search a storage unit that belonged to Nancy. I was there last night with Kim. Enya arrived just as we were leaving."

"If you were there yourself, why did you need her?"

"I couldn't exactly look at everything in detail while I was with Kim. She would have become suspicious."

"Fair enough." Pearce turned back to his keyboard. "I've got work to do. So, if you'll excuse me..."

"Uh... about that..." Manus started. "I need you to look into something for me."

Pearce gave him a sideways glance. "Don't rope me into this. I'm pulling double-shifts here, I haven't had a night off in months, and I'm getting a bit cranky."

"But you're the best at IT. Come on, it won't take you long."

Pearce narrowed his eyes. "That's what everybody says. You just don't want to do the legwork yourself."

True. Sitting at a computer, digging into data wasn't exactly Manus's favorite pastime. "I'll take over one of your shifts anytime you want me to, no questions asked."

Pearce tilted his head to the side, contemplating the offer. "Tell me first what you want me to do."

"I need to know what Nancy was working on in the months before her death, which guardians she was in contact with, what kind of information she provided, anything that could give me a clue as to why the demons were after her."

"*If* they were after her," Pearce clarified.

"Whatever. Just do it."

"You know that kind of assignment has to be authorized by the Council. You can't just re-open Nancy's case."

"It's already open," Manus corrected him. "By ordering me to make sure that her daughter stops digging into her mother's murder, looking for a supernatural explanation, the Council has already given me the authority to work this case."

Pearce tsked. "That's a bit of a stretch. You know the Council had no intention of letting you go that far. The order was clear."

Manus shrugged. He couldn't give a rat's ass about what the Council's order was. He knew better. "So, are you gonna do it?"

"Two shifts. You take over two of my shifts. Whenever I demand it." Pearce stretched out his hand.

Without hesitation, Manus shook it. "Good. And another thing."

"Don't push your luck," Pearce warned.

"Find out where Enya is. Trace her cell phone."

Pearce turned his head back to the monitors, his fingers already hovering over the keyboard, when he stopped in mid-motion. "Not necessary." He pointed to one of the screens: the closed-circuit security system for the compound. One of them showed Enya exiting the portal in the same clothes she'd worn the night before. "Look who's only just getting home."

Moments later, Manus rushed down the corridor, meeting Enya just as she came up the stairs from the basement where the portal was located.

"Where have you been?"

"The fuck!" Enya hissed, narrowing her eyes at him. "None of your fucking business. Who are you? Mother Superior? I don't live in a fucking convent!"

She tried to push past him, but Manus grabbed her by her biceps and stopped her. She ripped free and glared at him.

"You didn't reply to my messages."

"Yeah, well, maybe I was busy."

"Busy with what?" he grunted angrily.

Her jaw tightened, and that's when he noticed a red blotch on her neck. Was that a hickey? Shocked, he took a step back but couldn't rip his eyes off the revealing mark. "Oh." It appeared that Enya had a sex life outside the compound walls. And why was he surprised about that? After all, all the single male guardians had one-night stands, and those bonded to their mates now had sought distractions outside the compound before they'd met their mates. It was nothing unusual. He'd just never thought that Enya was doing the same.

Enya glared at him even more outraged now. "What I do in my private time isn't any of your business. You get that?"

Manus clenched his teeth. "Well, excuse me for being worried about you! Never mind. Next time, I'll know not to give a fuck."

Enya grunted unintelligibly. He wasn't sure whether it was a curse, an acknowledgment, or an apology.

"So, did you find anything in the storage unit?" he finally asked, calmer now.

"Nothing. Lots of worthless junk."

"How about the figurines? They were in a box."

"Extremely good replicas of some Viking artifacts. Nothing of interest to us or the demons."

"You sure?"

Enya gave him a stern look. "Do I look like I'm not sure?"

Manus knew better than to provoke her. "Fine. Guess that was a bust."

"Guess so." She turned on her heel and started walking away.

"Thanks, Enya," he called after her.

She didn't respond.

16

Kim brought the car to a stop in front of the office of the storage facility, her heart still beating like a jackhammer, and hopped out of it. She walked around it and marched into the office. Behind the counter, the kid from the previous night typed something on the computer and looked up.

"Mr. Songhurst left me a message to come here right away," Kim said before Brian had a chance to greet her.

"Oh, yeah, you're Miss Britton, right? From yesterday." He grinned. "I remember you."

She nodded impatiently. "Mr. Songhurst said there was a break-in?"

"He had to leave, but he said to show you." Brian walked out from behind the counter. "He discovered it when he made his rounds this morning. I told him it couldn't have happened yesterday; otherwise, you would have said something, right? I mean, you were there with your friend, and I was still in the office for a half hour. You would have told me if you'd found the unit broken into, right?"

Walking outside ahead of Brian, Kim said, "It was definitely fine yesterday when we left. And we locked the unit and put the key into the lockbox like you told us to."

"Yeah, I pulled the key out this morning," Brian confirmed. "I told Mr. Songhurst that it's not my job to check the units before I leave for the night. What are security cameras for, right?"

Kim sighed. The kid's incessant chatting was starting to get on her nerves. All she wanted was to get to the unit to see what had gone missing.

"Of course, the cameras," Brian said and pointed to the one near the office, "are just for show. They don't connect to anything. What a cheapo!"

Kim shot him a stunned look.

Brian slapped a hand over his mouth. "Oh, you're not gonna tell him what I said, are you? I mean, nobody is supposed to know that the cameras aren't hooked up. Oh shit, I'm gonna lose my job over this."

"No, you won't. I'm not gonna say anything to your manager."

Brian blew out a breath. "Phew! Thanks!"

Halfway down the path, Kim could already see the dented roll-up gate of her mother's storage unit. Somebody had used a crowbar or something similar to break the lock and damaged the door in the process, preventing it from closing or opening fully.

She had to duck slightly to step into the unit. When she reached for the light switch and flipped it, nothing happened.

"Yeah, light's burned out too," Brian, who'd slipped inside next to her, said. "I brought a flashlight." He switched on the flashlight and handed it to her.

Everything had been overturned and rifled through. Her grandmother's mirror was shattered, the upholstery of the rocking chair torn open, the stuffing removed. The boxes from the shelves had been tossed to the floor, its contents now strewn about haphazardly.

"Somebody was definitely looking for something," Brian commented. "I saw this old movie once." He pointed to the rocking chair. "About twelve chairs where one of them had a treasure inside, and some guy was looking for it, but the chairs had all been auctioned off to different people. Yeah..."

"Mmm." Kim dropped her head. Yeah, somebody had been looking for something. "Why now?"

"What?"

But she didn't reply to Brian's question. It wasn't meant for him. Why had somebody broken into the unit the night after she and Manus had visited it? Why now? Why not right after her mother's death?

She knew the answer to it: because nobody had known about the unit before. Kim had only found out yesterday. And the only other person who'd found out about it at the same time was Manus. Manus, the private investigator who had promised to help her.

But what if he wasn't helping her? What if he wasn't who he said he was? What if he'd come back after leaving her bed in the middle of the night, so he could search the unit thoroughly for whatever he was looking for? Oh God, she'd slept with him, had let him reel her in with his sob story, a story that was surely a lie. How stupid she'd been! How gullible!

She couldn't ignore any longer what was staring her right in the face.

Manus had just become the main suspect in her mother's murder.

"What do you want us to do with the unit?" she suddenly heard Brian ask next to her.

She turned to him. "I don't know yet."

"Mr. Songhurst said you'll need to vacate it soon." He pointed to the broken items. "You can use the big dumpster out back if you want to toss something."

"I'll decide on it later. I'll call Mr. Songhurst once I've arranged everything." Her mother's old things could wait. Right now, she had something more important to do.

The drive back to her mother's house seemed to take forever. It gave her plenty of time to think about her next steps. Unfortunately, the events of the previous night kept intruding, reminding her how foolish she'd been. How could she have fallen for Manus's lies? After he'd opened up about his past the previous night, she'd felt as if she'd known him forever. She'd trusted him like she'd never trusted any man before. And in his arms, she'd felt safe. And desired. He'd used sex to soften her up and lies to seal the deal.

What kind of man did that? What kind of man was so evil that he stopped at nothing to get what he wanted? Had he done the same with her mother? Had he tried to seduce her to get what he wanted and then killed her when she hadn't complied? The thought made her sick to her stomach.

Arrived at the house, Kim rushed inside. There was no time to lose. She needed to get to Manus before he found out that she was onto him and disappeared forever. In her mother's bedroom, she pulled out a metal box from the bottom of the closet and opened it. The 9mm gun her mother kept to defend herself from burglars was still inside. A whole lot of good the gun had done her. Kim would make better use of it.

She took the gun, loaded it, made sure the safety was on, then stuffed it into her handbag. Then she took a few steadying breaths and retrieved her cell phone. Manus's number was in her recent call list. She pressed it and let it ring.

Once. Twice. Three times. Was he not going to answer? Was she too late?

"Hey, Kim."

Did his voice sound apprehensive, or was she just imagining it?

"Hey, Manus." She tried to tamp down her pounding heart. She had to make this sound authentic, or he wouldn't go for it. "Can we meet?"

"Meet? Why, what's going on?"

"I found something. I think it's important. But I don't want to talk on the phone. There was a strange clicking sound in the line earlier when I spoke to a friend of mine. You know what I mean, right?"

There was a short pause, then he said, "Yeah, sure, of course, we can meet. Where?"

"The place where we met the first time," she said, continuing her ruse that she believed somebody was bugging her phone. "In an hour?"

"I'll be there."

"Thanks." She disconnected the call, set her cell phone to silent, and shoved it back into her bag. "Now, let's see who you really are."

She knew she should call her best friend to tell her what she was up to, but was afraid that Jennifer would talk her out of it. And this was something she had to see through.

17

———

Manus arrived at Auntie's Java Shop five minutes before he was scheduled to meet with Kim. When Kim had called him, he'd instinctively panicked, expecting her to be upset because he'd snuck out of her bed and her apartment in the middle of the night. He hated nothing more than clingy women who thought they had a right to him just because they'd been intimate. But Kim hadn't even mentioned the night of incredible sex. Did it mean she didn't care that he'd left her bed without saying goodbye? Had she perhaps welcomed that fact, so she didn't have to wake up next to him?

Fuck! How could Kim be so indifferent after he'd told her things he'd never told anybody else? Instead of at least telling him that she'd had a good time the night before, she'd immediately gone down to business. As if all he was to her was a means to find her mother's murderer. As if the sex had just been a by-product, something unimportant.

Manus ordered a coffee and sat down at the same table he'd met with Kim before. Only this time, he was alone. The two hybrids were back at the compound. If he needed their help with whatever Kim had found, he could call them discreetly later. But right now, he didn't want any witnesses. Seeing Kim again after their night of passion could turn into an awkward situation. Not because he regretted it—he didn't—but because it appeared that Kim had accepted his statement that he wasn't one for relationships just a little too easily. Was it a trick to lull him into a false sense of security, so she could dig her claws in, and he'd find himself in a relationship before he knew what was happening? Or was she not interested in him other than for a quick roll in the hay? He didn't know which option bothered him more. To be sure, he liked neither one. And that bothered him too.

He was about to take a sip from his coffee when his cell phone rang. He pulled it from his pocket and looked at the display.

"Kim?" he asked, answering it.

"Hey, sorry." She sounded out of breath.

"What's up? Where are you?"

"I hate to do this to you, but something came up, and I can't make it after all," she said.

"But you said you needed to talk urgently," he prompted her, hoping to get her to tell him over the phone.

"It'll have to wait. Building maintenance is here right now, water is dripping from the ceiling. That stupid idiot upstairs clogged up the pipes with cat litter again... Oh, I'm sorry. I'll call you as soon as I get this sorted. Promise. Bye."

Before he could answer, she'd already disconnected the call. Manus sighed in frustration and shoved the cell phone back into his pocket. He'd hoped for a lead in the investigation, and now all he could do was go back to the compound and see what Pearce had found in the meantime.

He left his coffee cup untouched and exited the coffeeshop. It was a busy afternoon with lots of people milling about downtown. While he could have ducked into an alley and made himself invisible, he rarely used his special skills during busy times. Being invisible did have its disadvantages. It made walking on the sidewalk a hazard. Since other people wouldn't see him, they wouldn't get out of the way, which meant he'd have to duck constantly, making for an awkward obstacle course. It was much easier to make his way to the nearest portal the old-fashioned way, by walking like a human.

He wasn't particularly keen on using the lost portal located in the red-light district of Baltimore, but it was the closest. For a long time, the Stealth Guardians had believed that portals only existed in their compounds, protected by not only the Stealth Guardian warriors but also by their collective *virta*, their lifeforce. But several years earlier, one of their own, Hamish, had discovered the existence of portals outside their own walls. Many of them had been mapped and catalogued since; others were still hidden, lost to their kind.

The guardians relied on the portals for fast and safe transportation between the compounds, preventing detection by the demons. Their locations were a closely guarded secret and could never fall into the hands of the demons, or their race and their world would be annihilated.

Manus cringed when he saw the big neon sign outside the inconspicuous building that invited its patrons in pink letters: *Touch our Junk*. Maybe entering invisibly would have been less embarrassing, but the box office employee had already seen him and feasted his eyes on Manus's body in a way that made him feel like he needed to take a shower to get clean.

Reluctantly, Manus paid the moderate entry fee and stepped into the dark interior. To his surprise, the place was busy even in the afternoon. The large room with its tiny bistro tables was filled with an equal amount of wide-eyed giggling women and horny old men. Clearly, some people had nothing better to do than watch half-naked men dance to cheesy tunes wearing frilly costumes that made the Village People look classy. A popular ABBA tune blared from the speakers while bits of clothing sailed into the audience, whose eyes were glued to the stage.

Manus ignored the goings-on on stage and made his way through the crowd. He felt many a woman's and man's eyes on him but ignored those stares too. He reached one of the doors leading backstage, made sure none of the wait staff was looking at him, and slipped through the unlocked entrance.

Now, all he needed to do was to get to the stairs that led into the basement and access the portal hidden there. Piece of cake.

KIM WAS STILL RECOVERING from the shock of seeing Manus enter a male revue in broad daylight but had swallowed away her embarrassment and bought a ticket to enter a few moments after him. Despite the fact that the place was busy, she was able to track Manus inside the club. He stuck out like a sore thumb. He was definitely one of the best-looking men in the audience. Not that there was much competition: most men watching the hotties on stage were heavyset, older, and most likely in the closet. While there were lots of women in the audience, it was clear that most of the men on stage were gay. Which begged the question: what was Manus doing here? Because she was pretty sure he wasn't here for the action on stage.

Making sure she always had an obstacle or a person ahead of her she could dive behind to hide, Kim followed Manus through the club. He made a beeline for one of the doors. She read the sign on it: *Employees only*. Undeterred, he opened the door and walked through it. Did Manus work here? She shook her head. No. He'd bought a ticket to enter just like anybody else, which meant he was going somewhere where he wasn't authorized to be.

Kim followed him, not thinking twice about the fact she was trespassing and would probably be arrested if caught. She could always say that she'd been looking for the restroom and hadn't been able to read the sign on the door due to the dim light. Perfect. Excuse in hand, she walked along the corridor lined with several doors, some of which stood open. Dressing rooms. Men in various states of undress milled about, seemingly unconcerned about who could see them.

Kim rushed past the doors to the spot where Manus had disappeared around a bend. When she reached it, she stopped and peered past it. All she could see was the back of his head as he disappeared down a staircase. Quickly, so as not to lose him, she hurried after him, using the boxes of supplies and hanging rails loaded with costumes for cover in case he looked over his shoulder. Once his head dipped below the landing, she rushed toward the stairs and looked to the bottom of them. Manus was gone. He'd descended the stairs faster than she'd expected. She ran down the stairs, the noise from upstairs still covering the sound of her footsteps.

At the bottom of the stairs, she had two choices: go right or go left. She had no idea which direction Manus had disappeared in. She looked down to the left and saw a light toward the end of a short corridor. There was only one door. It was closed. She focused her eyes and noticed the light above it illuminating the cobwebs a spider had spun across one corner. If Manus had exited that way, the spider web would have been destroyed.

To the right then, she told herself. She took a breath and inhaled the musty smell of the damp basement. The large area she entered was filled with crates and boxes, old furniture, and other props used for the shows upstairs. Between two rows of crates, she noticed a movement. Manus—he had to be back there. Stealthily, she walked on, aware that it was much quieter down here, and that Manus would hear her footfalls over the muffled sound of the music if she didn't tread lightly enough.

When she reached the end of the row of crates, she peered past them and froze. Manus stood facing a brick wall, his right hand braced against it. She focused her eyes, wondering what he was doing, when she noticed a glow emerge from under his flat palm. Odd. She blinked and focused her eyes again, but the glow was gone. As was a large portion of the brick wall. As if Manus had pressed a button and opened a secret passageway. A very dark passageway. Her eyes couldn't make anything out.

Manus was already stepping into the dark. Fuck! She'd lose him. She had to go after him. Taking a deep breath, she pulled the gun from her jeans and released the safety. At least she would be able to protect herself. Before she could change her mind, she bridged the distance between the crates and the secret passage with several steps and walked into the darkness.

Suddenly, it went pitch-black. The secret door behind her had closed.

Startled, she tilted forward and bumped into somebody.

"What the fuck!" It was Manus. He spun around and grabbed her with both arms.

Before she could free herself, she was tossed in the air, tumbling weightlessly in total darkness.

"Oh shit!"

"Kim?"

What was happening? Manus was doing something to disorient her. He was trying to subdue her, to bring her under his control.

This wasn't what she'd signed up for. But she had no choice now. He'd recognized her and saw her as an enemy now. Or why else was he grabbing her, so she couldn't get away, so she couldn't flee? Clearly, this passageway she'd followed him into was leading to a secret he didn't want to share with her.

Would he kill her for it like he'd killed her mother?

She couldn't let that happen. She had to fight him with all she had.

18

Manus had recognized Kim's voice the second she'd uttered a curse.

What the fuck was she doing here? How had she been able to follow him without him noticing? But more importantly, why?

However, none of this mattered in this instance because Kim was fighting him, trying to rip free of his grip. And if he let that happen during the journey through the portal, she could end up anywhere, forever trapped in the portal system, aimlessly flying through time and space.

"Stop it, Kim!" He tightened his grip, but it made her struggle even more fiercely.

"Let go of me!" she cried out.

"No! Damn it, Kim, hold still."

But the firecracker in his arms beat at him with her hands. Something hard hit him in the chest. Shit! Kim was armed with a gun. He switched his grip, wrapping one hand around her wrist, then the other around the second one.

"Let go of me, you bastard! You lied to me! You killed her!"

Light suddenly streamed into the portal. They'd arrived, and the door was open. But he didn't dare let go of her wrists. Instead, he yanked her out of the portal and willed it to close behind them. At least one danger was past. Now, he had to deal with Kim's inexplicable anger toward him. What the fuck had happened since the night before?

Kim glared at him, her jaw tight, her eyes narrowed. "Who the fuck are you?"

Manus tilted his head in contemplation, carefully studying her. "You know who I am."

"Yeah, a liar. That's what you are!"

She was right, of course, but he wasn't about to admit that. He had to first find out what she thought he'd lied about. He wasn't going to admit to anything more than she'd already discovered.

"I'm helping you find your mother's murderer, and that's the thanks I get? Insults?"

He loosened his grip slightly and immediately realized that it had been a mistake. Kim kicked him in the shin, making him yelp at the momentary pain, distracting him enough to free herself fully, her right hand still holding the handgun. A small-caliber pistol she now aimed at him.

"Step back!" she ordered firmly though he noticed her hand shaking.

Manus didn't move, but he lifted his hands in a submissive motion. "Don't do anything you might regret later."

"Don't worry, I won't regret this. All I regret is having believed your lies, having slept with you. How gullible I was!"

"Listen to me, Kim, you're obviously upset about something. Take a breath. Let's talk about it."

"When you left my place last night, you went back to the storage unit and broke in. Did you find what you were looking for? What you killed my mother for?" she spat.

In disbelief, he shook his head, ignoring her question, and instead homed in on her first statement. "There was a break-in?" It could only mean one thing. The demons were on their heels. "Shit." What if they'd followed Kim and discovered the entrance to the portal?

He took a step toward Kim. "We have to make sure nobody followed you. Give me the damn gun."

Kim shrank back a few steps, her retreat cut short by the wall. "How stupid do you think I am?"

"I admit I underestimated you," he hedged. "You set me up at the café, so you could follow me. Smart, I give you that. But you've set up the wrong person. I didn't kill your mother. And I didn't break into the storage unit. I had no reason to."

Kim tipped her chin up. "Maybe this will teach you not to lie to me," she said and made a movement with the gun, aiming for his shoulder.

Manus lunged for her, but she'd already pulled the trigger. The gunshot echoed against the massive stone walls. Simultaneously, searing pain shot through his left biceps. Blood splattered, and he crashed against Kim, taking her to the floor with him. With his good arm, he reached for the gun and wrestled it from her hand, tossing it as far as he could.

He tried to pin her down, but Kim punched her fist into his open wound and shoved him off her.

"Fuck!" he hissed. "Did you *have* to shoot me?"

When she picked herself up and veered toward the direction he'd thrown the gun in, Manus jumped up despite the pain and lunged for her, managing to snag the back of her jacket. Luckily, it was zipped up, so she couldn't slip out of it easily and he was able to yank her back.

At the sound of footsteps, Manus twisted his head and saw Aiden charging toward them. It had only been a matter of time until his brethren would come to his aid.

"Fucking demon!" Aiden screamed, his hand already aiming his dagger toward them. "Manus, duck!"

Shit! Aiden thought Kim was a demon. "No!!" Manus yelled.

Kim spun her head in Aiden's direction, freezing in mid-motion.

Aiden already flicked his wrist. The dagger flew through the air, perfectly aimed at Kim.

"Nooooooo!"

With every ounce of his remaining strength, Manus pushed Kim out of the way and dove after her, covering her with his body. He heard the dagger clatter to the floor several yards past them and breathed a sigh of relief. But the danger wasn't over, not as long as Aiden believed that Kim was an intruding demon.

He lifted his head. "She's not a demon, Aiden! She's human."

Aiden stopped just a foot away from them. "What?"

Slowly, Manus lifted himself from Kim. "She's human. She's Nancy Britton's daughter."

Aiden ran a shaky hand through his hair and exhaled sharply. "Fuck! You could have gotten her killed!" His friend shook his head. "Why the fuck were you fighting her?"

Clearly in shock, Kim tried to sit up, her eyes darting from Aiden back to Manus.

"Because she fucking shot me! And she was going for the gun again. That's why," Manus said, pointing to his bleeding biceps, which was starting to hurt like a bitch now. His previous gunshot wounds had never hurt that badly. "A little compassion would be nice right now."

Aiden furrowed his forehead, his gaze now trained on Kim. "So, may I ask why you were trying to kill my friend?"

Kim looked around her, apparently for the first time taking in her surroundings. And obviously looking for an escape route.

Aiden shrugged. "There's no way out, lady, so you might as well relax. You're lucky Manus is the forgiving type and pushed you out of the path of my dagger, or you'd be dead now. I never miss." Then he looked at Manus. "Leila can fix you up. You'll be as good as new in twenty-four hours."

Aiden was right. Only a dagger or sword forged in the Dark Days could permanently injure or kill a Stealth Guardian. All other weapons left only minor injuries that healed within a very short period of time.

"Okay," Manus said.

"You wanna lock her up in the meantime, given that she's a bit volatile right now?" Aiden asked, pointing at Kim while he helped Manus up.

When Manus caught Kim's frightened look, he shook his head. "We'll take her to the infirmary with us. Leila can check her out, make sure she didn't get hurt in the fight."

"Infirmary?" Kim asked, uttering her first word since Aiden had launched his dagger at her. Having escaped certain death had obviously stunned her into silence. She stood up stiffly, apprehensive about what would come next.

"You have nothing to worry about. Nobody here is going to hurt you, even if you don't want to believe that right now," Manus said. "But you will."

Once he had figured out how to tell her what she'd gotten herself into, and who he and his compound mates were. Because now that she'd traveled through one of their portals and was in their compound, he had no choice but to tell her the truth. How his brethren would take that news was an entirely different story.

By the sound of more men rushing toward them, it appeared he'd find out very shortly.

19

Believe him? Yeah, maybe Kim believed Manus that he wasn't going to physically harm her. After all, he'd just thrown himself in front of a dagger meant for her. But did that mean she would also believe whatever explanations he was going to serve up for the things that had happened?

Kim had no time to think on that any further because two men raced toward them just as she'd taken a few steps to join Manus and Aiden. Already on edge, she stared at the two young men. Her heart stopped, and the small hairs on the back of her neck stood up. The two men carried sharp daggers, the same kind Aiden had tried to kill her with.

Fight or flight? That was the question. Flight it was because the two looked bloodthirsty. Their eyes glared red, and their lips had peeled back from their teeth, revealing long, pointy canines: fangs.

"Where're the demons?" one of them yelled, still charging toward them.

"Did you leave us any?" the other added.

"No demons," Aiden answered rather calmly.

Heart still pounding, Kim shrank back, taking a couple of steps, when Manus's hand on her arm stopped her from retreating any farther.

He glanced at her. "They're with us."

She shook her head. No, this wasn't real. Nothing of this was real. She'd probably hit her head in that secret passageway when she'd been tossed around.

"But Pearce said you were fighting with an intruder," one of the bloodthirsty men said.

The two stopped in front of them, their eyes normal now, but their sharp teeth still protruded from their mouths. There was no denying it. "Vampires," Kim murmured to herself, trying to shake herself out of this nightmare.

"Put your fucking fangs away, guys. You're scaring our guest," she heard Manus order in an authoritative tone.

And just like that, the fangs of the two bloodthirsty monsters turned into normal teeth, making them look entirely human again. She blinked. No, she must still be dreaming.

"Hybrids, actually," Manus said in a more soothing tone. "They are half vampire, half human." Then he stared at one of them. "Grayson, I need you to go with Aiden and teleport to the strip club's portal and find out if any demon followed us there."

"Sure thing," the half vampire, half human Grayson said with a rather charming grin.

"We'll be back soon," Aiden promised. "Ryder, bring Manus to Leila and make sure she takes care of his wound." He turned halfway, then stopped and pointed at Kim. "Oh, and watch this one. She's got a habit of shooting people."

"I don't—"

His *get real* look was meant to shut her up.

"It's not a habit," Kim called after him, incensed. "It was one time. One fucking time!"

Manus tugged at her arm. "Let's make this time the last time."

To her surprise, the beginnings of a smile curved his lips upward.

For the fact that she'd just shot him and that his arm had to hurt like hell, he was surprisingly conciliatory.

As they walked along the corridor, Kim stayed as far away as possible from the vampire Aiden had called Ryder. He seemed to have noticed her apprehension because he cast her a sideways look and smiled.

"I don't bite," Ryder said.

"Ryder!" Manus ground out. "Bad joke, really bad joke."

Ryder dropped his head. "Sorry, I didn't mean it the way it came out." Then he shrugged and looked at Manus. "You could've prepared her. I mean, why bring Kim here and not warn her about us? Kind of a dick move."

At the sound of her name, Kim stared at Ryder. "You know who I am?"

"Yeah, sure, you're Nancy Britton's daughter. I was there when you met Manus at that café. But you probably didn't see me."

"Excuse me?"

"Yeah, when he was using his charm to make you think your mother's death wasn't related to anything super—"

"Shut up!" Manus cut him off, his voice sounding hoarse now.

Too late. She'd already heard enough. She stopped walking and glared at Manus, who looked rather pale now. "So, it was all a lie! You killed her, and you tried to make me believe that crap about the air conditioning system."

Manus opened his mouth. "I didn't k... The demons..." His voice died. Suddenly, his knees buckled, and he collapsed.

If not for the super-fast reaction of the hybrid vampire, Manus would have crashed to the floor. But Ryder caught him, then stared at her, stunned. "What's wrong with him? This shouldn't happen."

"He must have lost more blood than we thought," Kim said, feeling a little guilty for what she'd done.

Ryder looked at the back of Manus's arm. "No exit wound. The bullet is still inside."

With Manus in his arms, Ryder started running down the corridor. "Follow me!" he ordered without looking over his shoulder.

She could try to escape now, but something held her back. Instead, she looked at Ryder's disappearing form. "Ah, fuck it! In for a penny, in for a pound."

Kim charged after Ryder, worried she might lose him in the maze of corridors he was navigating, carrying Manus's two hundred pounds of muscle like he was a feather. Maybe he was really a vampire like they'd all claimed, like she'd seen evidence of, because no human had that kind of strength.

Finally, Ryder stopped and kicked a set of double doors open. Kim followed him into the large room. What she saw wasn't what she'd expected. The room was a mini state-of-the-art operating theatre any hospital worth its salt would have licked its chops for.

A woman in her late thirties, wearing a white doctor's coat, was waiting for them. Had somebody already notified her that they were coming? "He's out? What the hell?"

Ryder was already placing the unconscious Manus onto the steel table, the overhead lights glaring down at him, emphasizing the paleness of his skin.

"Something's wrong. Bullet's still in his arm. But he shouldn't have collapsed. It's just a flesh wound," Ryder claimed.

"I agree," the woman said, then briefly looked at Kim. "I'm Leila. I'm his doctor. Don't worry, I'll take care of him."

Kim nodded, her heart tying itself into a knot. Damn it, what had she done? Suddenly, her suspicions about Manus, about him being the one who'd broken into the storage facility, and about him being behind her mother's murder, weren't quite as strong anymore. What if he wasn't the bad guy here? What if he'd just been trying to help her like he'd promised?

A tear suddenly stole itself down her cheek. She wiped it away quickly but caught Ryder's look on her. He didn't make a comment, and she appreciated it. Suddenly, he didn't look that menacing anymore. He looked kind and full of concern for his friend.

Kim stepped closer and watched Leila work quickly and efficiently on Manus's biceps. "So much damage. Must have been a large caliber," Leila murmured.

"Just a nine-millimeter," Kim said.

"How would you know?"

"Because I shot him."

Leila lifted her head for a moment, meeting Kim's gaze. Then she shrugged. "Well, Manus can be a bit of a jerk sometimes." She took a pair of metal pliers from the tray next to her and dug into the wound. "Got it."

The sound of the bullet dropping into a metal bowl felt like a ton of weight dropping off Kim's shoulders. But her relief didn't last long.

"Oh shit, do you see this?" Leila asked, turning her face toward Ryder while pointing at the bullet.

Ryder perused the bloody bullet. "That can't be. That's impossible. We've gotta get one of the guys in here to confirm."

Leila shook her head. "There's no time. This isn't a commercial bullet. It's been hand-cast. If that bullet was made from metal from a weapon from the Dark Days, he's gonna die."

Die? Kim felt her throat constrict, her heart pounding as if it was trying to escape the confines of her ribcage.

"Ryder, you've gotta save him. There's no time to lose." She pointed to Manus's wound. "If we let this fester, it will infect his blood and spread through his body. It will poison him from within just like silver would poison you."

"Fuck!" Ryder hissed and extended his fangs.

Shocked and frightened, Kim shrank back when she saw the transformation from human-looking to vampire. "Oh God!"

Ryder didn't even look at her, too intent on his task. With his fangs, he pierced his wrist, then held the bleeding wound over Manus's wound.

"No!" Kim screamed. "You can't just turn him into a vampire!" Because by now she had accepted what Ryder was, even though she had no explanation for it. But if the common lore was true, then a vampire's blood could turn a human into one.

She reached for Ryder's arm, but the first drops were already dripping into Manus's open wound. It was Leila who stopped her from interrupting Ryder by snatching her wrist.

"It won't turn him. He's not at the brink of death yet. But if we wait too long, if his heartbeat drops too low, he will turn. It has to be done now."

Kim let out a shaky breath. "He'll stay human? You promise?"

Leila's eyes widened. "You don't know? He hasn't told you?"

Fear choked off her air supply. "Told me what?"

"Manus isn't human. He's an immortal Stealth Guardian."

"Not human?" Kim shook her head. "But—" She pointed to him lying on the gurney, his chest barely moving. How could he be immortal when just a moment ago Leila had said that he could die?

Leila seemed to guess her next question without Kim having to voice it. "There are few weapons that can kill a Stealth Guardian," Leila explained. "I believe that bullet is one of them. Where did you get it?"

"It was my mother's," Kim said automatically. "She kept the gun to protect herself. I took it when I..." Oh God, did it even matter now what she'd suspected Manus of? What were a few lies? Did whatever deception he'd used on her really matter now when his life hung in the balance? "I'm so sorry. I didn't mean for this to happen."

Leila squeezed her shoulder, then looked back to Ryder and Manus. Kim followed her gaze. Ryder had stopped dripping blood into the wound and was now prying Manus's mouth open to make him drink directly from his wrist.

When Kim saw Manus swallow, Ryder finally looked at her and Leila. "We need to wait now."

20

Manus felt as if he'd been drawn and quartered and then slowly been sewn together again. At least the lingering pain meant he was alive. And the reason for it appeared to be the metallic taste in his mouth. He recognized it: vampire blood.

He opened his eyes. Glaring hospital lights shining down on him blinded him for a second. Quickly, he turned his face to the side and sat up.

"Look who's awake."

He turned his head toward the female voice. Leila rose from her chair and placed her book upside down on the table.

"I feel like shit. How long have I been out?"

"Couple of hours."

That surprised him. "Did somebody knock me out while I wasn't looking?"

Leila chuckled. "You could say that. Your girlfriend shot you."

"I know she shot me. And she's not my girlfriend," he added quickly, not wanting any misunderstandings to crop up.

"Sure." Leila shrugged.

"Well, go on. What else happened? I wouldn't have passed out from a mere gunshot wound. It's ridiculous. I'm made of sturdier stuff than that." And passing out in front of Kim was embarrassing as hell. There had to be a good reason for it.

"Of course, you are. But the bullet wasn't an ordinary one. Somebody must have melted down a dagger from the Dark Days and forged bullets from it. Hence that bullet almost killed you."

Manus's heart raced. "Fuck!" He ran a suddenly trembling hand through his hair. "Did Ryder...?"

She nodded. "He drenched your wound in vampire blood and then made you drink some more. It worked."

"Guess I owe the kid big time."

"Yes, you do," Ryder said from the door, strolling into the room as if he owned the place. A confident smile on his face, he approached. "Good to see you're up."

Manus shook his hand. "Thanks, bro." It was the first time he'd called him what he called his Stealth Guardian compound mates. Ryder was like a brother to him now, somebody he could depend on with his life.

Ryder's smile widened. He understood. He was truly part of the gang now. "Anytime, bro."

"Where's Kim?" Manus asked.

Ryder tilted his head toward the double doors. "Pearce and Aiden are interrogating her."

Manus jumped off the gurney. "Interrogating? What the fuck?"

"Well, they said it's warranted under these circumstances."

"What fucking circumstances?" Manus growled.

"Let me see," Ryder said and lifted one hand, raising his thumb. "First and foremost, she shot you and you nearly died." He now added his index finger, counting. "Secondly, from the video footage Pearce pulled when you guys exited the portal, it didn't exactly look like you brought her with you voluntarily. And thirdly, she clearly had no clue that you're not human."

"Who told her that?" He should have been the one telling her the truth and not somebody else. He owed her that much.

"I did," Leila said firmly.

Manus opened his mouth to let her have it, but she cut him off instantly.

"And before you shoot your mouth off: she needed to know. She was worried about you. She thought Ryder's blood would turn you into a vampire."

That stopped him in his tracks. He stared at Leila. "She was worried about me?"

Leila nodded. "And very sorry that she shot you."

Manus tried not to be too obvious that this was a relief to him though it was. Kim regretting her actions meant there was hope. Hope that she would listen to him now, and that she would forgive the lies he'd dished up.

"Where are they holding her?"

Ryder motioned to the door. "Aiden and Pearce are in one of the offices with her. I'll bring you to them."

KIM HUFFED IN FRUSTRATION. Pearce and Aiden hadn't told her shit about what was going on. Instead, they'd been interrogating her for over an hour. As if she were a criminal! Asking her the same questions over and over again. Why she'd followed Manus. Whether she'd told anybody that she would be following him. Truth be told, right now she wished she'd called her friend Jennifer and told her about her plan of following Manus, at least then somebody would be looking for her.

Question after question Aiden and Pearce bombarded her with. They were particularly interested in the gun she'd used to shoot Manus. The gun she'd taken from her mother's bedroom. She answered truthfully; still, they didn't appear to be satisfied.

And whenever she asked questions of her own, they were stonewalling her.

They told her nothing about the two vampires she'd encountered, the demons she'd heard them talk about, or about Leila's claim that Manus wasn't human. Their answers were always the same.

"We'll get to that later."

"When?" she asked.

"When we can confirm your story with Manus. Once he wakes," Aiden said.

She shivered at the words. Did he mean *if*? "But Manus already told you who I am."

"Your identity is not in question," Pearce interrupted and tapped on a manila file folder in front of him. "We know who you are. What we don't know is if you're compromised."

"Compromised?" She furrowed her forehead, not understanding. "What is that supposed to mean?"

Pearce leaned closer. "Don't you think it's a little odd that a woman like you managed to follow Manus without him noticing and jumped into a portal right after him? As if you knew what to expect. We find that a little suspicious, don't we, Aiden?"

Aiden nodded. "Pretty fearless of somebody who claims she suspected Manus of being the bad guy."

Kim pounded her fist on the table. "I've been an investigative journalist for several years. That's what I do. I follow bad guys. I investigate shit!"

"Well, not here, you don't," Pearce said.

"Yeah, and exactly where is *here*?" she snapped.

"That's not for you to know," Aiden said.

Kim scooted back in her chair and crossed her arms over her chest. "Well, if you don't tell me anything, then I'm done talking too. I want to see Manus."

"We decide when you're gonna see him," Aiden said, sounding very protective of his friend.

"Actually, I'm the one to decide that."

Kim whirled around in her chair to look at the person who'd spoken: Manus. He stepped into the room and closed the door behind him. A bandage covered his biceps, but he looked better. The color was back in his face, and his eyes appeared clear and alert.

She shot up from her chair, happy to see that he was well, that he'd survived the ordeal. She was ready to throw herself into his arms when she stopped herself, freezing in mid-motion. This was the man she'd suspected of lying to her, of breaking into the storage unit, of killing her mother. This was the man she'd shot because she wanted answers. She couldn't just forget all that. Besides, he'd suffered because of her. How could *he* forget that?

"Manus," she choked out.

Manus nodded. "Kim." His voice sounded tight. Well, she couldn't blame him. He was pissed. And rightly so.

"What's going on here?" he asked, but he wasn't looking at her. He glared at Pearce and Aiden.

"Just doing our job," Aiden said.

"This is my case."

"Last time I checked, you were unconscious," Aiden said.

"Well, I'm fine now."

"Yeah, back to your usual charming self," Pearce said under his breath, but everybody heard it.

Manus didn't react to Pearce's dig. "I need to talk to Kim. Alone."

"Not gonna happen," Aiden said.

A low growl came from Manus. "You can't stop me from talking to her."

"We're not," Aiden corrected, exchanging a look with Pearce. "You can talk to her, but not alone." He pointed to her. "She shot you with a bullet made of metal forged in the Dark Days. She's too dangerous. We're not leaving you alone with her. Not until we can make certain that she means you no harm. End of discussion."

Kim witnessed the silent standoff taking place between the three men and didn't dare utter a word during the tense moment.

Finally, Manus said, "Fine. But not here. Let's go to the living room. The things we need to discuss and explain to Kim will take a while, and we might as well be comfortable. I for one don't fancy sitting on a hard chair right now."

Kim cringed at that. Manus was still in pain, and it was her fault.

21

Manus swallowed away his annoyance. He would have much rather spoken to Kim alone, come clean without any witnesses, but apparently his comrades weren't going to allow it. To keep him safe, they claimed. What bullshit! They wanted to be present to control how much he told Kim. Well, they wouldn't be able to stop him because the time for secrets was over. Kim was in the middle of this now, and he was in no mood to tell her more lies to explain what she'd just experienced. No, this time, it would be the truth, and nothing but the truth.

They were all seated in the living room. By Manus's estimate, he had about an hour before the whole gang would show up and somebody would prepare dinner. With three of the warriors now bonded—two to humans and one to a psychic—and one of the couples having five-year-old twins, the place could get crowded at times.

"Can I get you something to drink, Kim?" Manus now asked.

Kim shook her head, sinking deeper into the cushions of the large sectional. Manus sat opposite her in an armchair while Aiden and Pearce had spread out at the other end of the sectional.

"Well, then I guess it's time for me to tell you what you want to know," Manus started, his throat parched. He rose. "Maybe I need a drink."

He walked to the refrigerator and pulled out a bottle of beer, popped open the lid, and gulped down the cold liquid until he felt better. Taking a deep breath, he returned to the seating area and dropped back into the armchair.

"Yes, let's get this over with," Kim said. "I've waited long enough to get to the truth." She shot Pearce and Aiden an icy look. Apparently, being questioned hadn't gone down well. Manus would rectify this problem now.

"I'm sorry I wasn't able to explain things the moment we arrived here, but..." He glanced at his bandaged wound, then shrugged. "Anyway, since you've managed to follow me without me noticing, I suppose you deserve to know what's really going on. You've already seen too much anyway."

When a stunned gasp escaped from Kim's mouth, he lifted his hand to calm her. "That's not meant in a mafioso kind of way. What I mean is that considering that you now know of the existence of vampires and other preternaturals, there's no reason to keep the rest from you."

She nodded. "Leila said you're not human."

Manus cast a quick glance at his comrades, who watched in silence, then looked at Kim again. "We're Stealth Guardians, members of an ancient race charged with protecting humans from the evil influences of demons."

Kim tilted her head slightly. "When you say demons, I suppose you don't mean one's inner demons, one's bad impulses."

"I'm afraid I'm talking about demons made of flesh and blood."

"Green blood, actually," Pearce tossed in.

"Green? Really?" Kim said, sounding unconvinced. "Interesting." She still held her arms crossed over her chest.

Manus tossed Pearce a chastising look. "Let me handle this."

This was a delicate situation. Kim was skeptical. He could sense it, and if he gave her too many details that were hard to swallow—and frankly pretty incredible—he would have a difficult time making her believe. It was best to keep things as normal as possible.

"We have certain skills at our disposal. For example, we use a special mode of transportation," Manus continued cautiously. "You jumped after me, into one of our portals. You probably felt disoriented when we started traveling in it. As if you were being tossed in the air."

Kim's eyes widened. It was a good sign. "You said that we traveled. What do you mean? I'm pretty sure I didn't black out, and I'm also sure we didn't walk anywhere. All you did was open that passageway, that portal, on the other side, and we were here, underneath the strip club."

"We're not underneath the strip club," Manus said. "We're at the other end of town."

"No, that's not possible." She suddenly dug into her pocket and pulled out her cell phone. "And I'm going to prove it to you."

Manus pointed to her phone. "If you're trying to use the map app to get a location on where you are, you're out of luck. Our compound isn't traceable. Any GPS signal in and out of here is scrambled." That it was magic that prevented anybody from finding the compound, and not an electronic device, he kept to himself.

Kim stared at her phone, still tapping at her app, then lifted her head. "I see."

"I'm sure you've heard of teleportation," Manus said.

"Yeah, in the movies. It's not possible in real life."

"It is for us if we're using a portal. The demons use something similar, and you saw the tail end of it. The vortex in your mother's living room. You saw somebody disappear in it just before the vortex closed. That was a demon. Your mother's murderer."

KIM SUCKED in a slow breath of air, trying to digest the news.

"You've been looking for a supernatural explanation to your mother's death. I'm giving it to you. What you saw was real."

She didn't know whether to be happy that she finally knew she hadn't been hallucinating or whether to lament the fact that she'd stumbled into something she could barely comprehend. "You're telling me a demon killed my mother?"

He nodded.

"And you knew about this all along?"

"We figured it out shortly after she died."

Kim jumped up, angry now. "Then why? Why lie to me? Why come up with that stupid explanation about the air conditioning system?"

Manus rose. "I'm sorry about that. But we couldn't let you continue poking your nose into things that would have exposed us."

"It doesn't make sense," she spat. "If you say that's how it happened, then why would the police try to pin the murder on some dead guy? Did you bribe them?"

Manus shook his head, looking sheepish. "The police know nothing about that. I planted the evidence."

The implications of his words sank in immediately. "You killed a guy so you could pin my mother's murder on him? Oh my God!" She slammed her hand over her mouth.

"No!" Manus protested immediately. "Of course not. I merely found a dead body and planted the evidence on him. Why would you think that of me? I don't kill innocents." He appeared appalled by that idea.

"We'll all vouch for that," Aiden added. "We don't kill innocents. We protect them. That's our mission."

She tossed a look at Aiden. What did it matter that he vouched for Manus? They were all the same, all in it together. She needed an independent third party to verify what Manus was telling her. No journalist worth their salt believed a story based on just one source. "I need another source."

"What?" Manus stared at her, not understanding.

"I want to believe you. Because it would mean that I'm not crazy, that what I saw was real. But I can't. It's too fantastical."

"But you saw the vortex," Manus pressed. "You teleported through a portal with me. You saw the two vampires that live with us. You were there when Ryder saved me with his blood. And you still can't believe?"

She closed her eyes, recalling the memories of the vortex, the tumbling in the portal, the vampires' fangs. But what if she'd hit her head in the portal? What if she was still hallucinating and making up stories in her head to explain everything that had happened?

"I'm an investigative journalist. I need proof. I need a second source. Somebody with authority. Somebody whose identity I can verify." She looked into Manus's eyes and saw understanding in them. "I don't know your friends. I don't know any of you."

"You need the word of somebody you might recognize?" he asked.

Kim nodded.

Manus pulled his cell phone from his jacket pocket, unlocked it, and navigated to a screen, tapped on it, then pressed it to his ear. A moment later he said, "Hey, Hamish, you and Tessa getting home soon?"

To her surprise, she could hear the answer loud and clear. "Just walking in."

Kim turned her head and saw a tall, dark-haired man enter the great room, a woman with long brown hair and lavender eyes by his side. Kim blinked. She recognized the woman. In fact, she'd voted for her in the last election.

"Mayor Wallace?" Kim echoed.

Tessa Wallace walked toward her, a smile on her face. "Yes. Do we know each other?"

"What did you want, Manus?" Hamish asked. Kim recognized him now too. He was the mayor's husband. She'd seen photos of him and her in the papers.

"I need Tessa to vouch for me, for all of us," Manus said.

"Vouch?" Tessa asked. "What have you done now?"

"Nothing. All I need you to do is to explain to Kim here who we are and what we do. She doesn't quite believe me yet." Manus cast Kim a sideways look.

Tessa approached and stopped in front of the coffee table. "So, you're human?"

Kim nodded.

"How much is she allowed to know?" Tessa asked, addressing Manus.

"Everything," Manus said, "but give her the condensed version. We've got a lot more to discuss. And little time to do it."

Tessa nodded. "Kim, I'm sure there's a good reason why Manus brought you here. And probably also one why you don't believe him, but as somebody who was once in your shoes, let me tell you this: you can trust any of these guys here with your life. Because they will protect you from the demons with everything they've got." She reached for her husband's hand, and Kim couldn't help but notice the loving look they exchanged.

"My husband and the warriors in this compound are immortals. They have supernatural skills that I couldn't believe the first time I encountered them either, but they exist." She sighed. "And they'll do everything in their power to protect us. Without them, I would be dead now. They're men of honor."

"Thank you, Mayor Wallace."

"Call me Tessa, please."

Kim smiled at her, then turned toward Manus, looking straight into his eyes. She saw the truth now. And as incredible as it was, she wasn't scared anymore, even though she didn't understand everything yet. Vampires? Immortals? Demons? Teleportation? There was so much to absorb. And she was willing to listen now.

But she also had regrets. She needed to apologize. Because she'd caused someone pain.

"I'm so sorry I shot you."

Manus suddenly smirked, his eyes lighting up. "It was worth it."

22

Manus felt relief flood him. It had taken a bit of time and effort, but now they were on the same page. There was lots more to impart on Kim, but the first step was done. Kim trusted him.

"Shall we sit down again, Kim?" he asked. "I need to tell you something about your mother."

Slowly, Kim took her seat on the couch again, and Manus sat down opposite her.

"If you guys don't need me anymore, then we'll start preparing dinner," Tessa said.

Manus cast her a glance. "Thanks for your help, Tessa."

When she and Hamish walked into the kitchen, Manus took a deep breath and turned back to Kim. "Your mother worked for us. She was an emissarius, a messenger who'd alert us of anything that might be of importance to us or the demons. You might call it spying for us, but what she did helped us protect the human race."

Kim's lips parted. "My mother was a spy? But how? What would she know that could help you against the demons?"

"Her work in the museum often brought her in contact with artifacts that have significance to both us and our enemies. Whenever she came across something that she thought was important to us, she alerted us."

Kim shook her head, visibly surprised by that revelation. "Why did she never tell me? I mean, we told each other everything."

Manus sighed. "We made her promise not to. It's important that our secrets are kept. And the more people are let in on them, the more likely we'll be exposed. We can't risk that. So much so that when you started questioning the police's burglar theory and suspecting that there was a supernatural explanation for your mother's death, I was charged with intervening. We needed you to stop talking about what you'd seen."

Kim nodded in contemplation. "So, you told me that bogus story about the air conditioning system, and when I called bullshit, you planted fake evidence on that dead guy and somehow made the police connect the dots. But I identified the bracelet. It looked exactly like my mother's."

"Because it was identical," Manus said. "I had it replicated from photos and the original drawings we found in your mother's home."

"You broke in?" She furrowed her forehead. "But there were no signs of a break-in."

Manus exchanged a quick look with Aiden and Pearce. Both shrugged.

"Up to you," Aiden said.

Kim tossed them all a quizzical look. "What's going on?"

"I didn't have to break in," Manus finally said, having decided that there was no harm in telling her the truth, particularly since he'd have to use his preternatural skills in front of her soon anyway. "I can walk through solid objects such as a door or a wall."

"What?" Kim blurted out, her mouth dropping open in stunned disbelief. "You mean like a ghost?"

"Kind of. Stealth Guardians can dematerialize their body in order to pass through solid objects, then materialize behind said object. To the human eye it would simply look like a person walking through a wall, as if the wall didn't exist."

The implications of his words seemed to sink in. "So, you're saying you can enter any place, any building, any home?"

Manus nodded.

"So that's how the demon got in? The front door was closed. He didn't have to break in."

Manus shook his head quickly. Kim wasn't the first human to make the assumption that the demons had the same skills as the Stealth Guardians. "No, demons can't walk through walls. But they can teleport into a home if they can see where they're teleporting to, or if they've been there before. They use a vortex for that. That's how he got into your mother's home, and that's how he left."

Kim sighed and sank back into the cushion. "I always thought it would be a relief to find out who killed her and how he got in, but it's not." She met Manus's eyes, and he noticed the resignation in them. "If they can do that, if they can get into any place with their vortexes, then nobody's safe from them."

"That's why we do what we do, and that's why your mother and so many other humans help us in our mission: to keep them in check, to thwart their efforts, and to eventually defeat and destroy them. Unfortunately, the demons are hard to recognize."

"What do you mean? Surely, you can recognize a monster when you see one," Kim said emphatically.

Manus sighed. "Look at me. Do I look human?"

She nodded.

"Yet I'm not. Same goes for the demons."

"They look like humans?" she asked, shocked.

"Like ordinary humans, with two exceptions: they have green blood, as Pearce has already mentioned, and they have poison-green eyes."

"You mean all people with green eyes are demons?"

Manus chuckled. "No, of course not. In fact, the green eyes you think of are just normal human eyes. A demon's green eyes are entirely different. You'll recognize them when you see one, trust me. Unfortunately, they've gotten smart. They use sunglasses and colored contact lenses to disguise their eyes, making it impossible for us to spot them. That's why we've allied ourselves with vampires."

"You mean they can see through the disguise?"

"No. But they can smell the demons. Thus, they can warn us from an ambush."

"But you look like humans too, so how would they be able to ambush you? I mean, how would they even know you're Stealth Guardians?"

"We have an aura, and they, just like any other preternatural creature, can see our aura. That's how they recognize us."

"And you can't recognize theirs?"

"They have none."

"That's convenient," Kim said dryly.

"Yep, it sucks," Manus confirmed and shrugged. "That's why we borrowed a couple of vampires from our friends in San Francisco to help us detect demons."

Kim leaned forward and cleared her throat. "Yeah, about those vampires..."

"What about them?"

"Aren't you afraid that they'll turn on you and suck you dry? I mean, they seemed pretty bloodthirsty when I met them. No offense."

"Offense taken."

Manus whirled his head in the direction of the male voice, which he recognized as Grayson's. Grayson and Ryder marched into the room. Despite the harsh words, Grayson had a charming grin on his face.

"I'm not bloodthirsty," he said and approached the couch, but Manus rose and blocked him from getting too close to Kim.

"What do you want?"

"I just want to prove to our guest that I'm not bloodthirsty," Grayson said and peered past Manus. "Well, unless she likes it that way."

Before Grayson could push past him, Manus had him by the collar of his shirt. He couldn't tolerate the eternal womanizer making a pass at Kim. It was disrespectful. Besides, he would never allow some young buck to invade his territory and lay claim to something that had already been claimed.

"Hands off her," Manus hissed so low he knew only the two vampires in the room could hear him.

"You had your chance," Grayson replied just as quietly. "And we all know how that worked out. She didn't fall for your charm the first time. Now's my turn."

The young hybrid really thought he knew everything. Maybe it was time to update him on recent developments. "Shame you're about twenty-four hours too late." With a grin Manus released Grayson and added just as low, "I'm surprised you can't smell her on me."

Grayson's chin dropped in disbelief. Behind him, Ryder had difficulty suppressing his laugh.

Finally, Manus turned back to Kim and smiled at her. "It's all cleared up. Grayson was just joking. Weren't you?"

"Sure," Grayson pressed out through clenched teeth before turning toward the kitchen. "What's for dinner?"

As he walked to join Hamish and Tessa, Kim leaned over the coffee table and said in a low voice, "I thought vampires don't eat."

"Hybrids do, in addition to drinking blood. But let's get back to more important things," Manus replied. "Namely the reason why your mother was killed by the demons."

23

____

"Well, isn't that obvious now?" Kim asked, staring at Manus, who was still standing. "They killed her because she worked for you." And although she didn't mean to assign blame, she knew she sounded accusatory.

"No, she didn't," Manus said. "Being an emissarius doesn't automatically make a person a target for the demons. We're very careful, and so are the humans who work for us. It's rare that an emissarius dies in the line of duty."

"I didn't mean to accuse you or anything," Kim said in a gentler tone. "But what other reason would the demons have had?"

"The police were right when they suspected a burglar, only it wasn't a human burglar," Manus said. "The fact that the storage unit was broken into right after you and I visited it is a pretty strong indication of it. My colleague Enya searched the unit after we left."

"So, she rifled through my mother's stuff?"

Manus shook his head. "She looked through everything to see if your mother kept anything the demons could want. But she put everything back in its place."

Kim furrowed her forehead. She wasn't sure what that proved. "So?"

"If it was a demon who broke in afterwards, he was searching for something."

"But how would you know if it was a demon? The employee at the facility told me that the security cameras there are just for show. They don't work."

"We don't need security cameras. We just need to send somebody back to see if the overhead lights in the unit burned out. If they did, it means a demon was there. The gases in fluorescent lighting react to the presence of a demon by combusting." He glanced at Aiden. "Fancy going there and having a look, so we can be sure?"

"Not necessary," Kim interrupted. "I was already there earlier today, and I noticed that the lights had burned out."

"Then we have our answer."

Kim's heart sank. Had she known about the storage unit earlier, maybe she could have found whatever the demons had been after. "Then the demons now have what they were looking for."

"They don't."

"How would you know that?"

"Because Enya found nothing that could possibly have any value for the demons. And believe me, she's thorough and able to recognize artifacts that relate to our origin or have special meaning."

"Wow, Manus is handing out compliments. What a rare treat," a woman said from the kitchen.

Kim turned her head. A beautiful petite blonde leaned casually against the kitchen island. She was dressed in leather gear, and it looked good on her. Sexy, provocative, powerful.

"Enya," Manus greeted her. "How long have you been listening?"

Enya shrugged. "Long enough." Then she tipped her head up in Kim's direction, her gaze frosty, before addressing Manus again. "I see we're now admitting humans willy-nilly. Funny, I didn't get the memo that the Council relaxed its rules on humans in the compound. Maybe you want to clue me in on why you decided to break Council rules again by bringing Kim Britton here and risking the Council coming down hard on us this time?" She crossed her arms over her chest.

"Considering you're making us accessories after the fact, and I'm sick of paying for your infractions, I think I'm due an explanation."

"Enya!" Manus ground out.

"You're saying no humans are allowed here?" Kim interjected. "But the mayor is here. She's human." At least that's what she believed, but then, she could be wrong about that too.

Enya motioned to where the mayor and her husband did their best not to get dragged into the conversation and continued cooking. "She's also bonded to Hamish. Which makes her one of us."

Realizing that Manus was in trouble because of her, Kim said quickly, "It wasn't his fault. I followed him and jumped into the portal after him. He had no choice."

"She also shot him," Pearce piped up.

"He nearly died," Aiden added. "So, cut him some slack, will you?"

Enya raised an eyebrow, then uncrossed her arms. "I like you, Kim. You've got pluck."

Kim smiled involuntarily. "Thanks, I guess?"

"And for what it's worth, I agree with Manus," Enya added. "There was nothing in the storage unit the demons could possibly want. So, whatever they're after, they haven't found it."

"Yet," Manus said, nodding. "But it's still out there. So, we have to find it first."

"But we don't even know what it is," Kim said. "How are we supposed to find something when we don't even know what we're looking for?"

"Don't worry, I have some ideas. But in the meantime, we have to make sure you're protected. They'll be watching you," Manus claimed.

"She can't stay here," Aiden said, rising just as the door opened and Leila entered with two small children in tow.

Surprised, Kim looked at Leila and the children. She hadn't expected to encounter children in this place. Aiden swept both of them up in his arms and kissed them. They giggled and talked over each other.

"Aiden is right," Pearce now said, tossing her a regretful look. "I'm sorry, but the Council will give us shit if they find out. And they will. They always do."

"The Council?" Kim asked, turning to Manus.

"Our ruling body, our government. They make the rules. We're supposed to follow them." Then he addressed Pearce. "I wasn't planning on keeping her here anyway. The demons can't know that we're onto them. Kim has to be out in the open, acting normal as if nothing has happened. We don't want to tip our hand and make them suspicious. I'll be protecting her on the outside."

Kim shook her head. "But then they'll see you. Won't that make them suspicious? I mean, they can tell you're a Stealth Guardian. Won't that tip them off?"

Manus exchanged a grin with Pearce and Enya.

"Not if I'm invisible," Manus said.

Kim widened her eyes. "What?" Was he trying to tell her that he could make himself invisible?

He winked at her. "You'll see."

Enya chuckled unexpectedly. "Actually, you won't."

24

————

Kim let the door of her condo snap in behind her and flipped the light switch. "Are you still here?" she asked in a low voice.

"You don't have to whisper just because I'm invisible," Manus said.

She whirled in the direction of his voice, not having expected that he'd entered the apartment ahead of her.

"Let's close the curtains," he suggested, "so no demon can look in."

Quickly, Kim followed his suggestion, closing the drapes in all rooms. She'd had dinner with the Stealth Guardians and their wives and children at the compound before Manus had led her back to the portal. This time, they hadn't exited at the strip club but in an old abandoned warehouse. Once there, Manus had indeed made himself invisible while they'd walked to the nearest bus stop and taken a bus to her place. During the entire time, he'd held her hand to assure her that he was still there.

She'd never felt anything more unreal than feeling his hand in hers but seeing nothing.

"I still can't get over the fact that you can make yourself invisible," Kim now said, wandering back into the living room.

"It's a pretty handy skill," Manus said from behind her, sending a shudder down her spine.

She turned to him and watched him appear before her eyes.

"For tonight," he added, "I wanted to make sure that should the demons watch you, they'd see you return home without a Stealth Guardian in tow."

"Do you think they're watching me?" That thought made her shiver involuntarily.

"We have to assume it. They probably suspect that your mother told you about whatever was in her possession, which means they'll expect you to retrieve it at some point. They must have had you under surveillance when we went to the storage unit. Unfortunately, the demons are good. I didn't notice anyone following us."

"I don't blame you. Your priority was to stop me from exposing you and your people." And she hadn't exactly made it easy for him to fulfill his task. Instead, she'd caused him plenty of grief.

She sighed and stretched out her hand to touch his biceps. The bandage was gone now, but he was wearing a long-sleeved shirt, preventing her from seeing how well the wound had healed.

"Does it still hurt?"

He shook his head. "It's already healed. Vampire blood is the best medicine."

"I'll remember that for next time."

Manus smirked. "Oh yeah? Planning on shooting me again?"

Kim felt her face flush from shame. "I'm so sorry for doing that. I should have trusted you."

"You had no reason to trust me. I'm a stranger to you."

She moved closer, reducing the distance between them to a mere foot. "Not a complete stranger." She hoped he understood that she was alluding to the intimacy they'd shared.

Manus cleared his throat, his eyes now pinning her. "Sex doesn't necessarily make somebody trust you."

She placed her hand on his chest and moved it downward. "No, but intimacy does."

He inhaled sharply and put his hand over hers, stopping her from reaching his waistband. "What are you doing?"

"Making up for shooting you, for nearly killing you." Though it wasn't her primary motivation. What she wanted was to feel what she'd felt the night before. To be close to Manus, to feel connected to him.

"I'm not asking you to make it up to me," he said though his eyes said something different. There was desire in them and a hunger that turned her insides molten.

"But I want to." She pulled her hand free of his grip and slid it farther down, onto his pants, where she laid it over his zipper. A firm bulge greeted her. Big and hard, just like the night before. Oh, how she loved a man who responded so quickly.

"Kim..."

"No complaints, please."

"I wasn't complaining."

"Then what did you want to say?"

She saw his Adam's apple move as he swallowed hard. His lips parted to speak, but she already knew what he wanted, and what she was more than willing to give him.

"Let me do this," she murmured. "Let me make amends."

With both hands, she opened his pants and pushed them down to his ankles. Then she hooked her thumbs into the waistband of his boxer briefs and slowly shoved them down too. His cock sprang free, and she reached for it, wrapping her hand around his hard root.

"Fuck!" Manus hissed.

"Shhh," she whispered. "I'll never hurt you again." She dropped to her knees in front of him, bringing her head level with his hard-on. Nearly purple in color, pumped full with blood, his cock pointed right at her, the bulbous head glistening with pre-cum. She inched closer, bringing her mouth to within millimeters of his hard flesh. She could smell his heady scent now and inhaled the aroma. Heat suffused her and made her pulse race in anticipation. With her next breath, Kim wrapped her lips around the tip of his cock and slid down on him, taking him deep into her mouth.

Manus shuddered out a breath, and she reveled in the knowledge that this powerful warrior, this immortal guardian, was now at her mercy.

MANUS HAD to brace himself at the wall with one hand, fearing his knees would buckle for the second time today. This time, the reason wasn't blood loss from a gunshot wound but Kim's luscious mouth. He felt as if ascending into heaven. Everything around him faded away into oblivion; only the two of them existed.

When he'd brought Kim back to her place, he hadn't expected this to happen at all. He realized that she had lots of things to come to terms with now, lots of information to mull over. After all, it didn't happen every day that a human found out about the existence of immortals, vampires, and demons. Yet Kim had been a real trooper, not acting hysterically like many others would have.

He'd counted on spending the night on the couch, guarding her from there. Apparently, the couch would remain unoccupied tonight. Kim was making it abundantly clear where she wanted him to spend the night: between the sheets with her, making love even more intimately than they'd done the night before. And though he knew he should stop her, not take her up on the offer for so many good reasons, he couldn't recall a single one right now. Because her sucking him as if the world would end tomorrow had erased every sane thought from his brain.

Blow jobs were rare for him because most women shied away from it with a one-night stand. And one-night stands were all he ever did. No repeats, and certainly no relationships. But things with Kim were different.

He looked down to her kneeling in front of him, fully clothed while he was bare from the waist down. Everything about this situation screamed *forbidden*, yet he'd never found himself in a more tantalizing situation than he was in now. Kim's eyes were closed while she moved her mouth up and down on him, her tongue licking the underside of his shaft, caressing him with more tenderness than he deserved. Her head bobbed up and down, back and forth, and with it, her hair bounced against his skin, catching on the hair surrounding his cock and that covering his thighs. The contact was electric.

Manus reached for her, putting his hands to cup her face. Only gently, not to force her to suck him harder but to guide her. She opened her eyes and looked up at him. The look in her eyes nearly undid him. Unbridled lust shone back at him, making his heart pound like a jackhammer and his hard-on jerk forward involuntarily, seeking her heat.

"I've never felt anything this good," he said and meant it. "Oh, baby, don't stop."

He threw his head back, letting out a groan. He'd never had a woman taking such care of him, showing him such affection. He knew how ugly his scarred chest was; he wasn't blind. Many women shied away from him once he was undressed, but Kim had seen him in all his ugliness. Still, she sucked him as if to worship him, as if she really wanted him.

He rocked his hips back and forth now, adding to the friction Kim was providing. But he made sure not to ram his cock into her mouth, even though he was tempted to. She didn't deserve this, not when she was making him feel something so incredible: utter bliss. For the first time in decades, he felt free from the pain of his past. Free to allow himself to feel something again. To open his heart to another person. To love.

That thought sent a wave of heat from his chest down to his balls. "Fuck!"

If he didn't stop now, he'd come and shoot his seed into her mouth. And he couldn't expect her to accept that.

"Stop, Kim, I'm gonna come."

But Kim didn't stop. Instead, she put one hand to his balls, kneading them, while her hand on the base of his cock gripped him tighter, her mouth sucking harder and faster.

"Damn it, Kim! I can't stop it..."

She didn't heed his warning. With his last ounce of willpower, he pulled his cock from her mouth just as he orgasmed. His seed shot against Kim's chest, staining her shirt, but at least he'd avoided her face at the last second.

Breathing hard, he grabbed her shoulders and pulled her up to him. He slipped one hand onto her nape. Without a word, he took her mouth and kissed her deep and long, pouring his adoration and appreciation into the kiss to tell her what he couldn't put into words: that he was done with one-night stands and needed something more.

When he finally let go of her lips, he pressed his forehead to hers. "If that's what I get every time you shoot me, then you have my permission to shoot me every day."

Kim slid her hand onto his ass and pressed him to her. "I'm never gonna shoot you again, I promise."

He drew his head back. "Are you trying to tell me that this was the last time you sucked me?"

She chuckled softly. "I can think of many reasons why I would want to suck you again, and shooting you doesn't even make the top ten."

Manus let out an exaggerated sigh. "Phew. I was worried there for a moment."

Kim rolled her eyes. "Men!"

25

———————

Manus couldn't let Kim's comment stand and give the impression that all he was after was having his cock sucked. He was all for seeing to Kim's pleasure.

"Men, huh?" he murmured against her lips. "How about you let this man take you to your bedroom and make love to you?"

"Make love?" she echoed. "So not just sex?"

"No, not just sex. That was last night. We're turning over a new leaf tonight. I mean, with all that's passed between us, you following me, you accusing me of being the bad guy and shooting me, I guess we've gone beyond just sex. What do you think?"

She laughed softly, and the sound seeped into his heart. "So, that's all it took, me shooting you? That's crazy."

"Yeah, but crazy in a good way."

"Hard to argue with that," she said.

"Then let's not argue. Let's make love."

"You have a way of talking a girl into things..."

"It's a gift," he whispered and kissed her.

Minutes later, they were in Kim's bed, both naked. Manus looked at her gorgeous body. She was perfect. A woman like her could have any man; she didn't have to sleep with a man who had disfiguring scars, both inside and out. But he would be the last man to question Kim's choices. She was a woman not to be trifled with, strong-willed and determined. As well as adventurous both in and out of bed. He liked that about her. There was no shyness, no hesitation.

Braced on his elbow, lying on his side next to her, Manus ran his hand over her breasts. Her nipples were hard and rosy, her flesh firm yet pliable.

"You're beautiful," he said. "I could look at you all night." He rubbed his finger over one nipple.

"Mmm."

Taking his time, he kneaded first one breast, then the other, and felt Kim arch her back to thrust her chest toward him.

"Patience, baby. I'll take care of you."

He released her breast and moved farther south, caressing her flat stomach before approaching the apex of her thighs. There, a triangle of thin dark hair formed a canopy that hid her female treasure. Slowly, he combed his fingers through it and slipped them between her legs. She spread them wider, inviting him to explore her.

Manus pressed a kiss to her neck, then slid his fingers over her folds. Moist heat greeted him, and he let out a moan. He rubbed one finger along the slit and coated it in her juices. Kim moaned softly, and Manus stroked his finger upward again.

"Oh, yes!"

"Mmm," he hummed at her ear. "Teach me what you like, and I promise I'll give you anything you desire."

She undulated her hips, tilting her pelvis up so his finger slipped back down to her slit. He dipped the tip of his finger into her channel and felt her muscles grip him. His cock jerked at the sensation, already hard and heavy again, ready for more. But he could wait. Giving pleasure to Kim was more important Unt now. He had to show her how good he could make her feel before she woke up and saw the ugliness of his scars. Before she decided that she was wasting herself on him when she could have a man who was physically as perfect as she.

He pulled his finger from her and slid it to her clit. The tiny organ was engorged. When he swiped his wet finger over it, Kim moaned out loud.

"Yes!"

He smiled. Kim was even more responsive than he'd hoped. He scooted down next to her, then gripped her thighs and spread them even wider before moving into the space between them. Kim opened her eyes, staring down at him.

Realizing what he intended to do, a stunned "Oh" left her mouth.

"Oh, yeah," Manus confirmed. "Did you really think you could suck me like that and I wouldn't do the same to you? Now you'll be at *my* mercy."

He dipped his head to her center, already taking in the scent of her arousal. He inhaled deeply and looked back at her face. She was still looking at him, lust coloring her eyes now, a deep breath leaving her chest.

"Ah, how I love a woman who knows when it's time to let go and enjoy herself."

He brought his mouth to her nether lips and pressed a kiss to them, then snaked out his tongue and licked over her slit, gathering up the juices that oozed from her. He drank them down and felt his body harden, her taste infusing him with newfound vigor, just like the vampire blood earlier had revived him.

With his lips and tongue, Manus explored the passionate woman beneath him and teased moan after moan from her. He couldn't get enough of the sound nor the taste. Her flesh was rosy and soft, and her body twisted under his ministrations. It was rare that he had the chance to indulge in such intimacies. One-night stands generally didn't go this deep. But this was different, more intense.

Because the whole situation was different. He was Kim's protector now, and even if he wanted to, he couldn't just leave her the next day. There was no anonymity anymore, no hiding behind a persona he played.

What he was showing Kim right now was himself, the vulnerable part of him that wanted to feel something again, even if it meant risking losing everything again. Absent of the words to tell her what he wanted her to know, he hoped that she would be able to interpret his actions and understand that he was trying to let her in.

Eager to give her a night she would never forget, Manus poured every ounce of passion into his kisses and caresses. He listened to her body, to her heartbeat, to her breathing to recognize what she wanted from him and adjusted his touch to her needs. Under his hands, he felt her perspire. Her breathing turned erratic and ragged. Her heartbeat began to race.

When she placed her hands on his nape, he shuddered and intense pleasure shot down his spine and into his tailbone. His balls burned with the need to release their seed even though he'd orgasmed only minutes earlier. Kim was doing this to him just by allowing him to worship her with his mouth.

When Kim's movements suddenly changed, he knew she was close. He doubled his efforts, licking her clit with more pressure and a faster tempo. Moments later, he felt spasms charge through her body and travel to his lips.

Kim moaned out loud, her hips nearly lifting off the bed as she stiffened. Manus slid his hands under her ass and gripped her tightly, making sure to keep his tongue on her center of pleasure as she rode out her climax. When she let out a few deep breaths, he eased up and lifted his head from her center.

Her entire body glistened with a thin sheen of sweat and seemed to glow. He'd never seen anything more beautiful. As if they'd been lovers for a long time, he lifted himself up and rolled over her, bringing his cock to her pussy. He looked into Kim's eyes, seeing satisfaction and adoration in them, and slowly drove his hard-on into her, inch by rock-hard inch. She parted her lips and let a soft sigh escape, pressed her head back into the pillow, and thrust her breasts out to him. A sign of wordless acceptance if he'd ever seen one.

When he was seated to the hilt, he slowly withdrew and just as gently thrust back into her. Her muscles spasmed around him, a sign that she was climaxing once more.

"Again," she murmured and gripped his shoulders. "Do it again."

He repeated his movement, allowing the sweet torture of it to rob him of his breath. But he didn't speed up, didn't rush it, because he knew he'd come soon enough. And he wanted to make this last, to feel every inch of her, every fiber of her being.

Manus braced himself on his elbows and locked eyes with her while below, he continued his extraordinarily slow movements, drawing out the pleasure as long as he was physically able to.

"I've never felt anything this good," he said.

Her eyes were moist, and a soft smile sat on her lips. "I never thought it could be so... amazing."

Manus smiled to himself. Kim hadn't seen anything yet. There were things a Stealth Guardian was capable of that a human could never dream of. Intimacies reserved for lovers who had a future together. He pushed the thought away. It was too early to give such thoughts voice.

He had to concentrate on the present, the here and now. His cock inside her. Their bodies tangled. Kim wrapped her legs around him, demanding more now, enticing him to increase his tempo, tempting him to thrust harder. There was no resisting the urge now. After all, deep down he was only a man. He had desires. And the woman in his arms wanted him despite everything. Despite the lies, despite the scars.

He emptied his mind and thought only of Kim, of her beauty, her passion, and the loving look in her eyes. Everything else melted into the background. All he heard now were their heartbeats, their breathing, and the rustling of the sheets as they writhed against each other. He plunged his cock deeper and harder into her, riding her with such ferocity that he was surprised she didn't make him stop. Instead, she gripped him harder, her fingernails now digging into his back, forcing him to take her like a wild beast.

He wouldn't last much longer with her driving him wild like this. "Fuck, Kim!"

"Take me!" she called out.

It was the straw that broke the camel's back. He plunged deep and hard into her welcoming pussy, his cock exploding from the tip, filling her with his hot semen. He continued to thrust until he finally collapsed on top of her.

Acutely aware of his weight on her, he rolled off. He would have pulled her onto his chest, but he didn't want her to have to stare at that ugliness right now, not after what they'd just shared, so he rolled to the side and pulled her back against him, wrapped one arm around her front, and spooned her.

"Oh," she murmured, sounding pleased.

"Like that?" He kissed her neck right below her ear.

A visible shiver ran through her. "You're an amazing man."

He chuckled. "I'll try not to let this compliment go to my head." He shifted behind her, readjusting his still semi-hard cock to rest between her thighs.

"You can't possibly..." she started, but he interrupted her.

"Don't worry, I won't harass you again just yet. I'll let you rest first. I do have manners." Even though those manners were currently skating on very thin ice. With Kim's gorgeous ass tucked into his groin, anything could happen if he didn't keep himself on a tight leash.

Kim laughed, a sound so warm and soft, he wanted to hear it every day.

She turned her head to look at him. "I don't need the rest. But I'm concerned about you. Are you sure you've fully healed?"

"Vampire blood does wonders. But even without it, immortals heal from their wounds very quickly."

She seemed to contemplate his answer. "Hmm." Then she said hesitantly, "But those wounds leave scars nevertheless."

He nodded, knowing she wasn't referring to his biceps but his chest. "I was a teenager when it happened. As children, we're almost as vulnerable as humans. Once we mature, a fire can't kill or injure us."

"And even though you knew that, you ran into your burning home?"

He sighed. "My parents were all I had. The fire...it was a result of the explosion."

She furrowed her forehead. "Explosion? You said to me that your parents died in the fire. But how could they if as adults a fire can't kill a Stealth Guardian?"

"I couldn't tell you the truth back then without telling you about who we are."

She squeezed his hand. "What really happened?"

"The demons. They found our home, attacked my parents to get to our portal, because they knew if they could access one of the Stealth Guardians' portals, they'd have access to all of them and could destroy us from within. My father and mother fought bravely. They managed to get word out to other guardians. But we got there too late. Later, when the fire was out, we found their bodies. It was my mother who, with her dying breath, activated the self-destruct sequence so the portal exploded before the demons could gain control of it. The explosion caused the fire." He let out a breath, thinking back to that day. "In my heart I knew they were dead when I ran into the flames. I think I wanted to die too. But the other guardians, the adults who couldn't be harmed by the fire, pulled me out. They saved me even though I didn't want to be saved."

"I'm so sorry. It must have been terrible."

"It was. I lost my parents. The Stealth Guardians lost two incredible warriors and an irreplaceable portal."

"Irreplaceable? What do you mean by that? Didn't the Stealth Guardians build the portals?"

"They did. They used a tool, which in our history books is referred to as the source dagger." He paused for a moment. Did he trust Kim enough to tell her these things?

"How?"

"The dagger had magical properties and was used to carve our symbol into stone or wood. Once carved, the portal came into existence. The dagger had other powers too. It could heal any wound inflicted by a weapon forged in the Dark Days. It was truly a powerful artifact. But the dagger was lost a long time ago."

"Was there only one?"

"Yes."

"So, the guardians can't make any more portals?"

"I'm afraid not. We have to make do with the ones we have."

"Like the one in the male strip club," Kim said.

Manus chuckled. "Not an ideal location, I know. But we can't risk moving it. Too much can go wrong, and we could accidentally destroy it."

"Maybe it's not a bad location after all. I mean, who's gonna suspect a portal underneath a stage with half-naked dancing men?" She grinned.

"Oh, you enjoyed that view when you followed me, did you?"

"What if I did?"

Manus grabbed hold of her thigh and lifted it just enough so he could shift his cock to Kim's pussy. "Then I'll have to make you forget what you've seen." He plunged into her still wet channel with one single thrust, seating himself deep inside her.

Kim moaned at the unexpected invasion. "I can't even remember that there was a stage."

"Good girl," he murmured into her ear. "But just to be safe, let's continue."

26

Kim disconnected the call. "Okay, she's expecting me this morning."

Manus, freshly showered and looking even more handsome than the night before, nodded. "Great. Then let's do this. And don't worry: I'll be with you the entire time."

"Is it really necessary for you to be invisible?"

"It's better this way, at least for now until I can be sure you're not being watched by the demons."

"But didn't you say yourself yesterday that you can't tell a demon from a human?"

"That's right, but at least I'll be able to see if *anybody* is following you. And if somebody is, then it's most likely a demon. Nobody else has a reason to keep tabs on you." Then he smirked. "Besides, I like watching your ass."

Kim rolled her eyes but didn't take the comment as an insult. Manus had proven to be a very considerate lover and not the cold-hearted macho his colleagues apparently believed him to be. "You're incorrigible!"

Manus winked at her, oozing with charm. "Maybe if you try harder, you can correct my many faults."

She felt a flame ignite inside her. After everything she'd found out about Manus, she felt she knew him. And the many faults he referred to weren't really faults. Some of them were qualities. Loyalty and love had made him run into a burning house to save his parents. Not pride or foolishness. Loss and grief had turned him into a commitment shy man. Not callousness and coldness. But she also recognized that he wasn't quite ready to see that yet. Just like a hurt animal, he needed to trust again. And it was up to her to help him in that endeavor. But she was realistic too. Once all this was over, once they'd found what the demons were after, he would go back to his world, and she to hers. Yet that knowledge didn't stop her from dreaming of what could be if they both belonged to the same world and not to different ones. After all, Mayor Wallace and her husband, Hamish, seemed to make it work. She so wished she could ask her best friend for advice, but Manus and his colleagues had made it abundantly clear that she could never tell a soul who they were, what they were. And without telling Jennifer why she thought there was no future for her and Manus, there was no point in even telling her that they were intimate.

"Everything okay?" Manus suddenly asked, concern in his voice.

She quickly pasted a smile on her face. "All is good. Let's go then." She grabbed her handbag and her keys and headed for her apartment door. When she opened it and looked over her shoulder, she couldn't see Manus. "Are you—?"

A warm hand on her hip stopped her.

"I don't think I'll ever get used to this," she murmured, then left her condo and locked up.

She took public transportation, now and then feeling Manus's touch, reassuring her that he was still with her. It was a strange feeling but not an unpleasant one.

Arrived at her destination, Kim got off the bus and waited on the sidewalk for a moment, giving Manus a chance to catch up, then she walked the few steps to the entrance of the Museum of Antiquities, where her mother had been a curator.

At the info desk, she stopped and addressed the employee on duty there, "Hi, I'm here to see Emily Clyster."

The employee already reached for the telephone. "Is she expecting you?"

"Yes. Tell her that Kim Britton is here."

"Oh, yes, I'm sorry I didn't recognize you. I knew your mother. So sorry," the young man said.

"Thank you."

It took only moments for him to announce her to Emily, who'd been her mother's assistant for many years. When he put down the phone, he pointed to an elevator behind him. "Go to the top floor. Emily will be meeting you there."

"Thank you."

Kim walked past the information podium and pressed the elevator button. The door opened instantly, and she stepped in, taking her time. Slowly, the doors closed.

"Manus?"

"I'm still here, no worries," he said in a low voice. "And don't be so nervous. You're not committing a crime. You're just gonna look at a few things and ask some questions."

She fidgeted. "I know that, but it still feels wrong to snoop around when it's not technically my mother's office anymore."

Manus squeezed her arm. "You can do it."

A moment later, the elevator doors opened. In the hallway, Emily was waiting. She was a woman who should have retired a decade ago but always claimed she would get bored if she didn't have a job to go to. The last time Kim had seen her was at her mother's funeral.

Emily opened her arms, and Kim walked into the embrace, allowing the older woman to hug her tightly to her big chest and the warmth emanating from there to seep into her. It was a comfort she hadn't enjoyed in a long time.

"How you doing, hon?" Emily asked as she released her.

"I'm alright," Kim managed to say, wiping a traitorous tear off her cheek. "It's so good to see you, Emily."

"And it's good seeing you. I wondered when you'd be ready to come by and get your mother's things."

"I'm sorry it's taken me so long."

Emily made a dismissive hand movement. "It's no bother. You just weren't ready. All in good time."

Kim smiled at her, grateful for the kind words. "Could we go to her office?" She sighed. "I just want to see it one more time and remind myself of where she spent most of her time."

"Of course," Emily responded. "Come with me."

They walked to the end of the corridor, then turned left before Emily opened a door and stepped inside. Kim followed.

"You're in luck. The new curator is out of town today."

"Oh." Kim hadn't really thought about the fact that her mother had been replaced so soon. "Is she going to mind?"

"He," Emily corrected, "and he's not gonna find out. He doesn't need to know everything." She grimaced.

"Do you like your new boss?" Kim asked, sensing a trace of hostility in Emily's tone.

The older woman shrugged. "I think I might put in for my retirement after all."

"That bad?"

"It's just not the same without your mother." Then she took a deep breath. "So, let me see, I put all your mother's personal effects into a box in the office closet." She walked to a large built-in that covered one entire wall and opened a cabinet. "Ah, there it is."

Emily lifted out the box, and Kim immediately reached for it. "Let me help you."

"Thank you, hon."

Kim took the box and set it on the coffee table in the corner of the office that was equipped with a seating area. "Do you mind if I look through things quickly just to make sure I'm not taking anything that should really be given to her successor?"

"Oh, uh..."

"If you'll get into trouble for letting me in here, then I'll leave, of course. It's just..." Kim cast a look around the room to give Emily the impression that the memory of her mother was stronger. "...so much in here still reminds me of her..." She turned her face away and faked a sniffle.

"Oh, of course, hon. You take all the time you need. Why don't I get us some coffee from the kitchen?"

"You're the best, Emily. No wonder Mom loved you."

Emily smiled and left the room. The moment the door shut behind her, Kim heard the sound of somebody rifling through the box. She whirled around and stared at a snow globe floating in the air. She'd almost forgotten during her exchange with Emily that Manus was with her.

"Let's go through everything," Manus said, still invisible. "Here, start with the notebooks. I'll check out the calendar. The trinkets in here don't look like much." He placed the snow globe on the table.

Kim pointed to it. "I brought it back from a trip to Jasper National Park. I didn't realize she still had it."

"I didn't mean to diminish—"

She lifted her hand to stop him. "I know you didn't. But it's not gonna help us find a lead." She reached for the notebook and started leafing through it while she saw from the corner of her eye that the pages of the large paper calendar her mother had kept on her desk were being turned by an invisible hand.

For a few moments, there was silence between them.

"Have a look at this," Manus suddenly said, thrusting the calendar in front of her.

"What am I looking at?"

"This here."

"Manus, I can't see what you're pointing to since you're invisible."

"Oh sorry. Hazard of my gift," he said. "Look at the 4pm entry on the day of your mother's death."

Kim scanned the entries for that day and read. "Simon Kilgore, transl. celt." She looked up. "Looks like she had an appointment with a translator. Nothing unusual in her job."

"Maybe not, but if by *celt* she means Celtic, then I think we should look into it."

"Why?"

"Because that's our ancient language. So, if she saw an inscription on something that she believed to be Celtic, it could have something to do with us or the demons."

There was a sound at the door.

"Ask her assistant if she knew anything about it," Manus managed to say before the door opened fully and Emily reentered with two cups of coffee.

Kim put down the notebook she'd been looking through and walked toward Emily, reaching for the cup. "Oh, thank you so much." She took a sip. Emily did the same.

"May I ask you something, Emily?"

"Of course, hon. What is it?"

"I always thought that Mom wasn't working on the day that she died."

"That's right."

"But I just saw an entry in her calendar..." Kim picked up the calendar from where Manus had laid it down and set down the coffee cup. "Here it is. She was meeting with a translator. So, she must have been working that day after all."

Emily leaned in to look at the entry, squinting slightly. "Hmm. That's not an appointment I made for her."

"But weren't you making all appointments for her?"

"Most of the time, yes, 'cause it saved her a lot of time rather than her having to track people down and figure out when they could meet. I mean, that was my job. Must have been something private."

"That's odd. Why would she need a translator?"

Emily looked at the entry again. "It's definitely not for anything in the museum. If I'm not mistaken, her abbreviation means Celtic, and we haven't had any Celtic items in quite a while."

"Thanks, Emily. I guess you must be right. Maybe she found something on an antiques market."

"Yes, she loved those, didn't she?" A bittersweet smile crossed Emily's face. "I know she was raving about a find the weekend before her death."

"Oh? Do you know what she'd bought?"

Emily shook her head. "You knew your mother. She never let the cat out of the bag until she was absolutely sure she knew what she had."

"You're right." Kim sighed. "Listen, I shouldn't take up more of your time. All the things in the box are definitely personal items. I'll take the box home."

"You do that, hon."

A hug and a goodbye later, and Kim exited the museum.

"What now?" she whispered outside. "Do you think Mom found something at one of those antiques markets that she needed a translator for?"

"One way to find out," Manus replied just as quietly.

27

———

Simon Kilgore's office was located in a strip mall over a dry cleaner in a rough part of town.

"Are you sure you want to go visible this time?" Kim asked as they sat in the car a block away from Kilgore's office.

Manus turned his head to her and nodded. "I want to question him myself. Besides, I couldn't detect anybody following you when we went to the museum. It doesn't look like the demons have you under twenty-four-hour surveillance." Or if they did, they were very good, better than they'd been in the past. And maybe at this stage, letting the demons know that he was onto them wasn't all bad. It wouldn't be the first time a demon screwed up because he was under pressure. It could provide him and his brethren with a lead in the process.

"I must admit, seeing you makes me feel more comfortable than not knowing where you are," Kim admitted now. "I know this whole invisibility thing is cool and all, but it's also a little annoying for those who're not invisible."

"Well, then maybe next time I'll make you invisible too," he said casually.

"What?"

"Guess I forgot to mention that I can make others invisible, either by touch or with my mind."

"Really? I mean, we'd both be invisible?" She shook her head. "But then you wouldn't know where I was, and I wouldn't know where you were. That sounds a bit chaotic."

"It's not, because you'd be able to see me, and I'd be able to see you."

Her mouth dropped open. "And nobody else would?"

"That's right." He grinned and leaned toward her. "We could even make love in public and nobody would see us."

Her eyes widened. "Oh my God, that's your first thought? You're impossible!" Despite her words, mischief sparkled in her eyes.

Manus chuckled. "Don't tell me you wouldn't enjoy that." He slid his hand behind her nape and pulled her face to him. "I could take you right here, and nobody would be the wiser." He slanted his mouth over hers and kissed her, deep and hard, before releasing her. "Unfortunately, we've got work to do."

Kim's face was flushed, and she blew out a big breath. "You're such a tease."

"Don't tempt me." He pressed another quick kiss on her lips, then reached for the handle of the car door. "Let's do this."

Moments later they reached the entry to the lobby leading to Kilgore's office. The door was unlocked, as was to be expected during business hours. On the first floor, there were several doors, one marked *Mechanical Closet*, one without any inscription, and the last one saying *Employees Only*. This one appeared to be a secondary entrance into the dry-cleaning business.

Manus climbed the stairs, Kim by his side. On the landing, a sign directed them to the left, where three doors were located. The second one was Kilgore's. Manus knocked.

"Come in," a man answered.

Manus opened the door and entered. Kim followed close behind. The office was stuffed with books, magazines, and other papers. Bookcases lined the walls. Boxes stood waist-high off to one side of the room. Behind a desk with papers piled high on one side, a skinny man in his fifties pored over a book. A computer monitor took up the other side of the desk, and on the floor, an old desktop tower hugged the desk.

"Mr. Kilgore?" Manus asked. "Simon Kilgore?"

The man looked over his reading glasses. "Yes. How can I help you?"

Manus took a few steps closer. "I got your name from a friend, Mrs. Britton, Nancy Britton."

Recognition flickered in the man's eyes. "Uh, Britton, hmm, yes, I think I may have done some work for her."

Clearly, Kilgore wasn't searching his memory. He knew exactly what kind of work he'd done for Nancy.

"A Celtic translation, I believe she mentioned to me," Manus said, fishing for more information.

"Hmm, that's quite possible. Yes, yes, now I remember. I reviewed a short text for her." Kilgore glanced past Manus to where Kim stood, then back to him. "Do you need any translation work done?"

"Not exactly."

Kilgore raised an eyebrow. "Then, if it's not a translation you're after, I'm not sure..."

"You said you reviewed a text for her. You didn't translate it?"

The man cleared his throat. "I really can't talk to a stranger about work I did for another client. Confidentiality, you understand."

"Nancy Britton was my mother," Kim said, stepping closer. "And you were the last person to see her on the day of her murder."

Kilgore sat up straight, a look of outrage spreading over his face. "You're not suggesting that I had anything to do with—"

"Nobody is suggesting that," Manus interrupted quickly. "But since you were her last appointment that day, we're trying to get a sense of what her business was that day."

Kilgore seemed to relax a little. "Well, I mean, since she's dead"— he cast a quick look at Kim—"my condolences... I guess it doesn't hurt anybody to tell you what I did for her." He tossed a glance at his computer, then seemed to think of it otherwise. "She had sent me a copy of a short text she wanted me to review. It was in Celtic but a very old form of it. I gave her a brief overview over the content of the text, and she paid me for my time."

"That's all?" Manus asked.

Kilgore shrugged. "Pretty much."

"What was it about?"

"It was hard to make heads or tails of it. It started in the middle of something and then ended abruptly. Hard to really know what it was other than that it was some sort of fairytale or old myth."

Manus hummed to himself. Their history books could read like fairytales for anybody who didn't know what they were looking at. "You said a copy. Was it just one page?"

"Yes."

"But it seemed to be taken out of context? Perhaps a page out of a book?"

Kilgore looked away for a brief second, but Manus caught the action. The translator was trying to hide what he knew. And he knew more than what he was willing to tell. "Sure, yeah," he said non-committal. "But she never showed me a book or contracted me to translate one. Sorry." He stood up, a sure sign that he wanted to end the conversation. "I wish I could help you, but I don't know anything else."

Manus hesitated. He had to use other methods to find out what he needed to know. "Thank you for your help, Mr. Kilgore. We appreciate it." He turned to Kim. "Let's go."

He ushered Kim out of the office and down the hall.

"He was clearly lying," Kim said at the top of the stairs.

"Not here," Manus warned and took her hand to lead her down the stairs and out of the building.

Only once they were back inside the car did he speak again. "I know he was lying. He knows what was written on the page he saw. Even if it was an old form of Celtic."

"What do you think it was?" Kim asked curiously.

"I don't want to speculate."

"But then, what are we gonna do? We can't just give up."

"We're not giving up." Manus started the engine. "Did you see all the files and stacks of papers in his office?"

Kim nodded. "So?"

"He makes notes about everything. Which means there would be notes on that page that your mother gave him to review. Maybe even a full translation. We'll have to find it."

"You're not suggesting what I think you're suggesting, are you?"

"What do you think I'm suggesting?"

"To break in."

"You're learning fast. I don't know whether I should be proud of you or embarrassed that I'm corrupting you." Or turned on about the fact that Kim didn't seem to be scared of committing a crime to get to the truth.

28

———

All businesses in the strip mall were closed now, except for the Chinese takeout two doors down from the dry cleaners. There was steady traffic there despite the late hour, but Manus wasn't concerned about being detected. He and Kim had arrived cloaked, even though he doubted that the customers frequenting the Chinese restaurant would take any notice of them. However, since he had to break into the translator's office, Manus thought it best to be as inconspicuous as possible. And what was more inconspicuous than being invisible?

As expected, the glass door to the lobby, which was lit, was locked. Manus motioned to Kim—the only person who could see him—to wait for him while he passed through the door to get inside. He knew from his earlier visit that there was no alarm system. It was child's play to unlock the door from inside and open it.

He ushered Kim inside, then closed the door behind her, making sure nobody was watching and seeing a door open and close by itself.

"Just as well that you and your people aren't burglars," Kim said. "You'd be robbing us all blind, and we would never catch you."

Manus winked at her. "If this gig doesn't pan out for me, I might consider it as my second career choice." He put his foot on the first step. "I hear the pay is good."

Kim laughed softly. "Don't tell me they don't compensate you well enough for what you do."

He shook his head. "Money has no real meaning in our society. None of us gets paid."

He started walking up the stairs, and Kim caught up with him. "What? Then how do you live without money?"

"Oh, don't get me wrong. There's money. The compound has a budget, and everything a warrior needs comes out of that budget. But there's no personal property other than the furnishings in our private quarters. And even those were paid for by the compound."

"I didn't expect that. So, you're doing this job why?"

Manus smirked. "Being a warrior is a babe magnet." He met her eyes to make sure she knew he wasn't being serious. He didn't want to talk about the real reason why he'd become a warrior. Not just because he wanted to avenge his parents, but because being a warrior meant the chances of him ever loving somebody again were slim. Warriors in their society were in many cases foregoing having a family. Of course, his own compound mates were different in that aspect. Most of them had somehow managed to find a mate who hadn't asked them to give up their work. It was unusual to say the least.

A hand on his butt pulled him from his thoughts. "I guess it's not working for every warrior, is it?" Kim didn't quite manage to suppress her chuckle. The little minx was making fun of him.

"You'll pay for that later," he murmured back. "A warrior doesn't tolerate insolence."

Arrived at the landing, Manus turned to his left and marched toward Kilgore's office. In the upper corridor, the light was burning too. It wasn't unusual. Most businesses left the main lights on to deter burglars. At the door to Kilgore's office, Manus stopped and looked over his shoulder to Kim, who'd followed close behind.

"I'll open up from inside," he said, then turned back to the door.

He took a step closer when he noticed that the door wasn't closed. "Shit!" he hissed under his breath.

"What?"

He whirled his head to Kim and put a finger over his lips to silence her. Then he pointed to the ajar door. Kim followed his direction. Her eyes widened. He motioned her to remain where she was, then walked through the door without opening it any wider. If somebody was inside Kilgore's office, he had to surprise them.

Inside the office, it was dark. The blinds were open, allowing the faint lights from the parking lot to penetrate, throwing long shadows into the room. Manus allowed his eyes to adjust to the darkness and scanned the area. At first glance, nothing appeared out of order and the office was just as messy as earlier in the day. He listened for any sounds and held his breath to be able to detect if anybody else was breathing. But complete silence surrounded him. He was alone. Whoever had left the door open, and he didn't think Kilgore had been so careless, was long gone.

He walked back to the door and opened it. "Nobody here. You can come in," he announced to Kim.

Hesitantly, she entered the office and pulled the door shut behind her.

"I'll close the blinds, so we can use some light to do our search," he said and walked to the window. He passed the desk. Suddenly, his foot caught on something, and he would have stumbled had he not gripped the edge of the desk to brace himself. His gaze flew to the floor. "Fuck!"

"What? What is it?" Kim asked in panic, the sound of her footfalls indicating that she was coming closer.

"Don't!" he warned her. But it was too late. She was already shoulder to shoulder with him.

She gasped. "Oh my God!"

At Manus's feet, Kilgore's body lay frozen in death. He'd been stabbed in the heart. Manus crouched down to examine the wound. It was the one that had killed him in the end, but it wasn't the only one. Kilgore bore defensive wounds on his arms and torso.

"He fought with his attacker."

"Who would do such a thing?" Kim mused.

He looked up at her. "Would you close the blinds, please?"

Kim sprang into action and closed the blinds of the large window, allowing almost complete darkness to descend on the office. "Done."

Manus pulled out his flashlight and switched it on. "Thanks." He ran the light over Kilgore's body.

Kim stepped around him from the other side, where the chair had been pushed against the wall, and put her hand on the armrest for support as she bent down. Surprised that she didn't recoil from the dead body, Manus looked up at her.

"He looks scared."

Manus cast a glance at Kilgore's face. His eyes were open, and Kim was right: there was fear in his eyes. "He knew what was coming."

"Demon?"

"Would be my guess. He was stabbed. Demons always carry daggers with them."

"But my mother wasn't stabbed."

"No. There's another way a demon kills. One that leaves no outside trace."

"How did he do it? The demon that killed my mother. What did she feel?"

Surprised at the question, Manus sat back on his haunches and sighed. "Kim, it doesn't help you to—"

"No, please, tell me. I need to know. What did she feel? Did she suffer?"

Manus let out a long, deep breath. "Are you sure you want to know?"

She nodded wordlessly.

"Okay... A demon has to feed. We know they eat human food to nourish their bodies, but they need something else to feed their demon existence. They take a human's lifeforce, their essence, by sucking it out of their mouth or nose. I've seen it once. It's like a mist, like a fine fog that emanates from the human. The demon takes it in. It strengthens him, gives him power."

"How do they get to the lifeforce? How can it just leave a human's body?"

"By fear alone. They aren't called the Demons of Fear for nothing. They frighten the human so they can take their lifeforce."

"And the pain? Is there pain?"

"Physical pain?" Manus paused for a moment. "Not in the true sense of the word. Physically, your mother wouldn't have felt much. It's mostly psychological. The body itself doesn't experience true pain as the lifeforce is extracted."

"How can you know that?"

"Because we've encountered people who've had it done to them."

"They survived?"

Manus nodded. "Because we got to them before the demon took all of their lifeforce. Sometimes, they only take enough to feed and leave the human alive." He reached for Kim's hand and squeezed it. "Your mother was frightened of him, but she wasn't in pain when she died. I promise you that."

Kim sniffled. "Thank you." She rubbed her nose with the back of her hand, then pointed to Kilgore. "So, you think this wasn't a demon kill?"

Manus didn't answer immediately. He illuminated the area around the body with his flashlight. Papers were scattered on the floor, a water bottle had spilled and soaked the carpet, writing utensils lay under the desk. Something was peeking out from underneath Kilgore's right hip. With his free hand, Manus rolled the body toward the window, just enough so he could see what was underneath the dead man.

"A letter opener," Kim said.

Manus took it and let the light shine on the blade. "With green demon blood on its tip." He looked up at Kim. "He injured the demon who killed him."

"Why would the demons want to kill the translator?" Kim asked.

Manus rose. "Because he knew what your mother had given him to translate. And they didn't want us to find out."

"But why now? I thought you said we weren't followed."

"We weren't." He pointed at Kilgore's body. "Which means Simon Kilgore told them that we came looking for it. He warned them that we're onto them."

"You're saying he worked for them?"

"Possibly."

"Then why would they kill him?"

"Demons have no loyalties. He'd become a liability. They had to get rid of him."

Manus noticed her swallowing hard. "You think they took whatever Kilgore wrote down about the translation?"

"Most likely. But demons aren't perfect. They might have missed something. Let's look."

Manus stepped over the body to look to the side of the desk where he'd seen the computer tower earlier in the day. The old-fashioned machine lay on its side, its metal housing missing, the interior smashed up as if somebody had taken a sledgehammer to it. Manus examined it more closely.

"Motherboard's a goner." He knew enough about IT to know there was no getting at the data that was saved on the hard drive.

"Maybe there's a paper file," Kim suggested.

Manus scanned the desk and looked at the different trays. Despite the mess in his office, Kilgore had a system. Manus pointed the flashlight at the file drawers that stood along one wall and read the labels.

"Alphabetical files," Manus noted, then looked at the trays on the desk again. "And dated trays, going back a couple of months at least." He looked at Kim. "Go through the file cabinets. Start with B for Britton, then N for Nancy. I'll go through these trays in case he hadn't had a chance to file your mother's translation yet."

Kim followed his command, pulled out her own flashlight, and went to work. Manus plowed through the files, one after the other, but it became clear very quickly that Nancy's file wasn't among the ones on the desk.

"Anything?" He looked over his shoulder.

Kim closed the drawer marked with a large N. "Nothing. There's a hanging file in the Bs where Britton should be located, but it's empty." She sighed and leaned back against a side table, clearly frustrated. "We're too late."

"There are other ways of finding out what your mother found," Manus said though he was just as frustrated as Kim. If only they'd gotten here a few hours earlier.

"Let's go," Kim suggested and turned, walking toward the door.

The light of Manus's flashlight illuminated her back. Simultaneously, he heard a siren in the background.

"Fuck!"

29

Kim spun around, alarmed by Manus's curse. "What?"

He pointed at her. "Your clothes... they're stained with green demon blood."

"Yuck!" she let out. Could anything else go wrong today? "This had better come out in the wash." She pivoted back to the door but didn't get far.

Manus laid his hands on her shoulders. "That's not the point."

"Well, it is for me."

He turned her to face him, but she had a hard time making out his face. He'd switched off his flashlight. "Kim, I can't make demon blood invisible."

"Then we stay visible," she said. "There's not much going on out there anyway."

"There is." Manus let go of her shoulders and walked to the window, where he peeked through the blinds. "Police have just arrived."

"What? How do they know?" She pointed in the general direction of Kilgore's body. "There's no way."

Manus lifted his hand to stop her. "They're not here for Kilgore. It looks like they're here for the Chinese place downstairs. Probably a fight." He turned away from the window and walked toward her again.

"But we've gotta get out of here. If they somehow come up and find Kilgore's body, we're screwed."

Manus took her hand. "They won't have a reason to come up here. But I agree we've gotta leave. And we can't afford to be seen by anybody because tomorrow, when all the other businesses open again, somebody will find Kilgore's body, and we don't want sketches of us out there as suspected murderers."

"But you just said yourself that you can't make me fully invisible, not with the demon blood on me." Her throat constricted at the thought that she wouldn't get away.

"We need new clothes for you."

"Are you saying you'll leave me here on my own to go back to my place and—"

"There's a dry cleaner downstairs. We'll find something there." He tugged at her hand. "Come."

Relieved, she went with him. They walked down the stairs, Kim staying as close to the wall as possible, so if somebody looked through the glass doors into the lobby, the chance of them seeing green dots floating in the air was minimal.

When they reached the foot of the stairs, Kim was glad to see that none of the police officers outside was in sight.

"This way," Manus instructed and hurried to a door with a sign saying *Employees Only*. "I'll go through and open from the inside. But you'll have to give me a sign that it's clear and nobody is looking into the lobby when I'm opening the door. Okay?"

"Got it."

A second later, she watched Manus step through the door and disappear. She heard a lock flip from the inside and quickly flicked her gaze to the entrance doors. "Still clear," she said loud enough for Manus to hear, but not loud enough for anybody outside to register the sound.

The door opened toward her, and she stepped aside, then slid through the opening while Manus pulled the door closed behind her and flicked the lock shut.

It was dark, but they couldn't risk switching on a light or using their flashlights because the dry cleaning business had a glass front. If one of the police officers passed the store front, they would notice the light and take action.

"Let's go in the back," Manus suggested and took her hand to lead her through the rows of clothing hanging from long conveyor lines, all wrapped in plastic.

When they reached the back of the business, Kim could make out a large folding table, several stools and benches as well as cabinets built along the back wall. Above were several windows located close to the ceiling, letting in some light from the street running along the back of the strip mall. Nobody could see into the building from there, and the rows and rows of clothing provided ample coverage from the other side.

"Get undressed," Manus ordered and reached for a plastic wrapper. "Put your stained clothes in one of these. I'll toss them in the trash."

"Can't we just wash the stains out here?" She pointed to a sink and various spray bottles. "I'm sure they have stain removers here. I mean, it's a dry cleaner."

"Sorry. But demon blood doesn't come out."

She sighed.

Manus turned around and walked toward the rows of clothing. "Let me find you something suitable to wear."

While she heard him rummage through the dry-cleaned clothes, Kim shucked her long-sleeved shirt and shimmied out of her favorite jeans. The demon blood had even soaked through to her camisole, so she pulled it over her head and tossed it on the heap.

More sirens from outside sent a shiver down her spine. It was time to get out of here. Hurriedly, she stuffed the stained clothes into the plastic wrapper and made a knot at the top to close it. At the sound of some rustling behind her, she spun around.

Manus stood right in front of her, several hangers with clothes wrapped in plastic in one hand. He just stared at her, and she was suddenly fully aware of her nakedness. Another shiver raced down her spine, but this one wasn't caused by fear.

When Manus didn't say anything, she said, "I heard more sirens. Are more police arriving?"

He shook his head. "Worse. DEA. Looks like it's a drug raid."

"Shit!" she cursed under her breath.

The barking of a dog cut through the silence that followed.

"And they brought dogs."

Instinctively, Kim wrapped her arms around her torso. "They aren't gonna come in here, are they?"

"They have no reason to. They're focused on the Chinese restaurant. I guess they're involved with the Triad or some other Chinese drug gang. But I'm afraid we have to stay here until they're all gone. If we try to sneak by the police now, the dogs will go nuts. They'll smell us. Besides, with so much law enforcement out there, I'll never be able to open a door for you without them noticing it. And while I can keep us both invisible, you can't walk through a wall. There's no way out until they're gone. Sorry."

"How long?"

"A few hours for sure."

The thought of waiting in a dry cleaners shop with a dead body above them and law enforcement with a K9 unit searching the strip mall for drugs suffused her with fear. At the same time, she realized what Manus was risking for her. "Without me, you'd be able to leave through the back wall." She gestured toward it. "But with me, you're stuck. I'm sorry."

Manus reached for her arms and pulled her against his chest. "Don't be. I couldn't imagine anybody else I'd want to be stuck with at the dry cleaners." He chuckled. "In the dark. Naked." His mouth was suddenly at her ear. "I don't know about you, but I could think of something to while away the time."

Kim put one arm around his back and slid her hand to his nape. "You're a scoundrel, Manus. If I didn't know any better, I'd say you called the police with a tip yourself."

"You have a vivid imagination, Kim. Why don't you put it to better use and hop onto that table, so I can have my way with you, hmm?"

Her entire body tingled at the knowledge that Manus was intending to seduce her. At a dry cleaners of all places! She'd never done anything that forbidden. Never done anything that dangerous. Surrounded by law enforcement, in the middle of a drug raid, a dead body only a floor away—no, she'd never done anything like that. It made her feel daring.

She brought her lips to Manus's ear. "You want to fuck me?"

He let out a ragged breath and pressed his rock-hard cock against her groin. "That answer your question?"

She sucked his earlobe between her lips and gave it a tender bite. "Then you should just take what you want. Any which way you want it." She'd never given any man such license. Such free rein.

"You sure you wanna give me such liberty?"

She slid her hand down to his pants and laid it over the heavy bulge there. "If you don't, then I'll do what I want with you."

"And what might that involve?"

"Slow torture," she murmured into his ear.

He chuckled softly. "In that case, why don't I take the reins, and we'll reserve slow torture for a night when we have more leisure?"

Manus didn't wait for an answer but instead lifted her onto the table. Kim didn't protest. With expert hands, Manus stripped her of her panties and put them aside. Then he stepped back and undressed, first taking off his shirt, then his boots, his socks, and pants, and finally his boxer briefs.

Despite the dim light, she could see all she needed to see. His cock was hard and heavy, his gaze penetrating and filled with lust. When she felt his hands on her knees, pushing her legs apart, she let out a sigh. With his hands still on her knees, he rubbed his cock against her wet folds. A moan escaped her. There would be no foreplay tonight. She didn't mind. She couldn't wait to feel him inside her, impaling her, taking her.

With one thrust, he seated himself deep inside her, stretching her interior muscles to their capacity. It felt like he was even bigger tonight than before. Even harder. She clutched his shoulders and drew herself closer to him. Her breasts whipped, brushing against his chest.

A grunt was Manus's answer, then he drew back quickly, allowing his cock to withdraw from her sheath halfway before he plunged back in, faster this time. And with more force.

She gasped and gripped his shoulders more tightly.

"You said any which way," he said and repeated the movement. "So, I'm gonna fuck you the way you need to be fucked."

"Yes," was all she could reply before Manus took her hands and pried them off his shoulders, then eased her down to lie with her back flat on the table.

The next thrust made her body vibrate and turned her nipples into hard buds. Manus's hands were on her hips now, pulling her against him with each invasion, doubling the impact. She saw his silhouette move rapidly, heard his breathing, felt his strength, his power, his desire. There was beauty in his movements, and a confidence that she'd never seen another man display. As if he knew that no matter what he did, she wouldn't refuse him, would accept everything he was willing to give her. And she drank it in, the hard pounding of his cock, the relentless touch of his hands, the penetrating look in his eyes. A look that told her that he considered her his, that he'd never let another man touch her. That knowledge made her shiver. Nobody had ever wanted her like this.

Everything seemed to disappear around her. As if fog was rolling in and engulfing them. With it, her body began to tingle, and her arousal seemed to take on new heights. An orgasm hit her out of nowhere, crashing through her like an ocean wave. She gasped at the intensity of it and tried to catch her breath, but the next one was already cresting, burying her underneath it. The waves kept coming, kept driving her from one high to the next. She was floating, her body not her own anymore. She felt so much more than just her own cells. She felt Manus, sensed him as if she'd taken on animal senses, could feel something that she'd never thought was possible. As if she was connected to him by more than just his cock inside her. As if their souls were connected; as if they were somehow talking to each other.

Then she felt it, felt Manus's orgasm as his semen exploded from the tip of his cock, filling her, igniting another orgasm in her. Her body was shaking now, unable to come down from its high.

"Oh God!" What was happening to her?

"Fuck!" Manus cried out and suddenly pulled out of her. "What have I done?" He shrank back, panic in his voice.

Kim reared up from her position. The same panic she'd heard in his voice was reflected in his eyes now as he stared at her.

"What? What's wrong?" Her heart was pounding now.

Guilt replaced the panic in Manus's eyes as he continued staring at her. Something in his look made her glance down at herself. Shock jolted through her body. She stretched out her arms and stared at them in disbelief. "Oh my God, what's wrong with me?"

Her skin was shimmering golden.

"What's wrong? Is it the demon blood? Did it infect me?"

"No! No, nothing like that. You're fine. Trust me." Manus took a step toward her but stopped short of touching her.

"But—"

"It's my fault. I'm sorry." He ran a shaky hand through his hair. "I've never done this before."

She shook her head, confused and afraid. "Have sex? We had sex before."

"Yeah, but not like this. Not the Stealth Guardian way."

She furrowed her forehead but didn't get a chance to turn her confusion into a question.

"It's a way of making love that's unique to our kind," Manus explained quickly. "It's nothing to be afraid of. It's just—"

"It's just what? Is my skin golden from now on? I can't go out in public like that. People are gonna—"

"It'll fade. Very soon. In a few hours. I didn't pour that much *virta* in you."

"Virta? What's virta?"

"My lifeforce." He dropped his head and looked down at his feet as if he was ashamed.

"But I don't understand. Why? How? Why?"

He lifted his head and looked straight into her eyes. "Because I wanted you to feel *me*. To feel who I really am. I didn't want to hide myself anymore."

For a moment, she let it all sink in. That's what she'd felt. Him. His soul. His true self. He'd shared that with her. He wanted more than just sex. He wanted her to know him. A tear of joy in her eye, she lifted her hand to touch his face and was surprised when he shrank back.

"There's something else you need to know."

She swallowed hard.

"While your skin shimmers golden, every touch by me will result in you having another orgasm."

Her mouth dropped open. "Are you serious?"

Manus nodded. "Sorry. I don't know what came over me. I never—"

"You've never done this with anybody else?"

He shook his head.

Kim hopped off the table and wrapped her arms around him. Almost instantly, she climaxed again, and her knees buckled.

Manus caught her, pressing her firmly against him. "See, I told you."

"What are we gonna do now?" she murmured into his ear.

"What do *you* want to do?"

"Are the police still out there?"

"Yes."

She brushed her lips to his cheek. "Then maybe we should take advantage of this golden shimmer. That is, if you're up for it."

She felt Manus's hands descending to her ass, cupping her possessively. "Hmm, a woman after my own heart."

30

———

Manus still couldn't believe what had happened between him and Kim. Even now, more than twelve hours later, he was still in a state of shock. But no matter how often he told himself that it was wrong to have made love to Kim the Stealth Guardian way, he couldn't get himself to regret it. He'd never felt anything even close to the kind of bliss he'd experienced with Kim in his arms.

After the DEA, police, and K9 units had finally cleared the strip mall in the early hours of the morning, Manus had smuggled Kim into the compound and into his private quarters—he hoped without anybody noticing. Taking her to her own place while she was still shimmering golden hadn't been advisable. What if he lost his concentration and she suddenly became visible? If somebody saw her, questions would be raised. No, the best course of action had been to take her back to the compound. At least that's how he justified his actions to himself. That in reality he wanted her scent to rub off on his sheets was another matter altogether.

While Kim took a shower, Manus dialed Logan's number from the house phone and let it ring. He didn't have to wait long.

"Hey, Manus, what's up? Why are you here? I thought you'd be guarding Kim," Logan said.

"I am." He left it at that. "Listen. I need Winter's help."

"What for?"

Manus rolled his eyes. Logan was always protective of Winter, always looking out for her so that she wouldn't overexert herself by using her gift for useless endeavors. And if Manus were honest, if he had a mate who was a psychic, he'd probably do the same.

"We had bad luck last night. We broke into that translator's office who was doing some work for Nancy Britton. But a demon got there before us. Kilgore is dead. And there's no record of what he did for Nancy."

"Ah, crap. So, you're at a dead end?"

"Not if Winter can help us."

"What did you have in mind?"

"Can you bring her to Nancy's house? Maybe being around Nancy's things can trigger a vision. It's worked before."

There was a pause, then a sigh. "It doesn't always work that way."

"What doesn't?" The voice was fainter but definitely that of Winter.

"Manus wants to use your gift," Logan explained.

"Is it for something important?" Winter asked.

"Yes," Logan said.

"Give me that." Then her voice was louder as she was speaking directly into the phone. "Manus? I'll do it."

"Thanks, Winter. I really wouldn't ask you if there were any other way."

"No problem. But I can't promise it'll work."

"I know that. But I appreciate you trying. Have Logan escort you to Nancy Britton's house. Shall we meet there in an hour?"

"That works. See you then."

Manus disconnected the call.

"Who were you talking to?"

He turned his head toward the door to the bathroom, where Kim stood, fully dressed in the clothes he'd stolen from the dry cleaners.

"Have I mentioned to you that one of our warriors is married to a psychic?"

"A psychic? A real one?" she asked.

"Yep. The whole nine yards. Visions and all. She'll help us."

"How?"

"She'll try to force a vision at your mother's house. Maybe she can see what your mother had that the demons want so desperately."

"If they don't already have it," Kim said bleakly.

"They don't. If they did, they wouldn't have had to kill Kilgore to stop us from finding out what it is."

"I hope you're right."

He smiled at her. He was certain about it.

An hour later, they were inside Nancy Britton's house. Logan and Winter had arrived at the same time, both invisible just like Manus and Kim. Logan wasn't taking any chances with his mate, since the demons had once kidnapped Winter in order to use her visions to their advantage. They were still after her, but now she was under the constant protection of Logan and the entire compound and never went anywhere on her own.

Today, they'd even taken an extra step of protection and brought Grayson with them so the hybrid could sniff out any approaching demons.

"Okay then," Winter now said, letting her gaze roam in the living room. She sighed. "This is where she died, isn't it?"

Kim stared at Winter. The woman didn't look like a psychic, or at least not like Kim imagined a psychic to look. On the way here, Manus had told her that Winter had once been a tarot reader, unaware of her true gift, and that the demons had targeted her. Back then, Winter had played the part of the psychic differently: gypsy clothing, bangles on her wrists, large earrings, wild hair. All of that was gone now. She looked totally normal—and very pretty. No wonder Logan had fallen in love with her. They made a handsome couple.

Kim now nodded in reply to Winter's question. "Did Manus tell you about it?"

Winter shook her head. "I can still sense her." She ran her hand over the sideboard and smiled. "She had a sense for history, for preservation. I like that."

Kim smiled back, then hesitated. She wanted to ask how it worked, how Winter got her visions and what they looked like, but she didn't feel that she could ask such a personal question of a woman she'd only just met.

Suddenly, she felt Manus's hand on her arm, making her turn her head to him. "Let's give Winter a little space to explore."

"Sure," Kim said quickly, then addressed Winter, "I can also show you her bedroom, if that helps."

"Later. Let me see what I get down here first," Winter said and started walking around the room. Everybody else stepped back, giving her space and remaining silent so she could concentrate on whatever she needed to concentrate on.

Manus pulled Kim into the kitchen. "I know you're anxious, but there's nothing you can do right now. Winter can't force these things. Us standing around watching her every move is just going to put pressure on her."

Kim sighed. "You're right. I'm just worried about what we'll do if Winter doesn't have a vision. Because if we don't know what my mother found, then how are we gonna figure out where she hid it?"

Manus squeezed her hand. "We'll figure it out somehow."

Despite his calm exterior, Kim knew that Manus was concerned too. After what they'd exchanged the previous night, after the glimpse she'd gotten into his soul, he couldn't hide anything from her anymore. Somehow, she could tell what he was really thinking: that they'd be screwed if the demons found what had been in her mother's possession.

"Nothing down here," Winter suddenly said from the living room. "I'm not getting anything. Sorry."

Kim was already walking back into the living room. "Can we try the bedroom? There are a lot more things that are more personal to Mom. Maybe that will help?"

Winter gave her a kind smile. "Sure."

As she ushered Winter toward the stairs and everybody else made motions to follow them, Winter looked over her shoulder. "Just Kim and I, please." She looked at Logan. "You swept the place. There's nobody upstairs. So, don't look so worried."

Logan grumbled something to himself but remained with the other two men while Kim walked upstairs ahead of Winter and led her into her mother's bedroom, which overlooked the backyard.

"This is it," Kim said and invited Winter to enter.

"Do you mind if I sit down on the bed?" Winter asked.

"Go ahead."

Winter took a seat at the edge of the bed and ran her hand over the duvet. "Do you have the clothes your mother wore on the day she died?"

Kim shook her head, surprised at the question. "The police still have those in evidence."

"Hmm." Winter looked around. "Is there anything else she might have had on her on the last day?"

Kim swept her gaze around the room, looking for the jacket her mother had worn on cool days, when her eyes caught on her mother's handbag, which sat on a chair. She pointed to it. "Mom never left the house without her handbag. She said she felt naked without it."

Winter rose. "May I?"

Kim was already picking it up and handing it to Winter. "Here."

Winter took it, holding the handle with one hand while touching the leather on the outside with the other. "Hmm." A disappointed look crossed her face. "I thought since it's such a personal item... But nothing."

"Are you sure? There are other things inside, her wallet, her lipstick. Maybe if you touch those…"

Winter reached into the handbag and rummaged around in it. Kim blinked away the growing disappointment and looked at her feet to hide the rising tears.

A gasp jolted her back to awareness. She spun her head back to Winter, who dropped the handbag on the floor. A wallet, keys, and several receipts fell from it. A lipstick rolled under the bed. But Kim wasn't concerned with any of this now because Winter looked like she was about to faint.

"Manus, Logan," Kim called out as she jumped toward Winter to catch her.

But she didn't have to support Winter's weight because Winter was already opening her eyes again, steadying herself and breathing normally again.

"Did you… Was that…?" Kim didn't dare hope.

Winter nodded.

Simultaneously, Logan stormed into the room, closely followed by Manus and Grayson. Logan gripped Winter's arms. "Are you okay?"

"Of course, I'm okay," she said. "It worked."

"What did you see?" Manus now asked eagerly.

"It's a book," Winter started. "But I couldn't see the title or what was written in it."

"Then how are we gonna—?"

Winter interrupted Manus, "Because I know whom it belongs to."

"Who?" Logan and Manus asked in unison.

"There was an inscription. It said, *To my wonderful daughter, our future warrior, Virginia. Your father.*"

Logan and Manus looked at each other.

"You don't think that…?" Logan asked.

"If you're right, then we're in deep shit," Manus confirmed.

"Virginia is the only one who can confirm it."

"Who's Virginia?" Kim interrupted.

Manus turned to her. "I'll introduce you to her. Fancy a trip to San Francisco?"

"San Francisco?" Kim echoed.

"We'll take the portal," Manus said.

"Mind if I hitch a ride?" Grayson asked. "It's my mother's birthday, and I'd like to surprise her."

Manus sighed. "If you must."

"I must," Grayson said, grinning.

31

———————

It was after dark when Manus, Kim, and Grayson arrived in the lost portal that was hidden in one of the subway tunnels in the San Francisco Mission district, close to Scanguards' headquarters. While Grayson walked straight to his father's company headquarters, Manus hailed a cab and had Kim and himself driven to the Corona Heights neighborhood, where Virginia lived with her witch husband, Wesley.

He'd asked Logan to call ahead to make sure Virginia would be expecting them and to fill her in on the essentials without telling her too much either. After all, Virginia was a member of the Council of Nine, the Stealth Guardians' ruling body, and if she was made aware of how many rules Manus had broken when it came to Kim, she would have to report him to the Council.

The house was a Victorian like so many in San Francisco. Wesley had bought it many years before he'd met Virginia, and after they'd bonded, she'd moved in, though she had to split her time between San Francisco and the secret location of the compound from where the Stealth Guardians ruled.

Manus was about to ring the doorbell when the door already swung open. Virginia, dressed in a long black evening gown, stood in the doorframe to greet them.

"Come on in," she said while looking past them, vigilant as ever.

"We were careful," Manus said immediately.

"I know. Just a habit."

Manus ushered Kim inside ahead of him, then followed her. Virginia closed the heavy oak door behind them and turned to face them.

She extended her hand to Kim. "I'm Virginia."

"Kim. Nice to meet you." Kim shook her hand.

"Thanks for seeing us on such short notice," Manus said. He listened for any sounds in the house, but it was quiet. "Wes here?"

"He's at HQ. I'm supposed to go there too, so let's get down to business." She pointed to her dress then motioned to the open arch that led into the living room. "Take a seat."

Manus followed the invitation, sitting down on the couch, while Kim did the same. Virginia sat down in an armchair facing them.

"Since we're all under time pressure here, let me get to the point. Logan already filled you in on the background: the demons are looking for an item that was previously in the possession of an emissarius, Nancy Britton, Kim's mother."

Virginia nodded. "I'm sorry for your loss, Kim."

"Thank you."

Manus continued, "We don't know where this item is now. But we have reason to believe that whatever it was, it's written in old Celtic. The translator who was sampling it to give Nancy an idea of what it is was murdered by a demon. Most likely to make it harder for us to find out what it is. But we have Winter."

"Yes, Winter," Virginia said.

"She was able to force a vision related to Nancy. We now have reason to believe that the item is a book that belongs to you."

"To me? But if it's one of my books, then it can't possibly be lost."

"I can only tell you what Winter saw: a book with an inscription reading *To my wonderful daughter, our future warrior, Virginia. Your father.*"

For a moment, there was silence so thick that a pin dropping could have been heard in the room. Virginia stared at him, eyes wide, mouth agape.

"You're saying Nancy Britton had *that* book in her possession?"

Manus's heart began to beat excitedly. "You recognize it?"

Virginia nodded and rose, turning her back to them and looking out the floor-to-ceiling window. "The only book that was ever dedicated to me by my father doesn't exist anymore. It was lost in the explosion that destroyed my compound in 1968. Most likely burned and buried with the rest of my possessions."

And the bodies of her compound brethren. Virginia had been the only survivor. But Manus didn't add that. They both knew what the other was thinking. Instead, he said, "You can't know that. Not everything burned. It might have been found, just like the portal was later used in the building of the BART system here in the city. We have to assume that the book survived the explosion."

Virginia turned around to face them again. "Then if the demons ever get their hands on it, we're screwed."

Manus rose, realizing how serious Virginia was. "What was the book, Virginia?"

"A comprehensive history and training manual of the Stealth Guardian warriors."

"Oh my God!" Though he'd had his suspicion, shock raced through Manus, reaching every single cell of his body. "We've gotta find it before the demons do."

"Do you have any idea where Nancy could have hidden it?" Virginia asked.

Manus shook his head.

Kim spoke up. "We've searched everywhere. But now that we know what it is, I'll search the house again, and the storage unit."

Virginia shook her head. "It won't be there. As an emissarius, your mother knew that those would be the first places the demons would search once they found out she had it. She would have been smarter than that. She would have hidden it where nobody would suspect it, but where you, Kim, would eventually find it. As the only relative, you're the executor of her will. She would have known that as you close out her affairs, you would come upon the book. But it wouldn't be obvious to anybody else."

Kim stared at her, stunned disbelief coloring her face. "You're saying it's up to me now?"

"Manus will help you, rest assured. But you knew your mother best. You know her thinking, her reasoning. You're the one best equipped to figure out what she did with the book." Virginia sighed. "I wish I could help you, particularly since it was mine in the first place."

"It's nobody's fault," Manus said quickly. "I just don't understand why Nancy didn't bring it to our attention immediately."

Kim shook her head. "She didn't know what she had. Don't you remember what Emily, her assistant, said? That she never let the cat out of the bag before she was sure? She wasn't sure it was connected to the Stealth Guardians, and after she spoke to the translator and most likely pieced together what he translated and what she suspected, she might not have had enough time to contact your people. The demon killed her that night."

Virginia nodded. "That's good thinking. It means you need to figure out what your mother did between the time she left the translator's office and the time she got killed. Somewhere in that time span, she hid the book."

Manus nodded at Virginia. "Thank you, Virginia, you've helped us a lot. We'd better make our way back to the portal. I need to call Grayson to meet us there."

"Grayson came with you? You're not gonna be able to leave that early. He'll be at the party."

"Party?" Manus asked.

"Yes, Samson is throwing Delilah a big bash for her birthday." She waved them to follow her into the hallway. "Come, I'll give you a ride to HQ. You might as well say hi to Samson and the gang. They'll be upset if you leave without showing your face."

Manus exchanged a quick look with Kim then glanced at the clock. "It's past midnight in Baltimore. There isn't much we can do there right now anyway. Can I take you out for a drink and introduce you to some friends?"

"Vampires?" Kim asked.

"That, some humans, and a few witches."

"I'm not gonna say no to a drink."

"Well, then, let's go. We'll take my car," Virginia said.

32

———

"Security is extra tight tonight," Virginia said as she stopped in front of a large building with a glass-fronted lobby that was lit up like it was daytime. Two guards flanked the entrance.

Virginia turned her head to Manus, who was sitting in the passenger seat, then glanced back to Kim sitting behind him. "Normally, I'd be able to drive into the underground garage, but with two non-Scanguards passengers, they won't let me through."

"Samson isn't taking any chances, is he?" Manus asked.

"Not with practically all Scanguards' wives and children on the premises for Delilah's party," Virginia replied.

"So, how are we getting in?" Kim asked. After all, Virginia had made the suggestion to come to the party.

Virginia pulled a cell phone from her jacket pocket and made a call. "Wes will get you guys in, and then I'll park the car." She put the phone to her ear. "Hey, babe, I'm outside with Manus and his charge... Great, thanks." She disconnected the call. "He'll be right out."

Charge? Why had Virginia referred to her as such? Was that all she was? Manus's protégé? Now that Kim thought about it, she recalled that from the moment they'd arrived at Virginia's home, Manus had let go of her hand and hadn't made any physical contact.

Was he trying to hide from Virginia what had happened between them?

"There he is," Manus suddenly said and opened the car door. Manus exited and hugged a tall dark-haired man in his mid-thirties.

"That's your husband?" Kim asked.

Virginia turned her head back to meet her gaze. "Handsome, isn't he?" She chuckled. "Never thought I'd fall for a man so much younger than me."

"Younger?" Kim stared at Virginia, who didn't look a day over thirty-five.

"Yeah, he's barely over fifty, and I've already passed two hundred."

Kim's chin dropped open, but she didn't get a chance to reply. The door opened, and Manus offered his hand to help her out.

He introduced her to Virginia's husband. "This is Wesley. Wes, this is Kim."

Wesley shook her hand. "Any friend of Manus's is a friend of mine."

"Thank you. Nice to meet you too."

"Come on in, guys." He waved them toward the entrance, then said to the two guards, "They're with me."

Inside the elegant lobby, it was warm and smelled pleasant. Kim felt as if she was entering a spa, which was odd because Manus had explained to her earlier what Scanguards did: they were a security company run by vampires. She'd expected something different, something darker. Maybe black walls and red velvet curtains, a bunch of antique wall sconces throwing a dim light down the corridor they were entering now. But instead, the corridor was well-lit and could have passed for a hallway in a five-star hotel. Clearly, her preconceptions about vampires had to be updated.

"Party's in the V Lounge," Wesley announced, walking ahead of them. He turned his head and winked at Kim. "V stands for vampire, but then I'm sure you've already guessed that."

Kim nodded and smiled.

"You did prepare her, right?" Wesley asked Manus.

"That Scanguards is full of vampires? Yes, of course."

"And you're one of them?" Kim asked though she could see no outward signs.

Wes threw his head back and laughed. "Me? God, no! I'm a witch. An excellent one, actually."

"A witch?" Kim caught Manus rolling his eyes.

"Yes, Wes is a witch, and clearly a very humble one."

"Hey, somebody's got to do a little PR," Wes said, grinning. "And since nobody else is doing it for me, I'd better do it myself." He winked at her. "I'm really very good." Then he stopped in front of a door. "We're here. Word to the wise: if the drink is red in color, don't automatically assume it's wine."

"You mean they serve—"

"On tap, in a glass, very civilized," Wes interrupted. He passed an access card over the card reader next to the door.

Kim heard a beep, then a click, and Wesley opened the door inward, holding it open for them. "Ladies first."

Kim entered the room, Manus and Wesley on her heels.

The enormous room looked like an old-fashioned lounge in a fancy hotel, elegant yet comfortable and cozy with numerous sitting areas, a bar, a fireplace, and a big buffet toward the other end of the room. Pretty light fixtures hanging from the high ceiling threw a soft glow over the guests. The place was packed. Men were dressed mostly in dark suits while women wore cocktail dresses and evening gowns. Several kids milled around in one corner, where a play area was located. Soft music emanated from hidden speakers, and fragments of conversations drifted to the entrance, where Kim stood frozen.

She couldn't tell who of the assembled were vampires, witches, or humans. Everybody was behaving in a most civilized way and showed no outward signs of their nature. No wonder humans didn't know of the existence of vampires. If they looked and behaved like humans, how would anybody ever suspect them?

"Ready to mingle?" Manus suddenly asked, his mouth close to Kim's ear.

"Have fun," Wesley said and waved at somebody in the crowd, then paved a way through it and disappeared.

Kim turned her head to Manus. "How can you tell who's a vampire?"

"I just can. Every creature has a specific aura, but only preternaturals can see it."

"Every creature except a demon."

Manus laid his hand on the small of her back. "Let's forget about demons for a couple of hours. You're too tightly wound right now." He lowered his voice and brought his lips closer to her ear. "I know a good way of relaxing you, but I'm afraid that's not an option right now. So, how about a drink and enjoying an evening with friends instead?"

Kim had to smile. Leave it to Manus to realize that she was stressed out and needed a short reprieve before resuming the impossible task of searching for the book the demons wanted so desperately. "I think I could do with a drink." Then she remembered Wesley's words. "Nothing red though, okay?"

Manus took her hand, and they walked farther into the room, where he flagged down a waiter with a tray with ready-made drinks.

The man pointed to the various glasses. "Champagne cocktail? Whiskey? Martini?"

He didn't point to the fourth choice, which was a red liquid in a tumbler. Kim's eyes were drawn to it. Was this blood as she suspected?

"First time here?" the waiter suddenly asked in a low voice.

She nodded automatically.

"Don't worry, all the waiters are vampires. They won't offer you anything you're not supposed to drink."

"Thank you." She swallowed away her embarrassment for having been so obvious. "I'll have the champagne cocktail, please."

He handed her the glass while Manus reached for the whiskey. "Thanks."

As soon as the waiter was out of earshot, Kim whispered to Manus, "I feel like a fool. Please tell me when I'm staring, will you?"

"Just relax," he said calmly.

"Easy to say for somebody who's used to us," a deep voice said from behind her.

Kim spun around and stared at the face of a tall man with a ponytail. But it wasn't the ponytail or the intrusion in their conversation that made her shrink back but the long, deep scar that ran from his chin to his ear, marring his face. Shock paralyzed her. The man met her eyes. They reminded her of somebody, but unfortunately her brain had frozen too.

All of a sudden, he looked past her to Manus. "I think you're meant to tell her now that she's staring, Manus." Then he winked at her. "Don't worry. Everybody does it. I don't mind."

Manus reached past her, extending his hand, shaking the scarred man's. "Gabriel, good to see you."

"Likewise." He released Manus's hand. "Won't you introduce me to your human friend?"

"Of course. Gabriel, this is Kim. Kim, this is Gabriel, Ryder's father."

Now it suddenly clicked. That's who Gabriel reminded her of. "You have the same eyes as your son," she said, extending her free hand to shake his.

The contact was pleasant. She'd always thought that a vampire's touch would be cold, but it wasn't.

"Thank you, Kim. I hope he's been behaving," he now said with a glance at Manus.

"More than that, I should say. Ryder saved my life just a few days ago."

"He did?" Pride shone from Gabriel's eyes, and a wide smile curved his lips upward. "What happened?"

"Long story, but all you need to know is that your son acted without hesitating. He's a brother to me now," Manus said, and Kim was glad that he wasn't bringing up the fact that she'd been in fact the cause for Manus almost dying.

"He's a good kid."

"He's a man now," Manus corrected him.

"His mother will be very proud of him." Gabriel craned his neck. "I can't wait to tell her. By the way, Samson heard you were coming. Last I saw him was near the fireplace. Go and talk to him." With a nod, he walked away.

"Well, then let me introduce you to Grayson's parents," Manus said and pointed toward one corner of the room.

Kim took a quick sip from her glass, and together they started making their way through the crowd. "So, Grayson is the heir to all this? I mean the company?"

"Yes and no," Manus said.

"What do you mean?"

"Grayson isn't an only child, though with his attitude, you'd think he was. But he has an older sister and a younger brother. And Samson is a very egalitarian man. Knowing him, he'll either give the company to all three of them or to whoever is most capable of running it. And that might not necessarily be Grayson."

"Interesting. I thought a society of vampires would be much more patriarchal with clear lines of succession."

Manus chuckled. "You make it sound like it's a kingdom. Believe me, it's not. Everything Samson owns is because he worked for it. Unfortunately, Grayson is a bit of a spoiled brat." He winked at her. "But we're trying to train it out of him."

Kim had to laugh. "Any success?"

"The road to success is paved with lots of hurdles," Manus replied. Then he pointed to a seating area in front of a fireplace. "There he is, Samson."

At that exact moment, the tall man Manus had pointed to turned his head and looked straight at them as if he'd heard his name. And maybe he had. A vampire's hearing was supposed to be superior to that of a human.

Kim could have picked Samson out of any crowd without difficulty. He was an only slightly older version of Grayson: black hair, hazel eyes, a tall, well-proportioned body that spoke of authority and power. Suave was a word that came to mind when she ran her eyes over him. When Samson's eyes fell on Manus, Samson greeted him with a smile that conveyed genuine pleasure. Two more strides, and they'd reached the Scanguards boss.

"My friend," Samson said, "so glad you could join us." He squeezed Manus's shoulder and shook his hand firmly. "And I can't tell you how happy Delilah was when Grayson showed up here unexpectedly. Thank you for that."

"It was no bother." Manus turned slightly to the side. "May I—"

Samson extended his hand to Kim, his eyes warm and inviting. "Introductions aren't necessary. Grayson has already filled me in. It's a pleasure meeting you, Kim. Please call me Samson. We're very informal here."

Kim shook his hand. "Now I can see where Grayson gets his charm from."

"You flatter me," Samson said and looked over his shoulder. "Did you hear that, sweetness? Apparently, Grayson can be charming."

A woman in a long red evening gown, with long dark hair cascading over her shoulders, turned around from where she'd spoken to a tall bald man. She smiled at Samson. "I always thought so, but you only see his faults."

Samson reached for the woman's hand and pulled her closer. "Excuse me, Zane, I'm gonna steal my wife for a second."

"You can steal her for longer. I'd better check what trouble my boys are getting Portia into and rescue her."

As Zane stalked off, Samson continued, "This is my wife, Delilah. Delilah, this is Manus's girlfriend, Kim."

"Ah—" But Kim was cut off by Manus saying, "There must be some mis—"

"Grayson said..." Samson started, then exchanged a look with Delilah.

Delilah put a hand on her husband's arm, then looked at Kim, smiling. "I'm sorry. If you want to keep your relationship under wraps for now, don't worry, our lips are sealed. We know how the Council can get when a warrior starts seeing a human. Particularly one he was supposed to protect."

"Oh," was all Kim managed to squeeze from her tight throat. Was that why Manus hadn't touched her in front of Virginia? Had she gotten him into trouble with his superiors?

There was an uncomfortable pause, but thankfully, Kim remembered the purpose of this party and quickly extended her hand to Delilah. "I'd like to wish you a very happy birthday, Delilah. And whatever you're doing to keep looking so young, I'd love to know, because you don't look old enough to have a son of Grayson's age."

Delilah laughed softly as she shook Kim's hand. "I'm afraid it's not something you can buy in a store." She glanced at her husband, and the two exchanged a knowing look.

"There are advantages to being mated to a vampire," Samson said with a grin. "Apart from the hot sex, of course."

Delilah let out an embarrassed huff and slapped her husband on the arm. "Of which you won't be getting any if you make our friends feel uncomfortable." Despite the words, Delilah didn't seem to be too mad at her husband, because when he bent down to her and pressed a kiss to her cheek, she accepted the tender gesture with a smile.

"My apologies, sweetness," he murmured. "But you look just a little too ravishing tonight."

Kim could only stand there and stare. Too many things were going through her head. The powerful vampire in her presence seemed like a tame kitten when dealing with his wife, who seemed to have him wrapped around her little finger. But that wasn't everything. Had Samson just implied that his wife didn't age because she was mated to him, whatever mated meant?

"Don't worry, Delilah, your husband can't make us feel uncomfortable," Manus said. "Now, if Samson had said such a thing in front of Grayson, that would be another matter."

"If he said what in front of me?" Grayson asked from behind them.

Kim looked over her shoulder.

"You don't wanna know," Samson said to his son.

"I think I do," Grayson insisted. "I hate it when people keep things from me."

Manus put his hand on Grayson's shoulder. "Trust your dad on this one."

But Grayson didn't look like he wanted to let it go. "What—?"

Kim put her hand on his arm to distract him. "I'd love to dance, and your mother just told me you're a great dancer."

Confused, Grayson looked at Delilah, then back at Kim. "She did?" Then he grinned and offered his arm. "Well, then let's dance."

Kim winked at Delilah, then allowed Grayson to lead her to the dance floor.

MANUS WATCHED Kim walk away with Grayson, and while he would have liked to be the one to dance with her, he was glad to get a few minutes alone with Samson. He liked the over two-hundred-and-fifty-year-old vampire.

"Samson, do you have a minute to talk?" Manus started.

"I think I'll leave you guys alone," Delilah said.

Manus lifted his hand. "You don't have to—"

"I should mingle anyway," Delilah insisted. "You guys talk business."

Samson followed her with his eyes as she walked away.

"You're a very lucky man, Samson."

"Trust me, I know it." He tore his gaze from Delilah. "So, what's on your mind?"

"Grayson filled you in on what I'm working on?"

"He did."

"Well, we've just found out what the demons are after. A valuable book, one that recounts our history, customs, and training guidelines for our warriors. Should it fall into the demons' hands, then they've finally got the upper hand."

A concerned look crossed Samson's face. "What's the Council suggesting?"

"They don't know yet."

"When are you gonna talk to them?"

"Tomorrow morning. I can't really drag it out any longer, or they'll fry my ass for circumventing their rules, yada yada yada. You know the drill."

Samson's lips quirked, and he motioned in the direction of the dance floor. "Is she one of the rules you're breaking?"

Manus shrugged. Seeing her dance with Grayson made him realize instinctively that she was more than just a rule he was breaking. "She's got the best chance of all of us figuring out where her mother hid the book. If anybody can find it, it's Kim."

"Zoltan will be watching her," Samson mused. "Are you using her as bait?"

At the last word, Manus jolted involuntarily. "Bait? God no, I'm keeping her invisible as much as I can."

"You know that by hiding her, you're tipping Zoltan off to the fact that you're onto him, don't you?"

That boat had already sailed. Zoltan already knew that the Stealth Guardians were closing in; otherwise, he wouldn't have sent a demon to kill the translator. But to Samson he said, "I know, but it's gotten too dangerous."

"Or you've gotten too attached to her," Samson suggested.

"I've not—"

Samson lifted his hand. "I'm not judging. I'm not the Council."

Manus gulped down his whiskey. He wasn't looking forward to speaking to the Council, but he knew it was time. Now that he was aware of what Zoltan was after, and how this could put their entire race in danger, it was time to notify the Council and accept their wrath for keeping them in the dark for so long.

"Depending on what the Council decides tomorrow, there's a chance they'll ask for more vampires to support us until this crisis is over."

"I appreciate the heads-up. Considering the severity of the situation, I'm sure I can spare a few men to help you sniff out the demons. Have you had any recent demon sightings in Baltimore?"

"Nope. It's been a little too quiet. Basically nothing since Nancy Britton was killed. Almost as if Zoltan is curbing his underlings. He doesn't wanna rock the boat while he's looking for the book."

"And you're absolutely sure Zoltan knows what he's looking for?"

Manus nodded. "He knows. He's a very unusual demon. Smarter than the others."

"That may well be, but he's still a demon, and they have a fatal flaw: they are impulsive. They don't think ahead."

"Zoltan is different." Manus sighed. He couldn't put his finger on it, but he knew that Zoltan was already planning his next move. "We have to beat him."

"Then you have to start thinking like him."

Manus stared into the crowd. "Yes." He sighed. "But not tonight. There are too many people I haven't seen in a while."

Samson slapped him on the shoulder. "Then stay a while longer. Gives me a chance to spend some more time with my son."

"Then I'd better cut into that dance."

"You'd better, or he'll get some ideas. You know how he is."

"Like father, like son," Manus said.

"I'm a one-woman man these days. I'm afraid my son is still sowing his oats."

"Not with Kim." Manus would make sure of that. He'd already let them dance long enough. Time to intervene.

33

—————

Manus had gotten up early, letting Kim sleep in while he'd updated his brethren on the news he'd gotten from Virginia. He'd made it clear to them that Kim would stay at the compound from now on. It was too dangerous to let her go back to her own condo because if the demons got desperate, they might snatch her to use her to help them find the book her mother had hidden. He wasn't going to risk that.

Nobody had protested.

Pearce had communicated with the council compound and arranged for an urgent meeting for Manus, while the others left the command center to join their mates for breakfast. Manus nodded his thanks to Pearce and looked at his watch.

"Before you leave," Pearce now said. "There's something else."

"Regarding?" Manus asked.

"You asked me to look into what Nancy was doing for us in the weeks and months before her death."

Interested, Manus nodded. "What did you find?"

Pearce swiveled in his chair. "As was to be expected, she checked in with her liaison regularly, even if she had nothing to report. During one of those calls she mentioned that she didn't feel that she could defend herself with the dagger she'd been issued should she ever come in contact with a demon."

Manus was aware that many of their human spies received a weapon forged in the Dark Days to defend themselves should their work warrant it. It was a relatively new policy, implemented after many emissarii had lamented the futility of human weapons. "And?"

"According to the notes, Nancy was wondering if the dagger's metal could be used to make a more modern weapon. When the liaison warrior asked what she meant, Nancy said that it should be relatively easy to melt the metal into bullets."

Stunned, Manus stared at his compound comrade. "You've gotta be kidding me. Why did nobody notify us about this?"

Pearce grimaced. "Because the guardian in charge discouraged Nancy from trying it, telling her that it wouldn't work, that the potency of the weapon would be lost. And he told her that even if it worked, the bullets were something that could only be used once, whereas a dagger was good for many fights. He explained to her that we have a finite supply of weapons and can't afford to lose any." He turned back to the screen and read something. "Yeah, and apparently she said *fine*, and he figured that was it. So he didn't send it up the chain."

Manus shook his head. "She said *fine*? Does that guy know nothing about women?" He let out a breath. "When a woman says *fine*, she means anything but fine!"

"Yeah, well, what can I say?" Pearce said.

"That would explain why I never found the dagger when I searched her house after her death. I'd assumed that the demon had taken it." He shook his head again, surprised at what Nancy had done. "She must have used the workshop at the museum to melt down the dagger and make bullets from it." He sighed. "I wish she'd had them on her the day the demon followed her. She might have actually been able to kill him."

"Particularly since we now know that the bullets work." Pearce pointed to Manus's upper arm, where Kim had shot him with her mother's gun. "I think we should bring this up with the Council."

"Good idea," Manus agreed, "but not today. Let me get through this crisis first."

Pearce nodded. "Agreed." Then he glanced at this watch. "You'd better get out of here or you'll be late."

With a quick nod, Manus hurried out of the room and headed for the kitchen.

Kim sat at the kitchen island and was just starting her breakfast. She smiled at him. "Hey."

"Hey. I've gotta go. The Council is waiting for me."

She nodded. "Will they punish you?"

"Punish me? For what?"

"Delilah implied last night that the Council doesn't approve of relationships like ours."

"Don't worry about that. They've got bigger fish to fry than being concerned about what's going on between us." At least he hoped so. In any case, there was no reason for the Council to even know about it. None of his compound brethren would have told them. And Manus wasn't going to volunteer the information.

"I hope you're right," she said.

He nodded, feeling awkward because he wanted to reassure her by taking her into his arms, but they weren't alone. The kitchen was teaming with his brethren and their wives.

"I've instructed the hybrids to protect you while I'm gone. Stay in the compound. I'll be back as soon as I can."

"And what should I do in the meantime?" she asked, looking frustrated.

"Think about what your mother might have done with the book. If she hid it somewhere because she was afraid the demons were following her, she would have counted on you to find it if anything happened to her. When I'm back, we'll brainstorm together. We'll figure it out. Okay?"

"Okay." Kim rose and walked toward him, but he gave a quick

shake of his head. He didn't want any show of affection in front of his brethren. It all still felt too new.

"I have confidence in you. I know you can do it." Manus turned and left the kitchen.

He made his way to the lowest level, where the portal was located. His footfalls echoed against the thick stone walls, reminding him of how different his life was from Kim's. Had he really done the right thing by bringing her here, exposing her to a world that she couldn't truly understand? Not only had he broken a bunch of rules by doing so, he'd also broken his own rule: never to get close to anybody for fear that his heart might be broken again, just the way it had broken when his parents had perished. Or was it already too late for him? Had he already gotten too close and was just not ready to admit it to himself?

With a deep breath, he placed his hand on the carved symbol on the portal and willed it to open. The moment the heavy stone disappeared, he stepped inside the small cave that could accommodate eight people, ten if they didn't mind being squeezed together like sardines in a can.

His ride to the council compound was short despite the distance he traveled. A couple of years earlier, the original compound from which the Council of Nine ruled had been destroyed. Because of the constraint of not being able to build any new portals, the new compound had to be built at a location of one of the lost portals, a location that only warriors and the council members knew. The general Stealth Guardian population was unaware of it.

Upon his arrival at the compound, Manus made his way to one of the upper floors, where the council chambers were located. A guard stood sentry in front of two massive oak doors, adorned with diagonally laid iron bars.

"Identify yourself, warrior," the guard demanded.

"I'm Manus. I called ahead to speak to the Council."

The guard nodded. "They're expecting you, but only five members are present. Your request was too short notice. Next time—"

"Yeah, yeah, I know." Manus reached for the door handle, but the guard stopped him.

"Your cell phone, please."

Manus pulled his cell phone from his pocket and handed it to the guard, who placed it in a built-in box next to the door. No recording devices were allowed in the council chambers due to the sensitivity of the subjects discussed there. He was fully aware of that.

"May I now?" he asked impatiently.

"Go ahead, warrior."

Manus pushed the door open and stepped into the room. Just like the old council chamber, this one, too, had a half-moon-shaped table around which the council members sat. They looked up when they saw him.

Barclay, the head or Primus of the Council of Nine, and Manus's compound mate Aiden's father, waved him to step closer. To his left sat Riona and Wade, to his right Ian and Cinead.

Manus was glad to see that Virginia wasn't present. It meant there would be no awkwardness having to hide that Virginia already knew what was going on and hadn't disclosed it to the Council immediately.

"Manus, I must say, we're surprised you wanted to speak to us urgently. We're not aware that you have any sensitive cases on your docket right now," Barclay started.

"Primus." Manus bowed briefly. "Council members. I'm afraid we have a situation."

The council members' eyebrows rose.

"The demons have discovered the existence of a previously lost Stealth Guardian warrior training manual."

Stunned gasps echoed in the chamber.

"We need to mobilize our defenses," Manus added, "in case they find it before I do."

34

____

Kim sat at the kitchen island in the Stealth Guardians' compound, her mother's calendar lying open in front of her. The breakfast rush in the communal kitchen was over, and almost everybody was off to do whatever Stealth Guardians did. Only Grayson was keeping her company.

"What are you trying to do with that?" he asked.

"I'm trying to get into my mother's head. Figure out her logic," Kim said. Her best friend, Jennifer, would be a great help right now. She loved figuring out puzzles. But with this, Kim was on her own. At least for now.

"By going through her calendar?"

Kim nodded. "She always had a system to everything. Maybe it'll help me figure out what she did after she left the translator."

"What time was the appointment with him?"

Kim shrugged. "Let me see." She leafed to the page that contained the day of her mother's death. "4pm. Hmm."

"How long do you think the appointment lasted?"

"If I believe the translator, which I don't necessarily do, it wasn't a long meeting since the translator received the page to review in advance. So, I assume that Kilgore told her verbally what he could glean from the text. And that shouldn't have taken long. Hmm." Something was off.

"What?" Grayson asked.

"It's weird. When I got to Mom's place after the gym that day, she wasn't home yet. I assumed she'd gone grocery shopping, but I now know that she didn't. She didn't bring any shopping home, or I would have seen it later after she'd died."

"Wait, wait," Grayson interrupted. "What time did you get home?"

"At about six thirty. I was hungry and checked the fridge, but there wasn't anything I wanted. I figured Mom was out grocery shopping, so I went to take a shower. It must have been around seven o'clock when I heard the commotion downstairs and saw the demon disappear in the vortex."

"But you didn't hear her come home?"

"No, but it must have been while I was in the shower, sometime between six forty-five and seven." Kim stared straight at Grayson. "The demon must have been following her."

"From the translator's office?"

"I'm not sure. It doesn't take two and a half hours to get home from Kilgore's office. Not even with public transportation. No, she must have stopped somewhere."

Grayson pulled his cell phone from his pocket and hit the map app.

"I thought GPS doesn't work inside the compound."

"GPS works, but magic prevents it from pinpointing the compound. However, I can still get directions from one point of the city to another, like from Kilgore's office to your mother's house." He punched in the addresses, then hit go. "There. That's the route she would have taken with public transportation. Forty-five minutes max."

Kim pored over the route the app was suggesting. "So, why did it take her almost three times as long to get home?"

"Did she have any other appointments after Kilgore?"

"Nope. And we know she didn't stop at the supermarket either." So, what had her mother done during that time?

"Do you think she would have carried the book with her to Kilgore's office?" Grayson asked suddenly.

Immediately, Kim shook her head. "If she believed it to be valuable enough to get a translator, she would have put it somewhere safe." She suddenly knew what Grayson was alluding to. "But after what Kilgore told her, namely that it had something to do with fairy tales and such, she would have realized that she needed to get it to the Stealth Guardians. Which means she would have retrieved it from wherever she'd left it temporarily."

Grayson pointed to the app. "There are plenty of places you can hide a book for a few hours or a few days and nobody would know. Luggage lockers at the bus station, for example, or even her office. That would have been relatively safe. I mean, they have 24-hour security at the museum." He pointed to another spot on the map. "She could have gone back to her office, gotten the book, then made her way home."

"And somewhere on the way, the demon must have followed her," Kim said. "Probably alerted by Kilgore."

"Makes sense. But if she didn't have the book on her when the demon killed her, and it wasn't in the house, then where did she hide it, assuming she retrieved it earlier?"

Kim shook her head. "She must have known she was being followed, or at least suspected it." She pointed to the app. "Give me the route from the museum back to her house."

Again, Grayson punched in the addresses when the door suddenly opened.

Kim turned her head and saw Ryder entering, a small rectangular package in his hand.

Grayson didn't look up but said, "Hey."

"Do you guys need anything from the outside world?"

"Can't think of anything," Grayson said. "Where're you going?"

Ryder lifted the package in his hand. "Mailing this home. It's little sis's birthday in two days, and I finally found that first edition of *The Catcher in the Rye* she wanted so badly."

"Yeah, read that, couldn't really get into it. If you ask me it's over—"

"The post office!" Kim interrupted. "That's it. She must have mailed it somewhere."

"Excuse me, what?" Ryder asked.

"The book! When my mother realized she was being followed by a demon, she must have mailed the book to hide it."

"Brilliant!" Grayson said and looked at his app again. "Hmm. There's no post office on her way home from the museum."

"Doesn't have to be a post office," Ryder said, coming closer now. "I'm not gonna go all the way to the post office. There's a mailbox place not too far from here. They do the same thing as the post office. It's just a bit more expensive."

Kim jumped up and almost leapt into Ryder's arms. "Thank you, thank you, thank you!" Then she turned back to Grayson to explain, "The receipt. When Winter had the vision, she dropped my mother's handbag, and a bunch of receipts fell out. I'm pretty sure one of them looked like it was a mailing slip."

She hoped she wasn't wrong. She hoped that this was it, that this was what her mother had done to keep the book out of the hands of the demons: to mail it somewhere, where it would be waiting for her to be found. Somewhere, where the demons wouldn't suspect it.

"We have to go to my mother's house and get the receipt." She looked at Grayson, pleading with him.

Grayson hesitated. "Manus said not to let you leave the compound."

"Please, Grayson. We need to do it now. We can't afford to lose any more time. What if the demons figure it out while we sit here and twiddle our thumbs?"

Grayson exchanged a look with Ryder. "What do you think?"

Ryder nodded. "She'll be safe if we both go with her. I'm sure if

Manus knew what you guys just figured out, he'd say the same. We've gotta act quickly."

"Thank you!" Kim tossed both hybrids a grateful look and already headed for the door.

"Wait," Grayson said. "Fine, we'll assume Manus is okay with it considering the changed circumstances, but let's not advertise the fact we're leaving to the rest of the gang, okay? They might have different opinions."

Kim knew only too well from her first encounter with Pearce and Logan that they could be pretty hard-nosed about the rules. She didn't want to risk them delaying her. "Whatever you say."

"And as soon as we know whether your mother really sent the book somewhere by mail, we'll notify Manus. Agreed?" Grayson asked.

"Agreed," Kim replied impatiently. "Now let's go. Can we take the portal?"

Both Ryder and Grayson immediately shook their heads.

"No can do," Ryder said. "Only Stealth Guardians can operate portals. We've gotta leave via normal means."

Grayson opened the door. "Rock 'n' roll."

He stepped into the hallway, and Kim followed him. Ryder was right behind her and pulled the door to the kitchen shut behind them.

"This way," Grayson directed and pointed toward one end of the corridor.

As they walked along, Grayson suddenly said, "Shit. Someone's coming."

A couple of seconds later, Kim could hear the footfalls of several people approaching quickly. A moment later, two men came around the corner: Aiden and Hamish.

"Just who we were looking for," Aiden said upon discovering them.

Kim's heart beat into her throat. Did they know that she was planning to leave the compound against Manus's wishes?

"What are you guys up to?" Hamish asked.

"Nothing, just hanging out with Kim here," Grayson said as casual as possible.

"Good," Hamish said, "because we need you guys. There's been a possible demon sighting in a mall. We need you guys to sniff them out for us. Let's go."

"Uh, yeah, about that..." Grayson shifted his weight from one foot to the other.

"What?" Aiden asked sharply. "You guys have been complaining for weeks that you haven't had any demon activity, and now you're chickening out?"

"Hey, I'm not chickening out," Grayson protested, then pointed to Kim. "But I'm on protection duty for Kim. Manus made me swear not to leave her alone."

"I'll go with you," Ryder said quickly. "You only need one of us anyway to identify the demons. I'm up for it." Ryder motioned to Grayson. "Let him babysit."

Hamish and Aiden exchanged a look.

"Fine, you then," Hamish said. "Hurry."

Aiden and Hamish were already rushing in the other direction. Ryder tossed a quick look at Grayson and Kim and mouthed *Go*. Then he turned on his heel and followed the two Stealth Guardians.

Kim and Grayson didn't speak until the three were out of sight and earshot.

"What now?" Kim asked.

"We'll go, just the two of us. We'll be fine. Trust me, I can handle protecting you on my own. Piece of cake."

Relieved, Kim nodded.

"The exit is this way," Grayson now instructed and led her around the bend in the corridor, then to the left, where a small foyer opened up. He opened the non-descript door, and Kim followed him through. They were in a second foyer now, and the door they faced now was made of old oak and was adorned with iron hinges and ornaments looking like runes.

She pointed to the runes. "What are these?"

"Part of the magic that protects this place from being discovered." He reached for the door handle and opened the heavy door. "Come."

Grayson exited ahead of her. She followed him and stepped into the alley. Opposite them was a row of one-story buildings that looked like workshops, down one end of the alley was the entrance to a garage, and the other end led to a larger street. When Grayson pulled the door shut behind her, she looked over her shoulder.

Shock made her freeze in mid-movement. The building they'd just left, the Stealth Guardian compound, wasn't there anymore. In its place was an empty city lot with trash and overgrown weeds.

She gasped. "Where did it go?"

Grayson grinned. "Pretty cool, huh? When I first saw this, I was pretty stunned too, but Aiden explained to me that the building is still there, but it's cloaked. No human can see it. Heck, no preternatural creature other than a Stealth Guardian can see it either. But it's still there." He placed his hand on the spot where the door had been. "Here, try it."

Hesitantly, she put her hand next to his and felt the wood of the door underneath her palm. "Oh my God."

"Yeah, freaky." Then he motioned to the street. "Let's go. I've got a car parked a couple of blocks away." They were already walking in that direction when he suddenly added, "You know now where the compound is located. You can never tell anyone, or you'll endanger us all. Promise me."

Kim nodded automatically. "I'd never do anything to put any of you in danger." And she meant it. Despite her initial reluctance to trust a vampire, she'd come to see them for what they really were: honorable men, albeit with a thirst for blood. But then, who didn't have a flaw? Not even the noblest human was entirely without fault.

ARRIVED at the house about a half hour later, Kim quickly unlocked the front door and let herself and Grayson in. She locked the door behind them while the young hybrid quickly surveyed the property to make sure no demon was lurking in the shadows.

"All clear."

Kim pointed to the stairs. "The handbag is upstairs." She took the stairs two at a time, anxious to get to her mother's bedroom quickly. The fear that a demon could have gotten there before her seemed suddenly very real.

Inside the bedroom, everything was just as she'd left it. The handbag lay on the floor, some of its contents spilled. Kim crouched down next to it. She opened the bag and emptied it out completely, then went through the contents: wallet, pens, makeup, keys. Everything a woman needed. Where were the receipts she'd seen the day Winter had been here? She glanced around and suddenly felt a gust of air accompanied by the closing of a door. She looked over her shoulder and saw Grayson come toward the room from the other end of the hallway.

"Sorry, had to use the John. Have you found it?"

She shook her head. But the gust of air that had accompanied Grayson's closing the bathroom door told her that the receipt she was looking for couldn't be far. She bent down and peered under the bed.

"There!"

She reached for the two pieces of paper. The first one she examined was a shopping list. She tossed it, then looked at the second piece of paper. Exhaling slowly, she read it. It was from a mailboxes business and showed the sender's name, her mother's, as well as the recipient's name, also her mother's. Only the addresses differed. The sender's address was her mother's home address; the recipient's address was one she wouldn't have immediately recognized hadn't the field for *company* been filled in: ABC Storage.

"She sent it to the storage facility." She looked up at Grayson. "She sent it to herself, care of ABC Storage."

Grayson nodded. "That way the storage facility wouldn't open it. They'd just hold it for her. Brilliant."

"We've gotta call the manager." She rose, receipt in hand, and headed for the door. "I've still got their invoice downstairs. The telephone number was on there."

The invoice was indeed still sitting on the sideboard where the mail was kept. Kim grabbed it and reached into her pocket to take her cell phone out. But the pocket was empty.

"Oh, crap, I left my cell at the compound."

"Use mine," Grayson offered, unlocked his cell phone, and handed it to her.

"Thanks." She was already punching in the number and letting it ring.

A click on the other end, and then a male voice. "ABC Storage, Rick speaking."

"Yeah, hi, may I speak to the manager, Mr. Songhurst, please?"

"This is him. Who's this?"

"I'm Kim Britton. My mother has a storage unit with you. I was there the other—"

"Oh, yeah, the break-in. I'm sorry we won't be able to compensate you for anything that was lost. We advise all customers to carry insurance—"

"That's not why I'm calling."

"It's not?"

"I just found out that my mother sent a small package to your office about three months ago, right before her death. And it wasn't in the storage unit when I looked through it."

There was a short pause during which Kim instinctively held her breath.

"Ah, yeah, that's 'cause we don't enter the storage units." There was some rustling in the background. "But I remember something arriving for her. I was holding it until the next time she was visiting. Hmm. Where did I put it?"

"Could you look, please? It's very important." Kim exchanged a tense look with Grayson.

"Ah, yeah, now I remember. It's in the back office. Hold on a second."

All Kim could hear was the faint sound of footsteps and a door opening. "He's looking," she said to Grayson.

The hybrid nodded.

The seconds stretched to minutes, until Mr. Songhurst was finally back. "Yeah, I was right. It's still in the back office. Do you want me to mail it to you? I'd have to charge you postage though."

"No, no," Kim said quickly. "I'll come by in the next hour to pick it up. Could you please hold it for me until then?"

"Sure, I can do that."

"Thanks, Mr. Songhurst. I'll see you shortly." Kim disconnected the call and looked at Grayson. "Let's go."

"Hold it," he said. "We agreed to let Manus know about this."

Though she didn't want to delay any further, Kim knew Grayson was right. "Fine." She looked down at the phone when she noticed what was wrong with it. "Oh."

"What?" Grayson reached for his phone. "Damn it. Out of juice. I don't have my charger on me."

"Tell me you know Manus's number by heart."

"Of course."

"Good. I haven't disconnected the landline here yet. We can call him from it." She hurried into the living room and picked up the receiver there. "Can you dial?"

Grayson took the phone from her hand and punched in a number. "Here you go."

When Kim put it to her ear, the call was already connecting.

"You've reached Manus. Leave me a message."

"Voicemail, damn it," she said and waited for the beep. "Hey, Manus, it's Kim. Grayson and I have found where Mom hid the book. It's at the storage facility. She mailed it there, and the manager is holding it for me to pick it up. We're going there right now. Meet us there if you get this message within the next hour." She disconnected the call.

"We should wait for Manus to come with us," Grayson suggested.

Kim vehemently shook her head. "No, out of the question. Now that we know where it is, I can't just sit around and wait. We have to get it now and bring it back to the compound, where it'll be safe."

Grayson sighed and ran a hand through his black hair. "Fine. But once we have it, we go straight back to the compound, no other stops, no other delays. Is that clear?"

"Crystal," Kim said and was already heading into the foyer.

Grayson grumbled something unintelligible and followed her.

35

———

Zoltan looked up from his desk and stared at the demon who'd entered his private study. He didn't like to be interrupted when he was thinking.

"This had better be good news."

"It is, oh Great One," the demon replied, bowing low and sufficiently long.

"Report."

"We intercepted a call made from the house of the emissarius. Her daughter found the book."

Zoltan jumped up, excitement coursing through his green blood. He pumped his fist. "Finally!" The waiting had paid off. "Where is it? Does she have it in her possession?"

"Not yet," his underling said.

"Then where the fuck is it?" Zoltan interrupted, impatience tamping down his excitement.

"At the storage facility her mother had a unit at."

Zoltan made a dismissive hand movement, ready to toss his subject in the lava pit. "I've been to the storage unit. I've searched it top to bottom. It wasn't there. Get out of my eyes before I crush you with my bare hands!" Zoltan turned away, rage now blinding him. Could his underlings not get a single thing right? Could they not even do the simplest things like tapping an old phone? Did he have to do everything himself?

"But, oh Great One, I speak the truth."

Zoltan pivoted, glaring at the idiot. But the demon continued even though he trembled with fear. "She said it herself. She told the Stealth Guardian warrior over the phone that her mother mailed the book to the storage facility and that the manager confirmed that he's got it somewhere in his office."

Zoltan's rage evaporated. "The manager has it?"

The demon nodded. "Yes, and the woman is on her way to pick it up. Together with somebody she called Grayson."

"Hmm." Zoltan wasn't familiar with that name and was pretty sure it wasn't one of the Stealth Guardian warriors. Maybe some other friend?

"Do we know anything about a Grayson?"

The underling shook his head. "I'm afraid not, oh Great One."

"No matter," Zoltan said to himself. Whomever Kim was bringing with her to collect the book was of no consequence, because Zoltan would be at the storage facility before them and gone before they even showed up.

MANUS LET OUT a sigh of relief. The council meeting was finally over. They'd grilled him for far too long and discussed the action plan ad nauseum. But at least they'd agreed with him that this case was of the highest priority. And that Kim had to be protected while they were searching for the book. For once, the Council had praised him for his initiative and not reprimanded him.

Manus pulled the door of the council chambers shut behind him and turned to the guard standing in the foyer. His fellow guardian was already handing him his cell phone, and Manus switched it on immediately while already heading down the corridor. He was halfway toward the stairs when a beeping sound alerted him to a voicemail. He pressed *play* and brought the phone to his ear.

"Hey, Manus, it's Kim. Grayson and I have found where Mom hid the book. It's at the storage facility. She mailed it there, and the manager is holding it for me to pick it up. We're going there right now. Meet us there if you get this message within the next hour."

There was a faint click, then another one.

He pumped his fist in the air, excited that Kim had figured out her mother's hiding place, though he was less thrilled about the fact that she and Grayson were going to the storage facility on their own. He tried to tell himself that Grayson was more than capable of protecting Kim, despite the fact that he couldn't hide her from the demons.

He hit the play button of the voicemail once more, wanting to reassure himself that he'd understood clearly what Kim was telling him. Kim's message played in his ear again. When it ended, there was a click again, then a second one of the call ending. Odd. Two clicks. Why would there be two clicks? He looked at the number the call had originated from. He recognized it now: it was the landline at Nancy Britton's house. For some reason, Kim hadn't used her cell phone to call him.

However, that wasn't his immediate concern. There was something he'd heard in the landline, and he knew what it was. Recognized it from many decades ago. A crude device, for certain, but then not everybody went with the times, be it due to lack of skill or resources, Manus wasn't sure. But if he wasn't mistaken, somebody had listened in on Kim making the phone call from her mother's house. And he could guess who: the demons.

"Fuck!"

The demons now knew where the book was and were most certainly on the way there. Just like Kim and Grayson. He had to warn them, or they'd run right into the arms of the demons.

Without slowing his stride to make his way to the portal, he rang Grayson's number. It didn't even ring once but immediately went to voicemail.

"Shit!"

Rushing down the stairs to the level on which the council compound's portal was located, he called Kim. At the first ring, he sighed with relief. Her cell phone was switched on. By the second ring, his heart began to pound louder. Was he already too late? When had Kim called him? Had she and Grayson already arrived at the storage facility and encountered the demons? Another ring, and he began to perspire.

"Manus?"

It was Logan, who answered Kim's phone.

Panic charged through his cells. "Where's Kim? Why do you have her phone? Is she all right?"

"No idea. I just answered it 'cause it's charging in the kitchen. Why?"

"Fuck!" There was no way to warn her and Grayson about what they were running into. "Shit, shit, shit!"

"Wha—?"

"Kim and Grayson are in danger. Head to ABC Storage where Nancy Britton had her storage unit. The book's there. It was always there. The manager has it. But the demons know. They know. And Kim and Grayson are on their way there." The words were fairly pouring out of him. "They don't know that the demons are on their way. And Grayson's phone is off. I can't warn them."

"Fuck!"

"Get as many people there as you can. Now. As fast as possible. I'm on my way there."

"Even if I transport to the portal closest to the storage facility, it'll still take me at least twenty minutes from there."

Manus cursed.

"But Aiden and Hamish are out somewhere with Ryder. I'll call them. Perhaps they're closer. Go! I'll take care of everything else."

Manus was already pressing his hand against the portal's door and willing it to open.

Please don't let me be too late.

36

Zoltan marched into the office of the storage facility at the outskirts of Baltimore. The office shack was a functional one-story building with a glass door in the middle and windows to each side of it. On the door, the name of the business and the office hours were written in big white letters. The office itself was rather bare: a few visitor chairs, a clock on the wall, a door with the universal symbol for a unisex bathroom toward the left of it, and in the center of the office a high counter with another door behind it. The back office, Zoltan assumed, the one where the manager kept the book Nancy Britton had mailed.

A clever move by the dead emissarius, he had to admit that. And the demon who'd followed her that day and later killed her had neglected to mention that Nancy had dashed into a post office while he'd been trailing her. Idiot! Had he bothered to tell the truth and give a report that didn't omit anything, Zoltan would have been able to get his hands on the book months ago. Well, at least his underling had gotten his just desserts: a hot bath in the lava pit. Served him right.

Luck was with Zoltan as he looked around the front office. It was empty. A little bell on the counter invited with the message *Ring for service*, but Zoltan didn't accept the invitation. A glance at the clock confirmed that it was close to lunchtime. Was the manager out and had neglected to lock the office hut? Odd, but he wasn't going to look a gift horse in the mouth. This would be even easier than he'd expected.

He walked around the counter and searched the shelves and surface on its reverse side, which were hidden from visitors. Since the manager was expecting Kim to pick up the book, maybe he'd already brought it out from the back office and placed it somewhere easily accessible. But Zoltan didn't get the chance to rifle through the clutter that greeted him. The sound of a flushing toilet alerted him to the fact that he wasn't alone after all.

"Shit!" he cursed under his breath and rushed back to the other side of the counter, hitting the little bell just as a man stepped out of the restroom. The elderly man wiped his hands on his pants and looked at him.

"Oh, hello, how may I help you?"

Zoltan forced a smile. Change of plans. "Are you the manager?"

"Yes, yes, that's me, I'm Mr. Songhurst." He walked behind the counter, all business now.

"Ah, excellent. My friend Kim Britton sent me. She said she called you earlier to ask you about a package her mother mailed here... She asked me to pick it up for her," Zoltan lied without blinking.

Songhurst gave him a quizzical look. "She said she was coming herself, not that she was sending somebody."

"Yeah, well, plans change. She asked me to run this errand for her instead." If Zoltan had to hold his fake smile any longer, his face would crack.

"I'm sorry, sir, but I can't give you the package. Not without a signed authorization by Ms. Britton. There are strict federal laws when it comes to mail, you know. If she can't come herself, then have her email me a signed note or bring it with you next time you come."

Anger churned up in Zoltan. This little weasel was quoting laws to him? "A signed authorization, you said?" He reached into the inside of his coat. "Why didn't you say so in the first place? I've got one right here." He pulled out his dagger and pointed it at the insolent manager.

Panic in his eyes, Songhurst spun around and lunged for the door behind him. He managed to open it and rush through it, but Zoltan was already vaulting over the counter. He reached the door just as Songhurst slammed it shut from the other side and flipped the deadbolt.

It didn't matter. A little lock had never stopped him before. With his shoulder, Zoltan pounded against the door, once, twice. On the third attempt, the wood frame around the lock splintered and the door gave way. Zoltan swung it open fully, and Songhurst screamed. As he should, because he'd just pissed off the most powerful demon this world had ever seen. Now he would pay for it. Dearly.

KIM WAS glad that Grayson didn't mind breaking a few traffic laws in order to get her to the storage facility as quickly as possible. Despite the speed limits he ignored, Grayson was a driver who made her feel safe. The knowledge that he had super-fast reflexes due to his vampire genes certainly had something to do with that.

When they finally pulled up in front of the storage facility's office, only one car was parked in a spot clearly marked *Reserved for Management*. Grayson stopped the car and switched off the engine.

Kim reached for the handle and opened the door. "Wait here for me." She hopped out of the car, but Grayson wasn't listening and was already outside, coming around the hood by the time she'd slammed the car door shut.

"I'm coming with you," he insisted. "Protection, remember?"

"You'd do better staying out here, watching my back," Kim insisted, pointing to the road they'd come from and the paths leading to the rows of storage units. "Just in case a demon followed us."

Grayson gave it only a second's thought, then nodded. "Fine. Make it quick. I'll stay out here sniffing around."

She knew he meant it literally and nodded. "Back in a flash."

Kim headed for the entrance door and pulled it open. With a last look over her shoulder, she entered the building. The room was empty though she knew Mr. Songhurst couldn't be far. He knew she was coming, and the door was unlocked despite the fact that it was lunchtime. Arrived at the counter, she noticed the bell on its surface and rang it.

"Mr. Songhurst?"

She glanced around when she heard a sound coming from the door behind the counter.

"Mr. Songhurst?" she repeated. "It's Kim Britton. I called earlier."

The manager didn't reply, but she knew he was there. She could hear him rummaging through things in the back office. Impatient, she walked around the counter and gave a hesitant knock at the door. It creaked and opened enough for her to see a man bending over a cabinet, unwrapping something. She pushed the door open wider and made a step into the room.

"Mr. Songhurst, the door was open..."

The manager spun his head in her direction. "We're closed for lunch," he said in a brusque tone.

Somewhat taken aback, Kim froze in her movements. "But I called earlier. About the package for my mother, Nancy Britton." Her eyes were suddenly drawn to the item he'd been unwrapping, a book. It looked old. Was that the book her mother had sent to him for safekeeping? Why had he suddenly unwrapped it?

"Uh, the package, yes," he now said, "I'm afraid it's not here after all."

"But you said on the phone that you found it—"

"Honest mistake," he said, his voice now even colder. "Looks like my employee returned it to the sender without my knowledge. I'm sure if you wait a few days, it'll show up back at your mother's house."

Kim stared at the book in his hand. She knew Songhurst was lying. But she also realized that he was far too big and far too strong for her to engage in a confrontation with him. He didn't exactly look like the kind of man who would have a civil discussion about something, particularly if she accused him of lying to her. It was best to retreat and come back with Grayson. Surely, the vampire hybrid would be able to intimidate the man.

"I'm sure," she said as casually as she could and pivoted slowly. Her eyes fell on the doorframe. There, at eye level, the wood had splintered, and the remnants of a lock were still visible.

Cold fear raced down her spine and paralyzed her body. The man in the back office wasn't Mr. Songhurst. He had to be a demon, and this demon was now in possession of the book. If she left the office and alerted Grayson, the demon would have enough time to disappear through a vortex he could easily cast in the back office. She had to stall him until Grayson became impatient and followed her. Surely, the young hybrid wouldn't wait outside the office forever.

Slowly, Kim turned back toward the demon to engage him in a conversation. "Uh, Mr. Songhurst—"

He stood only a couple of yards away from her now, his gaze sweeping back from the doorframe to her.

Shit! He knew she'd noticed the broken lock, knew that she knew he wasn't the manager. The evil glint in his eyes confirmed it. And though they weren't green, she was certain he'd disguised them with colored lenses.

Kim opened her mouth and screamed at the top of her lungs, "Help! Grayson! H—"

The demon's hand around her neck cut off her cry for help. Would he kill her now the same way a demon had killed her mother? Was he perhaps the same creature?

"You should've just left. But no, you had to turn around, didn't you?" the demon hissed, his face now only inches from hers. "Now, come to Zoltan."

Her survival instinct kicked in. No, she couldn't let this happen. Couldn't let this evil monster suck the life out of her. She had to fight him, fight him until Grayson would come to her aid—if he'd heard her.

With all her strength, she drew her knee up and rammed it in the demon's crotch. The grip around her throat loosened, and she pulled free while the demon stumbled backward, groaning in pain, dropping the book in his hand to the floor so he could clutch his balls.

"Grayson!" she screamed again and tossed a quick glance over her shoulder. Through the open door, she saw the hybrid. He was still outside, but he wouldn't come to her aid—not until he'd defeated the two demons he was battling with. Zoltan hadn't come alone.

Fuck!

Knowing she had to help herself, she lunged for the book on the floor, reaching it just as Zoltan seemed to recover from the kick in the balls.

"You'll pay for this," he threatened.

"Not if I can help it," Kim vowed.

37

Manus turned into the entrance of ABC Storage barely slowing down the car. He'd teleported to the closest portal and stolen a car, then raced toward the storage facility without much regard for speed limits or traffic rules. He was glad for it now because the scene outside the storage facility's office shack confirmed his worst fears.

Grayson was battling two demons. Kim was nowhere to be seen.

Fuck!

Slowing down only marginally, Manus drove toward Grayson and the two demons. One of them turned his head, his green eyes gleaming in the sunlight. Manus veered toward him. He was only a couple of feet away from Grayson, but it would be sufficient. Manus kicked down the gas pedal and hit the demon with the front right bumper, catapulting him in the air.

In his rearview mirror, Manus saw the demon slam back on the ground behind the car. Though he knew the evil creature wasn't dead, he'd given Grayson a breather to more effectively battle the other demon. Manus stepped on the brakes. The car swerved and turned almost 180 degrees before it came to a halt. Manus jumped out of the car.

"Where's Kim?" he shouted in Grayson's direction but was already racing toward the office.

"Inside!" Grayson managed to call after him.

Manus stormed into the office. The front office was empty, but the door to the back office stood open, and he could see and hear what was going on. Kim was fighting with a demon, barely holding him off by kicking and thrashing. She was fighting for her life.

Manus charged around the counter and barreled into the back office. The demon snapped his head in Manus's direction and growled.

"Get away from her!" Manus yelled and lunged for the demon.

He now tossed Kim against the wall as if she'd been a mere toy he was done playing with. Kim moaned at the impact.

Furious, Manus tackled the evil bastard and together they landed on the floor. The demon was massive, an inch or two taller than Manus and probably twenty to thirty pounds heavier. And not from fat either. He was all muscle. The demon kicked back and managed to toss Manus off him. Manus rolled away and immediately jumped back up, ready to trade blows and kicks with the asshole.

The demon was ready, already delivering a punch that made Manus's head whip sideways. But Manus was prepared. He kicked high with his foot and pushed the demon backward. To his surprise, his attacker stumbled over something. When the demon gripped the desk to prevent himself from falling, Manus glimpsed the obstacle to the demon's feet: a pair of legs. Manus didn't have to be a genius to guess who was lying unconscious, or possibly dead, behind the desk: the manager of ABC Storage. But there was no time to check if the guy needed medical attention, just like Manus couldn't reassure himself that Kim's injuries weren't life-threatening, because the demon was already charging at him again. This time, he held a dagger in his hand.

Manus ducked away and reached for his own dagger, ready to plunge it into the demon. But his opponent was too agile for his massive size. He sliced into Manus's shoulder, making him wince at the pain and for an instant lose his concentration. But not long enough for the demon to do more damage. Manus made himself invisible to gain the upper hand and jumped past the demon. He stabbed his opponent, but the bastard had moved too fast, and Manus only grazed him on his left. Green blood spurted, staining Manus's clothes and giving away his position.

Shit!

The demon's injury was too superficial to slow him down. He kept coming, kept kicking with his feet and lunging with his dagger hand. And now with Manus's skill of turning himself invisible rendered useless, he'd lost his advantage, and they were about equally matched.

The sound of screeching tires outside suddenly drowned out their grunts. The demon cast a glance at the open door, and a look of panic crossed his face.

Manus didn't have to follow his gaze. Reinforcements had arrived. "Finally!"

But the knowledge of impending doom seemed to give the demon a new lease for life. Out of nowhere, he kicked Manus in the stomach and catapulted him back against a filing cabinet. In the process, Manus lost the grip on his dagger and it flew across the room and landed near the manager's body.

Meanwhile, the demon dove for the floor and picked up an item that had lain there. Though momentarily dazed from the impact, Manus managed to recognize it.

"The book!" he screamed.

The demon made a movement with his free hand. A vortex opened up in the middle of the room, the centrical force of it pushing Manus back against the filing cabinet.

"No!"

Suddenly, there was a movement next to the desk. Kim was lunging toward the demon's feet, Manus's dagger in her hand. Fearless, she stabbed the demon in the thigh before he could step into the vortex. When he cried out in pain, Kim jumped up, dropped the dagger, and reached for the book. She grabbed it with both hands, ripping it from him. He tried to grasp it, and it opened in the middle with Kim holding on to the front and back covers.

Manus barreled toward them and kicked one foot into the demon's wound. He stumbled backward into the vortex. As the demon disappeared in it, Manus heard a page ripping and watched the demon's hand clutch one page before he vanished completely and the vortex closed behind him.

Manus breathed hard. He crouched down to the floor to where Kim had sunk back, leaning against the side of the desk, breathing raggedly. Her hands were shaking, but she was clutching the book.

Manus took her face into his hands. He kissed her quickly. "You saved the book. You saved us all. I've never met anybody braver than you."

She tried to smile but groaned in pain instead.

"Don't move," he said. "I'm gonna get you help."

Manus rose and ran toward the front office. But he didn't get far. His fellow Stealth Guardians were already pouring in. Hamish was the first he laid eyes on.

"Need help?" Hamish asked.

Manus shook his head quickly. "Are the other demons dead?"

"Dead as doornails," Hamish confirmed.

Aiden appeared next to him and grinned. "There were only two out there. No big deal."

Behind them, Logan entered. "Did you get the book?"

Manus turned halfway, pointing at Kim. "Kim ripped it from the demon's clutches." He smiled at her proudly, then turned back to the guys and looked past them to where the two hybrids were standing. "Ryder, care to donate some blood to heal Kim? She's hurting."

"No problem." The young hybrid approached and kneeled down next to Kim. Then he motioned to the manager's body. "Do you want me to take care of him first?"

Manus rushed closer. "He's alive?"

Ryder nodded. "I can hear his heartbeat. Faint. But he's still alive."

Manus looked over his shoulder. "Grayson, you're needed. Make sure the manager survives."

"Piece of cake," Grayson said and approached with a swagger in his step.

While he moved behind the desk to heal Songhurst, Manus kneeled down next to Kim and Ryder. "It'll take the pain away and heal you faster," he said to Kim. "There's nothing to fear."

She looked up at him and handed him the book she'd fought so bravely for. "I know." Then she nodded at Ryder, who pierced his wrist with his fangs and set it against Kim's lips.

"Drink. I'll stop you when I know you've had enough."

Knowing that Kim would be okay, Manus rose and walked to his colleagues. "We have a problem." He sighed. "The demon managed to rip a page from the book."

All three of his brethren cursed.

"I have a feeling I know who this demon was," Manus added

"He called himself Zoltan," Kim suddenly said.

Manus pivoted and nodded. "The Great One. He's their leader. This won't be the last time we see him. And whatever information is on that page he stole, he'll use it against us."

"Then we'd better find out what we're up against," Logan said.

Hamish nodded. "Just as soon as we're done with cleanup here."

38

In the command center of the compound, Manus turned toward the opening door.

"Finally," he said with relief when he saw Logan enter with a book in his hand.

"Found it." Logan waved the book in the air and walked toward where Manus, Kim, as well as Pearce, Hamish, Aiden, and the two hybrids had been waiting for him. "I knew we had one in the vault that was the same edition as the one Kim's mother found."

Logan placed the book on the table next to the one Zoltan had managed to rip a page from.

"Then let's see what he's got." And whether they needed to be worried about what kind of information the Great One had obtained.

Manus leafed through the book to the page that was missing in the book Kim had so bravely ripped from Zoltan's clutches. He couldn't even express how proud he was of her for having risked her own life though he was still shaking at the thought of what could have happened.

"There." Aiden pointed at the page Zoltan had managed to steal.

Manus pored over it and started reading. "My Celtic is a little rusty, but if I'm not mistaken, this page is a reference to the source dagger."

Pearce leaned in and pulled the book closer, so he could read it. "I can run it through the translation program, but from what I'm reading here, you're right. It's about the powers it has. That it can create an unlimited number of portals." He pointed to a spot in the middle of the page. "And here it refers to its healing properties."

"Can Zoltan do anything with this information?" Kim asked.

Manus turned his head to her. "I don't see how. The dagger doesn't exist anymore." He pointed to the page. "It probably even says so in here, considering that the book was written well after the source dagger was lost. Right, Pearce?"

Pearce nodded. "Correct." He continued reading the Celtic sentences, then turned the page and stopped abruptly.

"What?" Manus asked and looked at the flipside of the page Zoltan had managed to snag. He didn't need to wait for Pearce's answer because he saw for himself what it contained: a drawing of the dagger.

Everybody drew closer to examine it.

"Can the demons make a replica?" Kim asked, her voice shaking. "I mean, like you made a replica of my mother's bracelet?"

"Sure, they can," Manus said, "but it won't help them. A replica won't have the powers of the source dagger. It's not how it works." He gave her a reassuring look. "Trust me on that. Right, guys?"

"Right," Pearce said, and the others nodded though they didn't look pleased.

Kim seemed to notice it and asked, "Then why are you all looking so concerned? What are you not telling me?"

"It's because we screwed up. Any piece of information the demons get about us can eventually bite us in the ass, even if it seems harmless now." Manus glanced at Aiden. "Your father won't be pleased that we let Zoltan get that page."

Aiden shrugged. "My father doesn't need to know everything." He looked at the other Stealth Guardians. "If we all stick to the same story, tell him that the book was recovered and is now safely locked away in our vault, he'll never need to find out that a page is missing."

Manus felt Kim fidget next to him. "Aiden's father? What does he have to do with this?" she whispered to Manus.

Aiden had heard her and looked straight at her. "My father is Primus, the head of our Council, our ruling body. He's the president, so to speak."

Kim's chin dropped. "Oh." Then her look bounced back and forth between Manus and his brethren. "And you're going to lie to him? What if he wants to see the book?"

"Good point," Hamish said.

"Not a problem," Manus insisted and lifted the intact book Logan had retrieved from the archives. "We'll show him this one. He's not gonna know the difference. I never told the Council about the inscription in it."

"What about Virginia? You said she's on the Council too," Kim continued. "What if she sees that it's not her book?"

"You worry too m—" Manus said.

"She's got a point," Hamish interrupted.

Manus sighed. "Fine. Then I guess we'll have to do a little cutting and pasting."

"Cutting and pasting?" Hamish asked, shaking his head. "You've gotta be kidding me. You want to take the missing page out of this book and glue it into the one we just recovered?"

"That's exactly what we're gonna do," Manus said. "Objections anybody?"

There were none.

"Good, then it's agreed. Let's get to work."

The door suddenly opened, and everyone fell silent. Enya entered and froze. She tilted her head to the side, regarding them suspiciously.

"Did I miss something?" she asked.

"Just a fight with the Great One himself," Manus said casually and lifted the book for her to see. "And we got what he was after, the book Kim's mother hid."

Enya stomped her foot. Her long blond locks cascaded over her shoulders. "Really?" She cursed under her breath. "Come on, that's so not fair! Every damn time you guys fight him, I'm stuck somewhere else. They really didn't need me in Seattle. There was no demon activity whatsoever. I was bored out of my skull all day long!"

"Don't worry," Manus said calmly. "You'll be there next time."

Because there would be a next time, for sure. There always was. The Stealth Guardians wouldn't stop until Zoltan was crushed and his demons annihilated.

"Oh, I'd better!" Enya vowed.

Pearce playfully boxed her in the shoulder. "You and me both! I had to man the command center while they got to have all the fun. We'll show them next time, shall we?"

"You're on," Enya promised.

39

Kim stopped at the door that connected the bathroom with Manus's bedroom, hesitating for a moment. For a week now, she'd spent practically every night at the compound with Manus even though there was no reason Manus still needed to protect her. The demons knew that the book was now in the possession of the Stealth Guardians again, safe and sound, locked away in a vault they would never gain access to. Kim was of no more value to them anymore and therefore of no consequence to the Stealth Guardians either.

Still, Manus had come to see her every day since he'd rescued her from Zoltan and taken her back to his private quarters at the compound, practically devouring her the moment the door closed behind them. But how long could this last? Sure, Tessa and Hamish were somehow making their relationship work, just as Aiden and Leila did. Logan and Winter were a different story. At least they were both preternaturals, and while Kim hadn't dared ask such a personal question, she assumed that as a preternatural creature, Winter was immortal like her husband. But Tessa and Leila? Wouldn't they eventually age and die while their husbands remained young and alive? How could such an unequal situation ever turn out to be satisfactory? How could they ever be happy?

Kim sighed. She couldn't face this prospect, a future where Manus would eventually lose interest in her because she would turn into an old woman, and he would remain a young man with needs she would eventually not be able to satisfy anymore. That's why she'd come to a decision. Tonight would be her last night with Manus. She would tell him that he had no obligations toward her, and that he shouldn't feel guilty if he broke it off with her.

She understood now why he'd never formed any emotional attachments after his parents' death: for him, love would eventually end in heartbreak. And she couldn't do that to him. At least now, this early in their relationship, his heart was still his, and therefore she couldn't hurt him. That she had, however, already lost her heart to him, he would never have to find out. A clean break was best now before their feelings for each other deepened.

With a steely resolve, Kim opened the bathroom door and stepped into the bedroom. She froze at the sight of what Manus had done to it. Dozens of candles gave the room a soft glow. Flickering shadows drew abstract pictures on the walls. And amidst all of it, Manus stood waiting for her. His robe stood open, giving her a clear view of his boxer briefs that stretched tightly over his groin. He was ready for her, just like he'd been ready every night since her rescue.

This would be so much harder than she'd expected.

"You look stunning," Manus said, his eyes roaming over her body.

She'd donned her sexiest nightgown, a concoction of red silk and black lace, wanting to make their last night a memorable one though she knew she wouldn't wear the expensive outfit for too long. But she also knew that Manus liked to feast his eyes on her, and she was more than willing to oblige him.

Kim ran her eyes over him now. He'd finally gotten more comfortable with presenting his bare chest, with not hiding it anymore, despite the ugly scars that marred it. She didn't really notice them anymore. They were part of who he was.

"Something wrong?" Manus slowly walked toward her.

She met his eyes, and he suddenly stopped in his approach.

"Did something happen?"

She didn't know how to broach the subject. How could she tell the man she loved that she was breaking up with him because they couldn't have a future together?

"Kim, you're making me nervous. Talk to me."

She swallowed hard. "I need to tell you something... We can't be..."

Two more steps, and he stood in front of her, placing his hands on her shoulders. "We can't be what?"

"Doing this... anymore. It's not... There's no..." Her voice cracked. She couldn't find the right words.

"Doing what? Damn it, Kim, what are you trying to say?"

"We can't have a relationship," Kim finally said.

Visibly startled, Manus pulled back until his arms were straight. "Are you breaking up with me?"

"It's best this way."

He tossed her an incredulous look. "Best? For whom?"

"For both of us." She dropped her gaze to her bare feet, unable to withstand his penetrating eyes for fear she would cry.

"I see," he said slowly and took his hands off her shoulders. "So, you've finally woken up and decided you don't want to be fucked by the scarred guy anymore. I should have known."

"Scarred—" She gasped involuntarily. "It's not your scars, it's—"

"Spare me the lies," Manus snapped, cutting her off. "I should have known."

"Manus, believe me. It's not that."

He pivoted, turning his back to her. "Why don't you get dressed and leave?"

"Not like this, Manus." She couldn't let him think that she was leaving him because of his scars. "It has nothing to do with your scars."

He huffed out a disgusted grunt.

"I can't be with you because I know we'll break each other's hearts."

She saw his shoulders stiffen.

"Because one day, you'll look at me and you'll realize you can do better. And with every wrinkle I develop, with every line in my face, every gray hair, I'll wonder when you'll trade me in for a younger woman."

He started turning, slowly. "A younger woman?"

Kim avoided meeting his eyes and continued, "Yes. Maybe not in the next five or ten years, but once the first signs of me aging show in my face, you'll wonder why you're still with me when you could be with somebody who's..."

"Younger?" he helped.

She swallowed away the bad taste that word created in her mouth. "Yes, while you're still looking the same as now." She sighed. "It must have occurred to you. I'm sure you're looking at your colleagues' wives and think the same. How long will it last? You and your brethren are immortal. You don't have to worry about aging. But I'm human. I'll grow old. And I don't think I want my heart broken in fifteen or twenty years when reality catches up with us."

"So, that's why you've decided to break my heart now." There was no anger in his voice.

Kim gave a slight shake of her head. "I can't possibly be breaking your heart. Manus, we've only known each other for a couple of weeks. Your feelings for me aren't that deep yet. You still have a chance to get away unscathed." Even though she didn't. She was already in too deep. "Take the chance. Do it for my sake. So that I know that at least I didn't hurt you. Because you deserve to be happy, Manus. You've gone through so much. I don't want to be the person who breaks your heart."

"Let me make sure I get this right. You want to break up with me because I'm immortal and won't age, and you're human and will age. Am I understanding this correctly?"

She nodded. "Yes."

"So, you're giving me a way out. It's generous, don't get me wrong, but I'm not gonna take it. I have a counteroffer."

Surprised at his words, she shifted her gaze to his face and looked into his eyes. "A counteroffer? This is not a negotiation. It's a breakup."

He chuckled. "Kim, if this is a breakup, you're not doing it right."

"Wha—"

"In a real breakup, you'd be tossing insults at me, telling me that you can't stand me, that I'm bad in bed, impossible to live with, emotionally abusive, and just not marriage material. I mean, you've done it, right? You broke up with Todd. I'm sure you told him that it just wasn't working between the two of you. Well, I don't hear you saying these things to me. So, it's not a breakup."

"But I have a legitimate reason," Kim protested. "I'll die, and you won't. I mean, that's a pretty big reason."

"Sure, it would be," Manus conceded. "If it were true." He stepped closer again.

"But—"

"You met Tessa, Winter, and Leila. They're mated to immortals. I thought you understood. In fact, I assumed you talked to one of them to ask about this. Women talk about all kinds of stuff. They could have told you that once you're bonded to me, you won't age anymore."

"Uh, what?" Now she was the one who didn't understand. "Are you saying Tessa and the others won't age because they're married to a Stealth Guardian?"

"Not married," he corrected, "bonded. It's stronger than marriage, and yes, it allows the Stealth Guardian's partner to draw from his immortality. Did you really think that any of my colleagues would have tolerated you staying here with me if they didn't expect me to make it official like they did? I wasn't going to just fuck you and then toss you aside when I had enough." He shoved a hand through his hair. "It's not possible because I'll never get enough of you."

Her eyes widened, and she felt her chest expand. Was this possible? If it was, they could have a future together.

"So, here's my counteroffer. Instead of breaking up, I want you to look into your heart and tell me what you feel for me. And if it's love, then bond with me, be with me for eternity. If it's not true love, walk away, because if we bond and one of us doesn't feel true love for the other, the ritual will kill us both."

Kim sucked in a quick breath and searched his eyes. "Both have to feel true love?"

"Yes."

"Are you saying you feel that for me?" She felt her eyes moisten with tears. Was it possible this warrior loved her the way she loved him?

Suddenly, Manus touched her cheek and caressed it softly. "Oh, Kim, I'm an idiot. I forgot to tell you the most important thing." He took her face into both hands. "I love you, Kim, with all my heart, my soul, with every fiber of my immortal being."

"Oh, Manus…" She didn't know what to say because her heart was overflowing with emotions.

MANUS FELT his heart pound as if it wanted to leap out of his chest. "If you need more time, if you're not there yet, I'll wait for however long it takes."

A tear loosened from her eye and rolled down her cheek. "There's no need to wait." She sniffled. "I know what I feel, what I've felt for a while now. I never thought it would happen so quickly. But when you showed me who you really are, what's really inside you… I fell in love with you in that moment. And every day, I love you more."

Manus let out the breath he'd been holding, allowing his heartbeat to normalize. "You make me the happiest man in the world by saying that." He brought his face close to hers, ready to kiss her, but Kim hadn't said yet what he needed her to. "Does that mean you'll have me? As your immortal mate? Forever and ever?"

"I can't think of anything I want more," Kim murmured and slid her arms under his robe, wrapping them around his back.

Feeling her hands on his bare skin ignited his passion for her in an instant. He pulled her against his chest and slanted his lips over her mouth, capturing it. Kim met him eagerly, responding to his kiss like she'd done the nights before though this time everything was different. This time, he knew that her kiss meant total acceptance of everything he was. Total acceptance of his scars, those outside and those inside.

Kim tasted of everything that was good in this world, everything that was right. Her scent and her taste seeped into every cell of his body, marking him, branding him so he would never want any other woman. He understood now what his brethren had experienced when they'd found their mates, when they'd secured their mates' affections. He'd finally found the one person who understood him and loved him despite everything.

He drew Kim closer to him, placing one hand on her backside to press her against his rampant cock, letting her know what he needed from her now. A moan was her response, and he gobbled it up like the greedy bastard he was. He rubbed his cock against her stomach, eliciting another moan from her, while he felt her heartbeat accelerate and drum against his chest to rival his own. Two hearts beating for one another. Soon they would be one.

Kim seemed as impatient as he because she now tugged on his robe and pushed it off his shoulders, forcing him to remove his hands from her. But not for long. As soon as his robe dropped to the floor, he pulled her back against his body. He reached for her ass again and hiked up her short nightgown. She wore no panties. Bare skin greeted his palms, and he ripped his mouth from hers and let out a breath.

"Babe," he murmured, "I can't promise you that I'll last long the first time tonight, but I can promise you that you'll never experience anything more amazing."

Kim chuckled softly, and the sound felt like warm water trickling down his spine. "Then get to work, warrior."

He didn't need another invitation. He gripped the seams of her nightgown and pulled it over her head, then tossed it to where his robe had landed. For a moment, he just feasted his eyes on Kim's naked beauty. She was perfect in every way. The perfect contrast to him.

When he suddenly felt her thumbs hook into the waistband of his boxer briefs, he realized he'd been staring more than just a few seconds.

Long enough for Kim to take matters into her own hands. She pushed his boxer briefs down, and he helped her and stepped out of them.

Cool air blew against his hard cock, but only for a moment. Kim was already wrapping her palm around him, making him hiss in a breath.

"Fuck!"

He was more than just sensitive tonight. Anticipation of what was going to happen tonight had made him hyper-receptive to Kim's touch.

"You're like a Roman candle," she murmured, giving his cock a slow tug while she brought her lips to his. "Am I doing that to you?"

He wrapped one arm around her waist and drew her against him. "You little minx, you know full well what you're doing to me." He kissed her hard and deep, then lifted her up into his arms and walked to the bed, where he slowly lowered her onto the mattress and caged her beneath him.

Her legs fell open, providing a space for him. And like he'd done the nights before, he accepted the offer and slid between her thighs while he braced himself on his elbows and knees.

When he looked into her face, Kim was looking right at him.

"How does the bonding ritual work?"

Manus brushed a few strands of hair from her face. "Remember the night we made love in the dry cleaners shop?"

"Yes."

"I poured my virta into you and made you shimmer golden. It's like that."

Her eyes widened. "Are you saying we already bonded that night?"

He laughed softly. "No, we didn't. There was one thing missing that night. One thing you'll have to do to make us one forever."

She lifted her hand to his cheek and caressed it. "And what is that?"

"When I give you my virta, you'll place your hand over my heart and send it back to me. It'll complete the cycle."

"But how do I do that?"

"Don't worry. You'll feel it." It was an instinct, even though she was human. His virta would guide her. "You'll feel me. My soul, my heart, my love for you."

He noticed a wet sheen draw over her eyes. "I saw your soul that night. I felt it."

Manus smiled at her. "And tonight, I'll feel yours." Slowly, he drew his hips back and adjusted his cock. A moment later, the tip of it touched Kim's moist folds. Without breaking eye contact, he pushed them apart and sank into her tight channel, allowing her interior muscles to squeeze him on his descent into pure bliss.

Kim's eyelids fluttered, and a breath rushed from her lungs. "Oh, yes."

Manus clenched his jaw. The feeling of being inside her, inside his mate, was quickly robbing him of his self-control. He'd thought that he would make love to her for a good while before he poured his virta into her, but he'd miscalculated. The urge to give his essence to her was stronger than the night at the dry cleaners, stronger because he knew that tonight they'd form their unbreakable bond. As soon as Kim had agreed to it, it couldn't happen fast enough for him.

With his Stealth Guardian powers, he willed the air around them to turn into a fog-like substance that cocooned them, protected them so nobody could harm them in their hour of deepest vulnerability. It shielded them from the outside and dulled everything around them, letting their surroundings melt into the background until it was only the two of them, floating on a bed of softness.

Manus began to thrust in and out of her, but with his third thrust, his control snapped and virta started to burst from him and seep into Kim. He could see it, feel how it permeated her cells, how it spread in her body, how it rose to her skin and turned it golden. The shimmer was tantalizing and made the air around them glow golden.

Kim arched her back, letting a deep breath escape from her throat. Wide-eyed, she stared at him, love and lust shining from her eyes in equal measure.

Without him having to prompt her, she placed her hand on his heart. He slowed his movements and watched his lifeforce travel from the center of her body to her shoulder, then down her biceps, and farther down still. When he saw the brilliant light reach her wrist, he braced himself. A second more, and his virta, now mingled with Kim's own lifeforce, reached her fingers. And from their tips, little electrical charges exploded and penetrated his skin, his muscles, his ribcage to find their way to his heart.

Shudders made his body tremble uncontrollably, spasms made him climax instantly, causing his cock to plunge faster and deeper into her. They were connected now, forever irrevocably bonded to one another.

He let out a moan and threw his head back, receiving more of their now shared virta. And with it he saw what he'd been craving for: a glimpse of Kim's soul. Pure and white, full of goodness and love. And he saw the grief for her mother, the grief that would always be there. Only now, it was surrounded by love, cocooned by it so it would never cause her pain again. And in his own heart he felt the same now. The pain the loss of his parents had caused him was now vanishing, but the memories remained intact, the love for them still potent. Because Kim had rescued him.

"And you rescued me," Kim now said, her gaze connecting with his. "From the demons, from my loss, my pain."

He smiled at her. Kim understood him because she felt him now. All of him.

"I'll always rescue you. Because without you, I'm only half a man."

Kim pulled his face to her. "You're more than I ever dared hope for. I love you, my warrior, my mate."

His heart full with love, he sank his lips onto hers, vowing to make this night one they would always cherish.

40

Zoltan closed the old, heavy book with the yellowed pages with a thud. Dust whirled up in the air. Leaning back in his armchair, he looked at the page he'd ripped from the Stealth Guardians' book. He'd finally translated the few paragraphs that had been written in an old Celtic dialect, one he didn't speak. After poring over book after book in his underground lair, he'd finally managed to decipher every word and make sense of the sentences.

And what a boon it was! The knowledge contained on this single page was worth a million books. He finally knew one of the most well-guarded secrets of the Stealth Guardians: their portals had been carved with what the book described as the *source dagger*, a dagger that wasn't in the Stealth Guardians' possession anymore. In fact, it hadn't been theirs for many centuries. They'd lost it. Where, how, not even the Stealth Guardians seemed to know. It meant not only that the guardians were unable to create any new portals, but that whoever found the dagger could create a portal that would automatically connect to all their existing portals.

If he, Zoltan, could find the source dagger, he would be able to create his own portal and invade the Stealth Guardians' domain with his demons, destroying them from within. He could attack all compounds and private residences of the guardians simultaneously, preventing them from coming to each other's aid. Total annihilation would be the result. He could wipe the Stealth Guardians from this world so completely that nobody would know they'd ever existed. His victory would be absolute. Nobody would ever question his rule again. Nobody would dare usurp him. His demons would be loyal to the death, worshipping him, because he had delivered them from the Stealth Guardians, defeated the only real opposition they'd ever had.

Finally, the humans would be as vulnerable as sheep without their shepherd. Just like he liked them: weak, unprotected, defenseless. There would be a feeding frenzy. And once all his demons had taken their fill, a new world order would commence. Humans would become slaves. Fear and pain would become their constant companions, turning their lifeforce into perfect nourishment for the demons. For him. He, Zoltan, would take the best morsels for himself, making sure he remained the strongest demon, cementing his power as the Great One.

He'd have a harem of women whose fear he'd feed on, whose bodies he'd ravish whenever it pleased him. He would be their master. Everybody would fear him, more than they feared him now.

And maybe then, when he was stronger, there would be no more debilitating migraines, no more crippling pain that threatened to crush his skull. He would be cured of whatever ailed him and threatened his very existence as the Great One. He was sure of it.

This time, he was certain that he would succeed because not only did the page contain a description of what the source dagger could do, there was also a drawing of what it looked like. It was more than he needed to go on a treasure hunt and find the dagger. And once it was his, once he held it in his palm, the world would be in his palm too.

Soon.

Very soon.

ABOUT THE AUTHOR

Tina Folsom was born in Germany and has been living in English speaking countries since 1991. Tina has always been a bit of a globe trotter.

She lived in Munich, Lausanne, London, New York City, Los Angeles, San Francisco, and Sacramento. She has now made a beach town in Southern California her permanent home with her American husband and her dog.

She's written 50 romance novels in English most of which are translated into German, French, and Spanish.

https://tinawritesromance.com
tina@tinawritesromance.com

facebook.com/TinaFolsomFans
instagram.com/authortinafolsom